BOUND
❧ — BY — ☙
BLOOD

HOUSE OF PAYNE SERIES
BOOK 2

IVY BLACK
AND
RAVEN SCOTT

YOUR EXCLUSIVE ACCESS

Thank you from the bottom of our hearts for your incredible support!

As a token of our appreciation, we've created an exclusive VIP newsletter just for you.

Immerse yourself in a world of raw passion, dark secrets, and unforgettable love. Sign up now at www.IvyBlackRomance.com to be the first to hear about new releases, exclusive discounts, and much more!

See you on the inside,
Ivy Black and Raven Scott

CHAPTER ONE

Mason

I stare from the gun to his face and back again. "We both know you're not going to shoot me."

Jack points the gun directly at my chest, his cold and cruel smile never wavering. "Let me ask you again, boy, are you willing to die for her? Because I can end you right here and let her watch you bleed out before I take care of her."

I fold my arms over my chest, and it takes every ounce of self-control I have not to lunge. "You are not going to lay a finger on her."

A muscle ticks in Jack's jaw. "I'm the one holding the gun."

I spread my arms out on either side of me. "And yet here I am. If you wanted to shoot me, you would've already, but we both know you're not going to."

His expression tightens as he presses his lips together.

"Like it or not, you need me," I add, in the same even tone of voice. "I'm the head of the Empire, remember?"

"Leaders can be removed."

I draw myself up to my full height and meet his gaze. "Go ahead then. Do your worst."

A part of me is wondering just how far I can push him before he cracks, but the other part knows it's pointless.

My father is many things, but stupid isn't one of them.

He knows that if he has any hope of winning the war, he needs me.

The bastard is just too proud to admit it.

My father can be cruel and dismissive, and he's never hesitated to discipline us, but if there's one thing I know, it's that he always pulls himself back from the edge when it comes to us.

Even if I can't understand why.

He's never been the warm or fuzzy type, and he still thinks he's God's gift to man, but you know he's more of a bully than anything.

Jack blinks, and his smile shifts and changes. In one quick move, he steps to the side and points the weapon at London. "There is more than one way to hurt you."

Anger, hot and potent, erupts within me. "You are not going to shoot her."

Jack laughs, and it sends another chill through me. "Or what, boy? Have I taught you nothing? Never make a statement you can't fully back."

He moves again and before I know what I'm doing, I react and knock the gun out of his hand. Jack barely has a chance to register his surprise before I throw myself at his middle. I throw him against the nearest wall, but my victory is short lived when a flash of silver catches my eye, and I jump backward.

A thin red welt forms on my arm and blood drips on the floor beneath me. "I see you brought a knife to a gun fight."

Jack straightens his back and levels me with a look. "A Payne always comes prepared."

I glance from London to the gun and back again. Slowly, I turn my attention back to my father. Out of the corner of my eye, I see her dive for it, her fingers trembling. "I couldn't agree more."

Jack holds the knife up to the light and makes a low humming sound. "What a disappointment you've turned out to be. All those years of

2

teaching…such a waste."

I spread my legs hip width apart and wait for him to strike.

He continues to circle me, his gaze occasionally darting over to London. "It is a shame to have to make her pay. Such a pretty face. Perhaps I'll put her to work in the club when we're done. With a body like that, our clients will pay good money."

"Your fight is with me."

Jack chuckles again and swings his gaze back to mine. "You stupid, ridiculous boy. What's the first thing I told you about teaching a man a lesson?"

"Take away everything he loves and then make him bleed," I reply, without thinking.

He stops moving and stares straight at me, his expression turning blank.

For a long moment, neither of us says anything, and I try not to twist to face London, even though I'm aware of her every breath and move.

Come on, you bastard. Do something already.

Abruptly, he lunges, and I intercept him with a quick swipe. He darts sideways to avoid it, and I throw a punch in, making him lose his footing. He growls and bares his teeth at me. Then I shove London back, and the two of us collide. Pain erupts behind my eyelids when he aims for the jaw and clips the side of my head. I blink back the tears and dive for his stomach, knocking him onto his back. He uses his legs to hold me in a headlock, and I buck against him.

Fear and fury pump their way through me in equal measure.

When I head butt him, he drops the knife and rolls away. I stand back up, adrenaline coursing through every inch of me, and offer him a grim smile. "We both know this only ends one way."

Jack straightens his back again, and there's cool calculation in his eyes.

I kick the knife away and curl my hands into fists. "Let's settle this the old fashioned way."

He looks from the knife to my face and back again. Finally, he straightens his back and gives me a cold and cruel smile. "No."

I frown. "What?"

Jack's expression is one of cold fury when he draws himself up to his full height and smiles. "You will be brought to heel, boy, one way or another."

Without waiting for a response, he spins on his heels and leaves.

I hold my breath for a few moments longer and stare at the space he occupied. When London releases a shaky breath, I exhale and cross over to the door. After locking it, I twist to face her, and London is leaning against the wall, the gun held away from her. As soon as she feels my eyes on her, she throws the gun away, and the cover falls into a heap on the floor.

She's still shaking when I take her into my arms. "What the hell was that?"

I draw back to look at her, and my eyes sweep over her. "We're fine. It's okay."

London licks her lips and rubs her hands up and down her arms. "Was that your father?"

I pause and nod, slowly. "Yes."

She runs a hand over her face. "He's going to kill us."

I take her hand and lead her back to the bed. After making sure she sits down, I bend down to retrieve her clothes and hand them to her. "He's not going to kill us because he needs us."

London pulls on her shirt first, and her eyes are still wide when she looks at me. "He needs you. He doesn't need me."

"I need you," I reply, a little harsher than I intend. "And he knows that if he makes a move against you, there will be hell to pay."

"Mason—"

"My father likes to play mind games," I interrupt, pausing to help her wriggle into the sweatpants. "He likes making people wonder what he's going to do next. His bark is worse than his bite."

Or at least that's what I keep telling myself as I wait for London to get dressed and splash some water on her face.

He's not going to make a move against his own son, not with everything else happening.

Still, there's a part of me that can't help but wonder.

How far is he willing to go to prove a point?

And what kind of punishment is waiting for me at the end of it all?

My chest tightens when London slips a hand through mine. I tuck her into my side and use my free hand to press two fingers against my temples. Slowly, she draws back to look at me, but I don't turn to face her. Instead, I step away and turn to the window.

"Fucking Mathew." I pause to drum my fingers against my thigh. My free hand clenches into a fist as I force myself to inhale. "He must've told him what happened."

As I exhale, I glance at London through the glass. She's gathered her hair into a bun on top of her head, and although she keeps stopping to sneak glances at me, I know she won't say anything else.

What else can she say?

I'm surprised she hasn't already run for the hills.

Half of me is tempted to join her.

Especially when I've just made things worse.

It's one thing to have my enemies gunning for her.

My father, on the other hand, likes to toy with people, relishing in dragging out their pain, and I have no doubt he wants to do the same with me.

Being his son and heir won't spare me from his wrath; if anything it'll make it worse.

I want to blame London for not being able to walk away when she had the chance, but I know it's more my fault than hers.

I should've known better.

I know how dangerous and volatile my world is, but I still let her get sucked in.

Fucking hell.

You better know what the hell you're doing because after what you just pulled with your father, he is going to do more than punish you.

I can imagine him pacing and fuming in the office downstairs, already picturing the many ways he'll make an example of me.

I can't blame him.

Even on his best day, Jack Payne isn't known as the forgiving kind, and having to haul ass down here to clean up a mess he told me to take care of must've put him in an even worse mood. I consider blaming my brother for not keeping his mouth shut, but I know it won't solve anything.

Not entirely, anyway.

The question isn't who told him, but who will fall in line out of loyalty to me?

I scowl. "I know you're worried about your father and Noah. I'll see if I can send someone to check on them."

Even though I hate the thought of having anything to do with her ex. As far as I'm concerned, the little shit is better off in her rearview mirror, but I know London won't turn her back on him.

Not when she feels responsible for getting him and her father tied up to lure her away.

London was the one who was kidnapped and starved, but she still feels responsible.

How long do you think it will take her to blame you for the mess they're all in? You didn't make her fall in love with you, but you didn't stop her, even when you knew what it would cost her.

London hides her trembling fingers behind her back and stands straighter. "I thought you didn't have anyone to spare? Because of what happened, I mean."

I stand up, and my fingers move to the buttons on my shirt. "I don't.

Not full-time, at least. They're going to have to look out for themselves, but I can have someone check in."

London swallows. "Your dad. He…"

"Is a real piece of fucking work," I finish. "Mathew is nothing compared to him. Try to avoid him while he's here."

London's hands clench into fists. "I can't hide from everyone, Mason. And how am I supposed to stay out of his way if we're staying under the same roof?"

Damn it.

Why does she have to be right?

Sending her away is the better option, but now that she's involved, I know my father won't leave her alone.

There's no corner on Earth she'll be safe in.

At least at the estate, I can keep an eye on her.

And do what? Play babysitter and ignore your responsibilities? Don't you think you've done enough damage? It's not too late to take this back. You can always claim she tricked you, and you found out she was working for your enemies.

I take one look at London's face and know I can't do that to her.

Condemning her by getting involved with her is one thing.

Marking her as a traitor is another, and as bad as my father is reacting now, throwing London under the bus to save myself and the empire is another.

You could set something up. Make it look like you punished her. Katia could help you come up with a fake ID and make sure she's settled somewhere far, far away.

It's a noble thing to do, but I can't bring myself to do it for the life of me.

Not even to make things easier.

Now that London has unlocked something in me I didn't even know existed, I can't shove it back in.

I won't.

Not even if it costs me everything I've worked hard to build.

I blink, and London is standing in front of me. Her expression is soft and open as she reaches for my hand. She laces her fingers through mine, and I pull her closer, the smell of her floral perfume intermingling with what we were doing, unfurling something in me.

I shouldn't be thinking that I can smell myself on her, or how it makes my blood turn molten.

There are a lot of things I shouldn't be doing when it comes to London.

When she wraps her arms around me, I'm startled to realize I can't remember the last time I've hugged someone. London's body melts against mine as she places her head in the crook of my neck. I squeeze my eyes shut and thread a hand through her hair to cup the back of her neck.

We stand there for the longest time, the air between us thick with emotion, everything building up within me.

You were right, Mom. Love does change everything.

With a frown, I pull away and cup her face in my hands. As London lifts her eyes to mine, I exhale. "You can still walk away."

London searches my face. "We already talked about this."

"That was before my father came. London, he… Mathew is a fucking *saint* next to him. My brother, he likes to gloat and rub it in your face. My father is a lot more… subtle in his approach, and he is meticulous."

London squeezes my hand, and her expression doesn't falter. "I can handle myself, and I'll be careful like you said."

The door to the room flies open, startling London. She glances over my shoulder, and I can tell by the tightening around her eyes that it's nothing good. Slowly, I shift, so London is half-shielded behind me.

Mathew lingers in the doorway, a bored expression on his face "Why is she still here?"

I release London's hand. "I should've known you'd try to have someone else clean up your mess."

He chuckles. "I'm giving you a chance to make this right. You know what our father is like, but I can convince him that even the best have lapses in judgment. For the right price of course."

I level my brother with a withering look. "Fuck off."

Mathew pushes himself off the wall, a smirk hovering on the edge of his lips. "I know she has her hooks in you, so I'm only going to say this once. Don't be stupid. For all we know, she could be working for the enemy. They probably sent her to stir up trouble and cause you to lose focus. I wouldn't say it's your fault, not really. Everyone knows you have a type."

I shoot my brother the dirtiest look I can muster and envision myself slamming him against the nearest wall.

It's not enough to quiet the roar in my ears.

Fucking weasel.

How far is he willing to go to get rid of me?

"As usual, you've proven that all you're good for us is lurking in the shadows and eavesdropping," I tell Mathew, my voice as hard as steel. "This doesn't concern you."

Mathew's grin grows, sending another wave of anger through me. "Anything to do with the family concerns me, *brother*."

I take a step in his direction, and satisfaction courses through me when I see Mathew's smug look falter.

He knows he can't take me without help.

"If you take one more step, you'll regret it."

Mathew's smile vanishes. "Fine. You have only yourself to blame for what comes next. Don't say I didn't warn you."

Then, he slinks off. Before he disappears, he tosses London a suggestive look, and a growl falls from my lips before I can stop it.

Once he's gone, I run a hand over my face and give London a quick look. She doesn't say anything when I unlace our fingers and leave the room. Katia appears as I leave, and a quick look passes between us before I round the corner and disappear. My father has his back turned to me when I find him in the study. He takes a sip of his drink, and I let the door click shut behind me and wait.

Taking care of betrayal, I can handle.

Storming an enemy warehouse, I know how to navigate.

Jack Payne is neither of those things.

He is something far worse, and I know that despite stepping back to allow me to run the empire, there's a reason our enemies still fear and respect him.

It's the same lethal calm he's turning on me now, and every alarm bell in my head is blaring.

What did you think was going to happen? Did you think he was going to welcome her into the family with open arms? Get a fucking grip, Mason. You know there's no way this ends well.

Silence settles over us.

After a long pause, he finally twists to face me, and I know the look on his face.

It's the one I used to bend over backward to avoid when I was little. The same one that reduces our enemies into blubbering messes.

I can't let him see how much she means to me, or he'll end us both.

Jack looks down at my arm and back up at my face. "It would be a pity to have to teach you a lesson, but it seems it's necessary. You've forgotten yourself."

I clench my hands into fists. "You handed me the reins, remember? And with everything else going on, I'm sure the last thing you want is for word to get out that we have trouble within our ranks."

He studies me. "You'd better be ready to back up your decisions."

I shrug and tense, every muscle coiled.

Do I really have what it takes to take my father on?

I like my odds in a one-on-one battle, but I know it won't be as simple as that. He's got men and women who are loyal to him and would come after me for a chance to curry favor with him. Having the upper hand in one battle isn't enough to end this. My mind races as I imagine all the ways this could spiral, and I wonder for the umpteenth time if this was our enemy's plan all along.

Maybe kidnapping London wasn't to spite me or make me find them another location.

Maybe it was about sitting back and watching as we tear ourselves from within, brick by painful brick.

Fucking bastards.

Why didn't I take care of them when I had the chance?

I should've put a bullet between their eyes, and now, I doubt I'll get close enough to try.

After I proved I could break into their warehouse, I'm sure they've shored up and gone underground, or heightened their defenses.

Getting to them again will be damn near impossible.

And you won't get the chance if you're too busy fighting with your dad. Think, Mason, and tread carefully. You've got an opportunity here.

Jack scoffs. "You always did have your mother's sentimental side. I thought we'd taken care of that. It seems I was mistaken."

"You're wrong about a lot of things."

Jack's eyes flash, making the hairs on the back of my neck rise. "Clearly. It's a good thing I have other options."

"I'm the only one for the job." My tone is cool and even. "You and I both know it's why you chose me."

My father chuckles humorlessly. "Is that what you've been telling yourself? That I can't find anyone else? I could walk out this door right now and find someone far more capable and a lot less troublesome."

I don't flinch. "Be my guest."

His eyes narrow further, but he says nothing.

For a tense moment, I wonder if I've pushed too far.

He did, after all, spend a good part of my childhood molding me into his image, and the better part of my adult years honing me as a weapon.

Even when my mom was alive, I still did as I was told, and as I stand here, searching my memory for the last time we were at odds, I'm coming up empty.

I have no idea if he's going to drag me out and make an example of me, or if he's going to step back into the shadows and let me ruin myself.

I don't know which option is worse.

How am I supposed to fight a war on all fronts?

Jack's eyes never leave my face. "Mathew was right to insist I come down here myself. This is far worse than I realized. Fuck her out of your system as many times as you want, and when you're done, you'd do well to remember who you are."

I press my lips into a thin line and say nothing.

Jack pushes back the leather chair. Then, he reaches for the glass decanter and pours himself a generous amount of whiskey. I watch the red and orange flames of the fire crackling and dancing, casting long shadows across the walls.

I stand a few feet from the door and watch my father carefully.

He eyes me over the rim of his glass. "When you came to me and begged me to put you in charge, I thought you had grown into the man I thought you could be. I had considered looking outside the family to ensure our future, but you insisted you were the only one for the job."

"I *am* the only one for the job."

Jack sets his glass down slowly and far more calmly than I expected. "The only job you're good for is fucking everything up. And for that cheap little plaything, no less."

I stiffen. "She's not cheap or a plaything."

Jack steps out from behind the desk and advances on me. "I don't fucking care what you want to call her, or what you want to do *with* her, but one of the first lessons I told you is to never let a woman distract you."

"I'm not distracted."

"The Fitzpatricks and Everetts are muscling us out of our business and forging alliances with other families." Jack continues as if he hasn't heard me. "I was under the impression the empire was in good hands, but you know how much I hate liars."

"I didn't lie. We've tripled our profit, and we've got people on the inside, manipulating the system in our—"

He slams me against the nearest wall before I can finish my sentence, baring his teeth at me. I hold myself still. After the little performance upstairs, I know he's trying to regain some of his dignity, some illusion of control.

For the sake of the Empire, I'll let him have it.

We both know he's been out of the game too long.

One strike, and I can send him sprawling back.

And one moment is all I need to prove my point and make him back off enough for me to do everything.

Still, I can't bring myself to do it.

Despite all the cruelty, and all the years he spent throwing me scraps, I don't want to hit him again.

Like it or not, Jack Payne is the reason I have the power I do today.

Because of him, I was given the chance to command fear and respect in every room I set foot in.

He's a bastard of a father, but that doesn't change what he's done for me.

Goddamn it.

"I knew you were all talk," Jack sneers. "All those years, and all those lessons I've taught you. What's the most important rule of survival?"

I shove him away, and he takes an uncertain step back. "Never let them see you falter."

His eyes move over me. "She's made you weak. I can smell it all over you. You are going to send her back to work in the club, and we're going to invite our enemies to see she means *nothing* to you. When sufficient time has passed, you can have her back, provided, of course, you keep her in check. I don't want to catch so much as a *whiff* of her name in our ranks."

I level him with a look. "And if I refuse?"

"You are a Payne." Jack's voice is steel. "You owe your allegiance and everything you are to this family. I am not in the habit of making an enemy out of flesh and blood, but don't push me. You have no idea what I'm capable of."

Except I do.

I walk a fine line between keeping our enemies in check and making sure my humanity survives.

My father, on the other hand, gave up any pretense of being human when we laid my mother to rest.

Sometimes, I wonder if he left more than his heart in the ground with her.

He reaches for his drink and takes a few sips. "You've worked hard to build everything up. It would be a shame to watch it all crumble."

He's right.

Whatever little crumbs of approval he's been throwing me, I've worked hard for. I've sweat, bled, and taken lives for the man in front of me, still as imposing and commanding despite the lines around his eyes and the smattering of silver in his hair.

You're still the little boy who wants his father to pat him on the head and tell him what a good job he's doing. You're always going to be that little boy, and you know it.

Do I have what it takes to go up against my father's wrath?

I'm not sure I want to.

As far as the empire is concerned, nothing has changed.

Except we both know it has.

The minute I went to save London against everyone's advice, I not only risked my father's wrath, I also painted a bright red target on my back and hers.

Michael and Lance were probably laughing at how easy it was to bait me.

Fucking assholes.

I can't afford to fight a war on all fronts, not even for London.

"And what if I told you it doesn't have to be one or the other?"

Jack raises an eyebrow and says nothing.

"You had Mom and the empire," I point out softly. "There's no reason I can't have both."

Jack's expression darkens again. "That woman is nothing like your mother, and I learned the hard way that I couldn't have both. Or have you forgotten the price we paid?"

"I could never forget."

I relive what happened to her every day, and the last promise I made while she drew her last breath, the light in her eyes growing dimmer.

Choosing London won't just affect me.

It'll impact my siblings, too, and I've spent too long trying to protect them from the chaos of this world to throw it all away now.

You made a promise to Mom to protect Olivia and Oliver, remember? Oliver, especially, would never survive this world, and you know Jack has been circling him like a shark for years, waiting for the moment to strike.

Now that Jack has found the chink in my armor, he won't let go easily.

Not unless I give him something worth far more than the satisfaction of watching London pay.

"I haven't forgotten my duty to the empire," I add in a stronger voice. "Or my duty to this family. I will make our enemies pay. I won't stop until I have them kneeling before us and begging for forgiveness."

Jack scoffs. "And how do you plan to do that when you're so busy playing house?"

"By cutting them off at the knees. Since they saw fit to go after something of mine, all bets are off. I can do whatever I want as retaliation, and they know it."

There's a hint of approval in his eyes. "Good to see she hasn't made you completely worthless. I was planning to pay Oliver a visit. It's high

15

time to bring him into the fold, don't you think?"

Ice settles into my veins. "There's no need. Mathew and I can handle things."

Even as a spineless coward, Oliver is one of the few things Mathew and I can agree on.

He needs to stay as far away from the family business as possible.

I don't want it to cost him his life like it did with our mom, and if that means my youngest brother hates me for what I've become, it's a small price to pay.

I will shoulder it without question to keep him safe, because that's what I promised my mother.

Jack shoots me a chilling smile. "Show me you can handle this, and I won't be forced to deal with your little problem."

I know he'd take pleasure in that.

London doesn't stand a chance against him or anyone else from my world.

And whose fault is it that she's in this mess to begin with, huh? You had to get attached.

I clear my throat and cross over to the desk. After pouring a drink, I raise the glass in his direction. "I'll make our enemies regret the day they crossed us. I'm gathering intel and preparing for a strike as we speak."

"I look forward to it," Jack says. "Now, tell me—"

The door to the office bursts open and Carlisle hurries in, blood caked on one side of his head. He skids to a halt, and his eyes widen when he sees Jack. Then, he bows his head.

"I'll come back later."

Jack crooks a finger in his direction. "Speak."

Carlisle lifts his eyes. "There's been an attack, sir. In one of the warehouses. We're working on getting it contained."

I slam down my glass. "What the fuck do you mean there's been an attack? How did this happen?"

And why did it have to happen with my father here?

Are they trying to send a message, to prove that even Jack Payne doesn't scare them anymore?

I glance in his direction, and I can already see his wheels turning. Whatever leeway he's giving me is contingent upon my success, and Carlisle bursting in here like a madman talking about an attack on one of our warehouses isn't helping.

Fucking Carlisle.

"You came highly recommended, Carlisle. Your father and brothers know how to keep their own," Jack adds. "I can see my son hasn't molded you the way he should have."

Without warning, my father whips out a gun and presses it to the side of Carlisle's temple.

His eyes dart between us. "All due respect, I didn't have any orders to be on the lookout for warehouse attacks—"

"All I hear are excuses," Jack snaps. I hear the click as he removes the safety, causing a muscle to tick in Carlisle's jaw. "Give me one good reason why I shouldn't put a bullet through your head."

I give Carlisle a meaningful look. "You heard my father. Talk."

Carlisle is a brute, but I chose him for a reason.

He is far less skilled and tactful than his brothers, but he was much more eager to prove himself.

I know he feels indebted to me for giving him a chance.

When push comes to shove, his loyalty won't be called into question.

Even now, he doesn't falter as he turns to Jack Payne, who moves the gun so that it's pointed at the center of his head. Carlisle faces the barrel unflinchingly, and I know it has less to do with fear and more to do with control.

The kind he's spent years honing.

The kind that could get a man like the great Jack Payne killed.

My right-hand man looks ready to rip into my father with his bare hands, but he's not stupid enough to take that risk when he knows I'll have to retaliate.

"I'll bring you their heads on a platter," Carlisle offers after a long pause. "And I'll send a clear message to their loved ones."

Jack pulls the gun away and pretends to examine it. "Things have gone to shit since I've been gone. It's a good thing I arranged to stay a while."

"Carlisle will make it right," I say without looking at him.

Jack unfastens a button on his jacket with one hand and uses the other to put his gun away. "Make yourself useful and bring the car around. Let's see what kind of mess my son has created now."

Carlisle nods tersely and exits the office.

On my way out, I spot Katia at the top of the stairs, her face smoothed into an impassive mask. She looks at Jack and then back at me. I jerk my head toward my bedroom, and she nods in return.

Outside, I duck into the car after my father and drum my fingers against my thighs. "I know where to hit them so it bleeds. I'll make sure they pay for this."

My father gives me a bored look when he looks up from his phone. "I'm sure you'll find a way to make sure this doesn't go unanswered."

"It won't."

We both know we can't start a war with our allies without cause.

Whatever tightrope they were walking, they gave me what I needed to blow them out of the water if the need arose, and I'm glad they did.

As far as my dad is concerned, it gives me a good excuse to get my hands dirty.

CHAPTER TWO

London

"What do you mean I'm not allowed to leave the room?"

Katia spares me a quick bored look before glancing away again. "I know you're not deaf, princess. You heard me."

I throw my hands up and scowl. "I'm not a princess."

"You're certainly getting treated like one, so if you want my advice—"

"I don't."

"—enjoy it while you can." Katia's bright eyes linger on me for a brief second. "It's not every day someone like you gets to enjoy these perks."

"What the hell is that supposed to mean?"

Katia steps into my field of vision, dressed in head-to-toe black, her dark hair twisted into a tight braid. "It means we both know you're not going to last, so do yourself a favor and milk it while you can."

I fold my arms over my chest. "I'm not that kind of woman."

"I don't care," Katia replies. "We're both stuck doing things we don't want to do."

"I want to talk to Mason."

"He's not here."

I step outside the door and raise my voice. "I'll go and find him then."

Katia swings back to me and raises an eyebrow. "I wouldn't try and leave this floor if I were you."

"Are you threatening me?"

Katia throws her head back and laughs, and it makes me want to throw something at her. "When I threaten you, you'll know."

I take another step, and Katia moves quickly, her eyes flashing in warning. "You can't stop me."

"How much you want to bet on that, Princess?"

I narrow my eyes further. "Stop calling me that."

The corner of Katia's mouth twitches with amusement. "Why would I do that?"

"Because it's fucking annoying."

Katia's eyebrow climbs. "Mason's little pet has a potty mouth. Maybe you're not that spineless after all."

"Fuck you."

Katia laughs again, and it makes me clench my hands into fists. "I know you aren't a fan, but trust me, I'm the best option you have right now."

I picture Mason's father towering over us, the unmistakable promise of pain and rage in his eyes, and it makes me pause.

"He's not going to lay a finger on me."

Katia gives me a look that borders on pity. "I wouldn't underestimate Jack Payne if I were you. He's not the kind of man you want to piss off."

"Too late," I say.

Katia steps toward me. "He's nothing like Mason. Whatever you think you know is nothing compared to what happens in the shadows."

I stare at her. "I'm well aware of that."

Being in the man's presence has left my stomach in cold, hard knots.

I've been trying to shake the feeling for the past hour, but the harder I try, the more worried I become.

I know I need to be strong, especially if I'm going to survive in this world, but I have no idea how to do that when there's danger around every corner.

Without Mason around, who will have my back?

Katia might be on watch duty now, but I know she won't hesitate to turn the other cheek.

All Mason's father needs is to promise her Mason on a silver platter, and she won't hesitate to throw me to the wolves.

I almost wish Mason had left me to fend for myself.

I've heard enough whispers about Katia to know she's not the kind of woman you want to mess with.

You wanted to be a part of Mason's world, remember? You can't get cold feet at the first sign of trouble.

Mason needs someone smart and strong who can hold her own.

But I can't stop thinking back to the ice in his voice when he left me in the room, and the dismissive look he gave me.

It reminds me a little too much of the ruthless man who made me sign the contract.

Don't forget that he's still there, lurking underneath the man you're trying to pull out.

Katia gives me another infuriating smile, prompting me to step back into the room and slam the door in her face.

When she laughs, I toss her a dirty look through the wood and begin to pace.

I know I don't have a lot of options, especially when Mason's father could be waiting for me to be left vulnerable.

He looks like the kind of man who would slice my throat without batting an eye and then drag me out to be made an example of.

How is Mason even related to him? He can't be his father.

A sliver of fear winds its way up my spine as I wonder just how much trouble Mason is in, and how I can help if I'm being kept under lock and key.

How am I supposed to prove myself if I'm not being given the chance?

How can I keep Mason's father from driving a wedge between us?

Jack Payne has only been here a few hours, and he's already pierced our little bubble and shoved us, unceremoniously, into the real world.

I shudder to think of how far he'll go to get rid of me.

As soon as the thought crosses my mind, I reach for the phone Mason left behind and dial my father's number from memory. My heart is pounding and my palms are sweating as I wait for him to pick up. The entire time, I'm imagining a car driving by the house and opening fire on anyone in the vicinity.

I picture my father knifed in his driveway, calling out to me as he bleeds out.

Then I see them drag him here, binding his hands and legs as he is forced to his knees for my mistakes.

He's the reason you're in this mess, remember? And he made a deal with Mason's enemies in exchange for you. He doesn't deserve your pity or your worry.

The phone stops ringing, and it slides out of my hands, shame burning a hole in the pit of my stomach.

My father might be the reason I'm in this mess, and a main factor behind me getting kidnapped, but I know I'm far from blameless.

I didn't walk away when I had the chance, and a part of me knows I should have.

What right do I have to blame him when I've only made things worse?

I told myself I was doing this for the right reasons, and here I am, unable to walk away because I've seen a glimpse of the man behind the mask.

The kind Miss Deveroux insists isn't worth saving.

But she's wrong. She has to be.

I haven't given up my freedom and normal life for a lie.

I scoop the phone off the floor and dial my father again. I continue to pace the room. When I reach the window, I push the curtain and look out at the afternoon sun, casting a golden glow over the Mason estate.

"Come on, Dad." My heart is pounding uneasily in my chest. "Pick up, please."

It stops ringing again, and I throw it against the nearest wall. It bounces off the wall and falls to the floor. I rake my hands through my hair, cross over to where the phone fell, and pick it up again.

Noah answers on the fifth ring, his voice gruff and thick with sleep.

I clear my throat. "It's me. I know I have no right to call—"

"You have a lot of fucking nerve, London." Noah's voice rises in anger. "After what you put me through, what the hell do you want? You want to get me tied up and beat again?"

I wince and squeeze my eyes shut. "That wasn't my fault."

"That doesn't help," Noah snaps, and I hear a door open and shut in the background. "Nothing you can say or do is going to help."

"I know that." My voice grows smaller. "It was never meant to get this complicated, okay? I'm sorry, Noah. I didn't want to hurt you. I still care about you."

"Look, I am glad it worked out. At least Mason is good for something, but come on." Each of Noah's words drips with exhaustion and confusion. "He's using you, London. I don't know why you can't see that. You need to snap out of it. Even if you won't do it for me, at least do it for your parents. It's not too late."

I grip the phone tighter and count backward from five. "I'm not calling to talk about him. I need you to check on my father."

Noah doesn't reply.

"I know you don't owe me anything, but he loved—*loves* you like a son, and you told me you've always thought of him as a father. I can't tell you what's happening, but he could... he could be in danger."

Noah exhales. "Why are you coming to me with this? Shouldn't you go to Mason?"

"I'm coming to you, not him. I know this is shit, and I know I screwed up, but I don't think he should have to pay the price. I know you agree with me."

Noah's voice is quieter when he answers, and it makes my chest tighten. "You know I do."

I turn my back on the window and squeeze my eyes shut. "I know I don't have the right to ask, but I'm doing it anyway. You told me I once meant the world to you. *Please.*"

I hate that he's hearing the crack in my voice, but Noah and I have been through a lot.

I refuse to believe that the man I spent all of those years with is gone.

He's still somewhere inside, buried underneath layers of hurt and betrayal.

Noah is still a good person, and I'm choosing to believe he'll do the right thing.

Mason is not going to be happy about this. Then again, he's not here, so how you choose to defend your family is up to you, not him.

Noah lets out a deep sigh. "What am I supposed to tell him? We haven't exactly spoken since those thugs tied us up."

I press two fingers to my temples. "You can tell him that I'm worried. I don't know if that'll help…"

"Lo…." The longing in his voice is a punch to the gut. "I know I was hard on you when I first found out about the deal you made, but it's not too late. We can still have the life we wanted. I'm willing to overlook the past few months. Just come home, please."

I want to grab the lifeline he's offering with both hands.

Noah is offering me stability and normalcy, and a life I can already picture, right down to the matching Christmas outfits.

But sometime in the past few months, it stopped being what I wanted.

Mason is all I can think of, and all I can imagine for myself.

He's everything I never knew I wanted, and I ache at the thought of leaving him, even if it means having to look over my shoulder all the time.

24

It's a small price to pay for the chance to be with Mason, even if I am scared to admit it.

There's a lump in my throat when I answer. "I'm sorry, Noah."

There is only silence on the other end.

I pull the phone away from my ear, check it, and put it back again. I clear my throat and speak again but in a quieter voice. "Are you there?"

"I don't know what you want me to say."

I ignore the pounding in my ears. "We've been through a lot together. I don't want it to end this way."

Noah sighs. "It's hard for me to believe when you say that, London. Especially because of how easily you're throwing everything away and turning your back on us. I thought I knew you."

"You did know me," I whisper. "But it turns out I didn't know myself all that well."

"I'll check on your father, but don't call and ask for any more favors." Noah's voice trails off toward the end. "I'd say I hope it works out for you, but I wouldn't mean it."

My breath hitches in my throat. "Noah—"

"Goodbye, London."

The line goes dead, and I'm left with an ache in my stomach and bile in my throat. For a long time, I stand in the middle of the room, listening to the dull thudding in my ears. Finally, I leave the phone on the bed and stumble into the bathroom. After switching on the lights, I grip the sink and avoid looking at myself in the mirror.

I cup my hands together and splash cold water on my face.

When I pat myself dry, I tell myself that I'm doing the right thing and that ripping the band-aid off now is better than down the line.

Noah will thank me when he has a woman who loves him with everything in her and has no doubts.

Someday, he'll be surrounded by children and a doting wife, and I'll be nothing more than a passing memory.

Still, it's hard to ignore the twinge in my chest as I step out of the bathroom and cross over to the door. I yank it open, and Katia is standing there, examining her nails. I snatch a leather jacket from behind the door and shove my arms into it, taking comfort in Mason's familiar spicy cologne. Then, I square my shoulders and close the door behind me. Katia doesn't look up as she steps in front of me, blocking the hallway.

"Look, we both know you don't want to do this."

Katia's expression gives nothing away. "No?"

"Come on. I'm not an idiot, and I'm not blind. I know there's history between you and Mason."

Katia says nothing.

"Without me here, you have a chance at winning him back. All you have to do is look the other way while I sneak out."

Katia's eyebrows draw together. "He gave you a chance to leave, and you didn't, and now that he's stuck out his neck and risked everything else he's worked hard for you want to leave?"

"I just want to check on my family."

Katia's expression is hard and resolute. "That's not an option."

"I'm not asking," I tell her through gritted teeth. "You can either get out of my way or tackle me. Either way, I'm going."

Katia makes a sweeping hand gesture.

My heart is in my throat as I take one step forward and then another. When I'm far enough away to breathe a sigh of relief, I tell myself that I'm doing the right thing. Although the last thing I want is to cause more trouble for Mason, I can't sit around and let the guilt eat away at me.

I have to see my dad.

I need to do something.

I round the corner to find Katia by my side. Wordlessly, she stands in front of me, an intimidating figure in her dark ensemble. I give her an incredulous look and try to sidestep her, but she throws out an arm. Frowning, I shove it away, but it comes right back, and she pushes me backward.

I stumble and scowl. "What the hell? I thought we had an agreement."

"I am not going to betray Mason." Katia lifts her chin. "I owe him so much more than my life. He asked me to keep you safe, and if I have to do it against your will, I won't hesitate."

"I can sneak back in before anyone knows I'm gone."

Katia snorts and doesn't release her grip on my arm.

I try to pry off her fingers, but she's got a vise-like grip.

I struggle in earnest. Katia doesn't break a sweat when I throw both arms around her and try to pull her to the ground. Then, she abruptly releases me, and I fall onto my back, staring up at her in a daze. A moment later, I push myself up to my feet, but Katia has me flat on my back again, and spots break out in my vision.

"I thought you were supposed to keep me safe." I pant and give her a withering look. "Let me go, Katia. I have to check on my family. It's not like you care. You'd be doing yourself a favor."

"Your family is fine," Katia says. "You, on the other hand, have a habit of getting yourself in trouble, and if the look on your face is anything to go by, you'll thank me later."

"I doubt that." I gingerly get back to my feet.

After Katia knocks me down a third time, I use the back of my hand to wipe the sweat from my face and launch myself at her middle. Her mouth forms a surprised O, and her slow blink gives me a surge of satisfaction as we fall to the floor with a thud.

Adrenaline rushes through me as we roll on the carpet until I get the upper hand.

Katia shifts, and my punch lands on her side, sending a sharp pain up my arm.

Red-hot anger pumps through me as she throws me off, and I stumble to my feet.

Without warning, she kicks my feet out from under me and climbs on top of me. Then, she pins my arms behind my back, so I'm left staring at the wall and breathing through my mouth.

"Stop fighting me." Katia's voice is laced with a warning. "I told Mason I'd keep you safe, but even I have my limits."

I stop struggling. "Go ahead, then. Give it your best shot."

Katia releases me and dusts herself off. "I don't think so."

My eyes widen in disbelief as I watch her turn her back on me and leave. Several moments pass before I storm back to the room in defeat. A short while later, there's a knock, and I wrench the door open, an angry retort on my lips, only to find a silver tray of food. After a quick glance around the hallway, I take it in and leave it on the table in the middle of the room. Then I wander over to the window and peek through the curtains at the smattering of clouds gathering on the horizon.

What have I gotten myself into?

I'm still turning the idea over in my head when the door opens, and Mason is there, wearing a button-down shirt and a pressed pair of pants, with his hair disheveled. He glances from the uneaten plate of food to me and back again before strolling into the room.

"I heard you tried to give Katia a run for her money."

I scowl. "It's not funny."

Mason stops in front of me, and there's very little of the warmth I saw earlier in the day. "I'm not laughing."

I hold his gaze. "I'm not a prisoner, Mason. You can't keep me locked up."

"You're not locked up. You can go anywhere in the house—"

"Provided I stay out of your father's way and let Katia shadow me, you mean," I interrupt hotly. "How is that not being locked up?"

"You're not in a cage, London." Mason's eyes narrow. "It could be a lot worse."

"I'm aware of that, but I didn't agree to stay just so you could keep me in a cage while you go out and take care of business."

Mason stares at me and says nothing.

"We're supposed to be in this together. Don't shut me out. Let me be there for you."

"You know what would help? It would help if you did what you're told."

I throw my hands in the air and glare at him. "I'm not a disobedient child who needs to be told what to do and where to go. I'm your… I don't know what I am, but I didn't agree to this."

Mason's eyes glitter, and my pulse skitters. "You wanted to be a part of my world, London. This is part of the territory. While I'm off taking care of business, as you put it, I need to know that you're not causing problems."

"Checking on my family won't cause problems."

"It is when it involves leaving the house, when I told you it isn't safe, and when our enemies are circling. Or do you feel like getting kidnapped again?"

"Isn't that what Katia is for?"

Mason barks out a laugh. "Katia is good, but there's only so much she can do. I have to focus, and I can't do that if I'm worrying about you."

"I don't need you to worry about me."

Mason cups my face in his hands, and his eyes are stormy as they search mine. "I always worry about you. Since the moment I laid eyes on you, I've had an urge to protect you and keep you safe, even when I didn't understand it."

I lace my fingers through his and don't look away. "I'm fine, Mason. Like you said, you have bigger problems to worry about. Is that why you ran off earlier?"

He gives me a curt nod but doesn't release my chin.

I exhale. "Tell me."

Mason searches my face and then drops his hand. "There was an attack on one of the warehouses. They're trying to send a message."

"The same allies who kidnapped me?"

"There might be another player in the mix, but we're not sure yet."

I frown. "What makes you think that?"

"It doesn't add up." Mason backs up, leaving a few more inches of space between us. "I'll get to the bottom of it. In the meantime, you need to let Katia do her job."

I sigh. "I'm not one of your employees."

Mason turns to face me, and a suggestive smirk plays on his lips. "Trust me, I'm well aware of that. You'll never be able to work for me again. You'll cause too much of a riot."

"You're changing the subject."

Mason takes another step, and I don't move. "You don't seem to mind."

"I do. I just don't think now is the time to push it."

Mason covers the distance between us and crushes me to him. "You're right. I've got far better uses for our time."

I tilt my head back to look up at him. "We're not done talking about this."

Mason lowers his head. "I've got other ways to convince you. Sooner or later, you'll see things my way."

The breath leaves my body as he hoists me over his shoulders and slaps my ass.

He sets me down on the bed, silencing my protest with a searing hot kiss that makes me forget what I wanted to say.

CHAPTER THREE

Mason

"Are you going to need backup?"

Katia stiffens and levels me with a look. "I can handle her."

I down the rest of my drink. "At least she'll keep you entertained."

Katia mutters something unintelligible. I step out from behind the desk and stroll past her. In the doorway, I pause to spare her a glance over my shoulder. Katia turns to face me, and a long moment passes when neither of us says anything.

Her face softens. "It's bad, isn't it? The warehouse thing?"

"Not as bad as not knowing who the enemy is."

Katia's expression darkens. "I should be out there, hunting people down, and making them give up information. I'm more useful that way."

I shake my head. "I need you here."

"To protect her." There is an undercurrent of anger in Katia's voice. "She doesn't even appreciate what you're doing for her. Yesterday, she tried to get me to look the other way by telling me that I want to."

"She wanted to get to her family."

Katia's eyes move steadily over my face. "I think you need to keep an eye on her and make sure you know where her loyalties lie."

I raise an eyebrow. "Are you questioning her loyalty or her motives?"

"Both," Katia replies without preamble. "You already know how I feel about this whole thing."

"I'm aware," I reply tightly. "You're also aware of how important she is to me. I'm trusting you to keep her safe. Is that a problem?"

I know it's selfish of me to force this on her, but other than Carlisle, she's the only one I trust with London.

In the short amount of time I've known London, she's come to mean a lot to me, and I can't be fighting a war on the front lines while worrying about her.

Keeping her safe isn't negotiable.

But if Katia can't be the one to do that, I'll find someone else who can.

Katia's expression turns impassive again as she straightens her back. "I know how to do my job."

I give her another meaningful look. "Good. Get it done then."

With that, I spin on my heel and stride out of the office. My father is waiting by the front door in a crisp custom Armani suit, not a hair out of place. He glances up when he sees me, and his eyes move over me steadily, leaving a trail of unease in his wake.

He hasn't stopped judging me since setting foot on the estate, and I know that's not going to change anytime soon.

Between keeping an eye on my father's men and keeping his ear to the ground to figure out what's happening with our allies, Carlisle has his hands full.

I wonder if my father knows that having him here only makes things worse.

I shouldn't add worrying about my father's motives to my long list of things to do, but I also know I can't turn my back on him for one second.

Father or not, Jack Payne won't hesitate to take me down if I get in his way, and there are plenty of ways to make people suffer.

He doesn't have to stick a knife in my heart to make me bleed.

Especially now that he's seen me with London.

As soon as we get in the car, he slams the door shut and turns to me. "There are better uses for the assassin's time."

"Katia has other things to do." I pause to pour myself a drink. "You don't need to worry about her. We should discuss strategy."

Jack drums his fingers against his thigh and looks out the window. "There is no strategy to discuss. The plan is clear. We make it clear that your lapse in judgment has no impact on our continued partnership, nor should it."

I eye him over the rim of the glass and grip it tighter. "I'd prefer it if you didn't refer to London as a lapse in judgment."

He makes a vague hand gesture. "When it comes to the empire, certain decisions need to be made for the greater good."

I take a long sip of the drink, and it burns a path down my throat. "They still need to be taught a lesson."

Jack turns to me. "I have every intention of making sure they do, but we're still going to the meeting to smooth some ruffled feathers. Better to have them in our corner."

I take another sip and sit up straighter. "What are you planning?"

"That's not your concern," Jack replies coldly. "All you need to do is make sure to look apologetic for taking down the people at that abandoned house."

I don't like being kept in the dark, especially not where the empire is concerned, but I know better than to push.

Whatever punishment my father has for me, there are far worse things than sidelining me when it comes to business matters.

He's toying with you. Taking charge of the meeting is child's play compared to what he can do, and you know it.

Still, I'm relieved London isn't tied up in a basement somewhere at his mercy.

I set the glass down with a little more force than necessary. "I will not apologize for protecting my own."

33

Jack gives me a bored look. "We have nothing further to discuss."

"We're not done talking."

He raps on the roof of the car, and it slides to a stop. The door opens, and he steps out. Then, I hurry after him, the protest dying on my lips when I see the group of men standing with their backs erect and guns bulging under their shirts.

What has my father agreed to?

I catch up to my father at the top of the stairs of the abandoned building, and he gives me a slow and meaningful look. Together, we step inside, our men sliding into place. Every nerve is heightened as a damp smell wafts up my nostrils and makes my stomach tighten.

The entryway is dark, and our footsteps are soundless against the carpet.

The lights flicker on, and I blink as the room shifts into focus, revealing an airy space with a high ceiling, big windows, and a wooden table in the center. I recognize some of the men in attendance, and my mind races.

Michael Everett and Lance Fitzpatrick are standing on the other side of the room, engaged in quiet conversation.

As if sensing my eyes on them, they glance up.

I don't realize I've taken a step forward until my father puts a hand on my arm.

He leans sideways and pretends to brush lint off my shirt, his voice dangerously low. "Either keep yourself in check, or I'll have someone do it for you."

I tear my eyes from Michael's face and look at my father. "You're just going to let what he did to the warehouse stand? What happened to making our enemies pay?"

A muscle ticks in Jack's jaw. "We have nothing on them, so unless you have the men to launch a war, I'd suggest you keep your fucking mouth shut."

As much as I hate to admit it, he's right.

My father didn't come out on top in a world as dangerous as ours by making baseless accusations and reckless decisions. While he might have operated in the shadows more in recent years, underneath the cool, composed exterior is a man who knows how to be slow, methodical, and precise.

And he will surgically remove me before allowing me to ruin everything he's built.

Again, I remind myself that being his son won't spare me from his wrath if I don't keep my anger in check.

The last thing either of us needs is to be seen bickering in full view of our enemies.

It's exactly why he's making a power move like this here, where he knows I'm less likely to push back.

Conniving son of a bitch is showing our enemies he can bring me to heel.

It's humiliating in all of the right ways, but I have to give him props.

There's more than one way to strip a man of his defenses, and Jack is nothing if not creative.

At least he hasn't chosen violence.

Another long moment passes before he leaves my side and goes to greet some of the people in attendance. Someone pulls out a chair with a screech, and he offers them a bored look. Then he sits down, and the air in the room changes. Several pairs of eyes are on me as I join him at the table and avoid looking at Michael.

I'm determined not to let him get under my skin.

That's probably what he's hoping for. Don't give him the satisfaction of seeing you lose your shit in front of all these people. You know how hard it is to exhibit strength once they've caught a whiff of weakness.

I've worked too hard to be the weak link.

I school my features into careful neutrality as Michael pulls out a chair opposite me, and after a brief hesitation, Lance does the same. One by one, everyone sits, and the room quiets. Slowly, my father leans forward, and every eye in the room is on him as he clears his throat.

"I know you all know why we're here." His voice is even and controlled. "We've all been allies for a long time, and that partnership has served us well. Look how well we're all doing."

A murmur of agreement rises.

Jack links his fingers together and looks over the room slowly. "I know there have been some disagreements, but with everything happening, I wanted to remind you all of how much easier it is to work together."

Another murmur rises.

Lance shoots me a look. My face gives nothing away until he begins to squirm. Eventually, he shifts and looks away, sweat breaking out on his forehead.

I'm going to make you bleed, you little rat. If you thought things were bad before, you haven't even come close to what I'm capable of doing. Just wait until I can get my hands on you.

One way or another, Lance and Michael are going to find themselves alone with me, and by the time I'm done with them, they're going to wish they'd stayed hidden.

"… the terms of our partnership have been in place for a while, but they are open to renegotiation under the right circumstances," Jack finishes with another look around the room. "Let it not be said that we are unreasonable."

Silence meets his statement.

Jack's expression hardens as he pushes back his chair to stand. "Let me be perfectly clear that I will find out who was behind the attack on our warehouse and the incident with the girl, and I'll make the person responsible wish for death."

Behind closed doors, he might give me grief about London, but I know he won't let anyone sense the tension in our ranks.

I don't know whether to be relieved or worried.

Jack leans against the table, and his expression turns to stone. "Make no mistake that while we value our continued partnership, any attack on a Payne is an attack on all of us."

I don't miss the brief panic that crosses Michael's features.

My father clears his throat. "Now that that has been settled, there is the matter of the location that was promised. We have several lined up."

"This isn't about the location anymore."

Jack looks at Michael, who doesn't flinch. "I understand there's been some reservations about how things have been handled—"

"Especially by your son," someone mutters from next to me.

I wheel in their direction, and a balding man with a protruding belly sinks into his seat and avoids my glare. "Anyone who has a problem with me can speak up directly."

Jack places a hand on my shoulder and keeps it there. "We all know my son has done well in leading us into a better and more profitable future. His reputation speaks for itself."

"You mentioned renegotiating the terms of our partnership."

My father removes his hand and looks at Lorenzo Moretti, whose silver hair glistens underneath the fluorescent lights. His dark, rheumy eyes give nothing away, but I know he's assessing everyone in the room and determining the best way to get himself to the top.

I've heard the rumors of how he's spilled blood within his ranks to maintain power, and how he's silenced even his family.

Lorenzo Moretti isn't a man to be trifled with, and something about being in the same room always makes me uneasy.

Lorenzo is a man who enjoys the kill, a formidable enemy and ally, and a man I'd rather not piss off.

"We can renegotiate, yes," Jack replies. "Though I was given to understand that the purpose of today's meeting was something else entirely."

I begin to wonder if we are here to smooth some ruffled feathers.

Or are our allies abandoning ship?

Fuck.

How did everything spiral out of control so quickly, and how had I not noticed the cracks and fissures?

Had I been so focused on getting London that I'd missed the signs?

You need to make this right. Whether or not you meant to set a chain of events in motion is beside the point. This is your fuckup.

I stand, feeling every eye in the room sizing me up. "We're prepared to offer several of our prime locations in the interest of maintaining the continued partnership."

It's the one thing my father and I agreed on.

For the sake of the empire….

Michael Everett laughs. "I never knew it would be that easy to make a Payne yield."

A flash of anger surges through me. "Most of this mess is your fault. I suggest you sit the fuck down."

Michael remains defiant. "You going to storm my office again?"

I have my gun out before the words leave his lips.

The room grows tense as I step out from behind the table and cross over to Michael. The men who are positioned against the wall step forward, their hands on their guns. Without looking over, I know Carlisle, and a few of our men have formed a barrier between them and Michael.

I'm tempted to end him then and there, consequences be damned.

"Nothing to say?" I press the gun to his temple. "Here I thought you'd finally stopped hiding behind your name like a coward."

Michael's face remains calm and impassive. "At least one of us has."

I lower my voice. "I should've taken care of you when I had the chance."

One corner of Michael's mouth twitches upward. "And who's to blame for that?"

"I won't make that mistake again." I fire a warning shot into the wall behind him, and all hell breaks loose.

Someone tackles me from behind, and we fall forward with a thud. I throw my weight back, the back of my head connecting with something solid. There's a loud grunt, and the arms around my waist go slack. When I spin around to face my attacker, all I see is red.

I pull my hand back and land a solid punch to the stomach.

My nameless attacker grunts again and launches himself at me.

We crash into a nearby chair, and the wood digs into my back.

Then we're rolling on the floor, and there's the metallic taste of blood in my mouth. I growl as fury burns through me. I'm battling to gain the upper hand when I hear another gunshot, and a bullet clips my hair and lodges itself into someone behind me.

The smell of sweat and gunpowder fills the air.

And all I can think about is getting my hands on Michael Everett.

Once I finally have the upper hand on my assailant—a blond, muscled man with a tattoo peeking out from under his shirt—I force myself to my feet. My heart is pounding in my ears, and every inch of me is alert and on edge as I glance around the room to see my father locked in a heated exchange with Moretti.

There's a flicker of movement to my right, and Michael lunges for me, his fingers closed around the grip of a gun. Carlisle materializes out of nowhere and knocks the gun from Michael's hand. It only slows his advance long enough for me to throw myself at his middle.

I place one leg on either side of Michael and land a solid punch to his face.

I throw another punch and hear the satisfying crunch of bone as blood sprays from his nose. Somewhere in the chaos, I hear Lance's voice. Then I see him stumble toward us, cradling his arm to his chest with his eyes wide. Carlisle tackles Lance, and I turn back to Michael, whose blood stains my knuckles and my shirt.

Slowly, I lift him by the scruff of his neck, so we are eye level. "Not so smug now are you, you piece of shit?"

Michael pulls back his lips and offers me a bloody grin. "It's a little pathetic how easy it is to rile you up. The great Mason Payne. I expected more."

I shake Michael hard enough to make his teeth rattle. "In case you haven't noticed, asshole, you're on the receiving end of my anger, so you might want to reconsider your strategy."

"Yeah?" Michael says. "Look at what you've done with only a little bit of goading."

I slam Michael against the nearest wall. Then I place my arm against his chest, restricting his air supply. "I maintain what I said. You didn't think this through, and I will enjoy watching you bleed out. Once I'm done with you, I'll move on to Lance. Maybe I'll even go find that sister of yours."

Michael tilts his head and spits out a mouthful of blood. "Do whatever the fuck you want, Payne. You and I both know that you're not in control anymore. After today, everyone else will know it, too."

I punch Michael in the stomach, and he doesn't flinch. "What the fuck is that supposed to mean?"

Michael leans in so close that I can smell the alcohol on his breath. "It's going to be so fucking good to watch you burn. Knowing you'll take the Payne empire down with you is just a bonus."

I throw another punch and pin Michael again. "That's not going to happen."

Michael raises an eyebrow and uses his free hand to gesture vaguely. "Look around you. It's already begun."

A sick feeling spreads through my stomach as I glance away to take in the carnage around me. A few people are bleeding out on the floors, and many others are cradling their arms or hobbling on their feet. My father has Moretti pinned against the other side of a table, and they're still circling each other, but I know that look on his face.

He's out for blood.

All his tightly wound control is about to snap and unleash the side of him everyone whispers about, and it's all my fault.

Shit.

I've played right into Michael's hands.

My mind whirs to assess the damage. I see Carlisle holding Lance and a few others at gunpoint, and my stomach sinks. The real purpose of the meeting wasn't to mend fences and make amends. The only reason we were lured here is to tear each other limb from limb.

I have a sinking feeling this whole fiasco was orchestrated by Michael and Lance, with the full support of their families.

The Fitzpatricks and Everetts aren't just hoping to strong-arm us into submission.

They won't even give us the courtesy of engaging in a direct war, not with how we outmaneuver and outgun them.

Fuck, fuck, fuck. This was set up to make sure everyone sees you spiral.

I've enabled them to thin out the herd.

After today, anyone who survives won't want to side with the Paynes once word spreads of how quickly the meeting got out of hand, and how we instigated it.

I swing back to Michael with a growl. "This isn't over."

Michael laughs. "Isn't it?"

I release him, and he crumples to the floor. "Get up, you pathetic son of a bitch. The only way you're going to win this is by having other people do your dirty work. You can't even take me on. I wonder what your father thinks of the coward he raised."

Michael snarls and throws himself at me.

We spin in a half-circle, and I throw another punch in Michael's side.

There's a flash of silver as he whips a knife out and swipes at me.

He slashes me across the side, and as I watch a few drops of blood stain the hardwood floor beneath me, something in me snaps. I growl and throw myself at Michael again. Only this time, I throw punch after punch and don't hold back.

His face is a bloody pulp, but it's not enough.

I keep seeing London's face when I saved her. Each blow feels better than the last, but it doesn't quiet the roaring in my ears.

After days of quiet planning and thinking, it feels good to take my anger out in its rightful place.

I have no idea how long I stay on top of Michael, but my knuckles are raw and throbbing when a pair of arms wrap around me and yank me back. I twist to shove the person away, but stop short when I realize it's my father. He glances past me and gives me a pointed look when I look back again.

Sirens slice through the air in the distance, forcing several people to their feet.

Everyone glances around, and no one says anything.

"I'd suggest we all leave while we can. Our friends in blue can't overlook this." Jack's tone is calm and even. "We can deal with this later."

There's a chorus of grumbles and shoving as the sirens move closer.

Then, we race out the back door with Carlisle and a few others on our heels.

We throw ourselves into the black car at the end of the alley as it peels away from the curb. I take out a napkin to wipe my hands and exhale sharply. Once we're far enough away, Jack takes his gun out and points it at me.

My heart skips a beat. "Another repeat of earlier? Aren't you getting tired of—"

Using the butt of his gun, he strikes the side of my head, sending a sharp slice of pain through me and cutting off the rest of my sentence. I glare at him through narrowed eyes as he draws his hand back and strikes me again, hard enough to make stars break out in my vision.

When he draws back a third time, I move my hands to stop him.

His eyes widen.

Jack flexes his fingers and moves closer. "I should take care of you myself. Since you've been such a liability."

I don't release his hand. "You won't."

"You're not untouchable."

I look at his hand and then back at his face. "Neither are you."

His nostrils flare, and his expression contorts into one of malice. "A man doesn't make empty threats."

I release his hand and roll my shoulders. "Who said anything about them being empty?"

"You have more of your mother in you than I realized." Jack turns to the compartment in the center and pulls out a decanter. He pours himself a generous amount of amber liquid and glances out the window. His gun remains in his lap and is pointed at me.

I stare at the shadows and lines of his face, and a pang of longing hits me.

Suddenly, I'm a little boy hiding in the hallway and listening to my parents fight. When I blink, I'm nine years old again, and I'm sitting at the top of the stairs, my feet dangling from the banister. My parents are standing opposite each other in the foyer. My mom's eyes are red-rimmed, and her voice is thick with emotion.

My father's face is silhouetted in darkness, and I remember how cold and emotionless his voice was. That night, as I sat there, holding my breath while I watched them, my mother pleaded for her family as tears streamed down her face. I blink again, but this time, I see my father's impassive face reminding her of what she signed up for.

Though he had softened a bit and done his best to keep her away from the more dangerous aspects of his life, my father had never lied to her.

She had always known, or at least suspected, the kind of man she married, the one she had joined her life to, and no amount of love and wishful thinking would change that.

My mom probably thought she would be enough to save him.

The wrought-iron gates shudder open, welcoming us to the sprawling Mason estate, and I push away the memory. While having London around has made me think more about my mother and the sacrifices she made, I also don't like that it brings up the feelings I've kept hidden under lock and key.

I keep replaying the promise I made myself as a lonely but determined nine-year-old.

One who told himself he wouldn't put a woman through what my mother went through.

I had grown up believing love was a weakness, a tool to be used against you, and something that crippled your defenses.

But as the car pulls to a stop outside the estate, and I catch a glimpse of London's outline through the upstairs curtain, I realize how wrong I was. When London comes downstairs to greet me, stopping at the last step and glancing uncertainly at my father, I take her into my arms.

Her familiar, comforting smell, like soap and freesia, washes over me.

I made that promise long before I knew London, when the thought of her was easy to dismiss as unrealistic.

Now that I have her in my arms and my life, I know I can't let her go.

If I've doomed us both by not being able to do the right thing, then so be it.

CHAPTER FOUR

London

I run my finger over the small, angry welt on his brow and frown. "I don't understand why he hit you."

Mason shrugs. "Because he can."

I exhale and reach for the first-aid kit next to me. Slowly, I dip a piece of cotton in some disinfectant. I hold my breath and press it against his wound, but Mason doesn't react.

Knowing he's surrounded by ruthless and cunning enemies is one thing.

Seeing how volatile his father is leaves a bad taste in my mouth and an ache in my chest.

I was up half the night tossing and turning as Mason slept soundly next to me.

How can he be okay with having a father like that?

Based on everything you know about him, does it seem like he has a choice? He probably doesn't know any better.

It makes me miss my father with a fierceness that surprises me.

In spite of everything he's put me through, I want to put it all behind me.

I want to believe we can still be in each other's lives even if he's turned his back on me.

He hasn't abandoned you for good. He wouldn't.

A hard knot settles in the center of my stomach as I turn the thought over and over in my head, growing sadder and sadder with each passing moment.

I miss my father's Sunday morning pancake-and-egg breakfast while we sat in the backyard, talking about everything. I miss camping under the stars and him showing me how to trace the constellations. I miss family movie night when the three of us built a fort in the living room and hid inside and watched movies until the sun came up.

Tears spring to my eyes as it dawns on me how much I've left behind, and how much has been taken from me.

The longer I stay with Mason, the more I realize how little I know of his world.

Mason takes my hand in his. "It's not as bad as it looks. I'm fine."

I sniff and continue cleaning the wound. "I know."

Mason's fingers close around my wrist, and he tugs me onto his lap. Then he cups my face in his hands and waits for me to look at him. "What's wrong?"

I avoid his gaze. "Nothing."

"I thought we agreed we wouldn't lie to each other," Mason murmurs. "You can tell me."

I meet his eyes. "Can I?"

"You've got the heart of a lion. The way you stand up for yourself, and the fact that you're still here... you can tell me anything."

I blow out a breath. "There's nowhere else I'd rather be."

Mason found his way into my heart against all odds and repeated warnings, and I have no one to blame but myself for not heeding the signs when I could have.

Mason's hands drop to my waist, and he presses his forehead to mine. "It won't always be this hard. This life, I mean, and missing how everything could've been."

My chest tightens at the ache in his voice. "I hope you're right."

Mason moves back to look at me, and the soft glimmer in his eyes makes me melt. "I know this isn't the life you imagined for yourself, but I will do my damnedest to make sure you know how lucky I am to have you."

Someone knocks on the door, and Mason scowls. Slowly, and with a great deal of reluctance, he sets me on my feet and moves to the door. He blocks the view, so I can't see who's there, but I recognize Carlisle's voice. There's a whispered conversation, and then Mason turns around, holding a gun in his hand.

He crosses over to me. "Do you know how to use a gun?"

I shake my head.

"Katia will teach you." Mason shows me how to turn the safety on before handing it to me, the cold steel feeling strange against my flesh. "This is just in case you need to use it. You shouldn't ever have to."

I hold it awkwardly away from my body. "Right."

Mason runs a hand over his face. "I'm going to take a shower and go. There's a lot of damage control that has to be done after what happened."

Gingerly, I set the gun on the nightstand and turn to face him. "You said you've all had a partnership for years. I'm sure one bad night won't change that."

At least I hope it won't.

If what Mason said is true, the people who kidnapped me are the least of our problems.

There are a lot more dangerous allies lurking in the shadows, and everything is held together by a thread.

One spark is all it'll take to set the whole thing on fire, and I can't understand why anyone would risk getting caught in the crosshairs.

Mason pulls me into his arms for a rough kiss.

I thread my fingers through his hair, but before I can deepen the kiss, he releases me and steps into the shower. He peels off his clothes and shoots me a heated look. After a brief hesitation, I glance at the gun on the nightstand. Then I hurry in after him, the bathroom already steaming up.

Mason doesn't waste any time when I slide the curtain behind me and turn to face him.

Sometime later, when he leaves, I perch on the edge of the bed and link my fingers together. I toss glances at the gun and ignore the hammering in my chest. Finally, I pry an empty drawer open and shove it there.

Katia is in her usual spot against the door when I come out, only this time she's admiring her blade, bright sunlight dancing off the smooth silver. She doesn't say anything when I step in front of her and clear my throat.

"I want to go check on my dad, and before you say no again, I have a proposition."

She doesn't say anything.

"I will try not to make it hard for you to keep me safe at the house and anywhere else I have to go if you let me go."

Katia snorts. "I don't care if you make it hard for me."

My heart jumps into my throat. "You can come with me to see my dad."

"Why would I want to do that?"

"So you can tell Mason that you tried to stop me, and just in case things go sideways."

Katia stops examining her blade to look at me. "So far, I don't see how any of this benefits me."

I throw my hands up. "I'll put in a good word for you with Mason."

Katia curls her lips in disgust, and I resist the urge to step back. "Let's get something clear here, Barbie. I don't need you to put in a good word for me. I've been around a lot longer, and I'll be around long after this whole thing blows over and you're either collateral damage or on the run for your life."

Her words feel like I've been stabbed through the heart.

But I know she's not wrong about my odds of staying, assuming I even survive Mason's cutthroat world long enough to run for the hills.

Katia is a constant in his life, and I will always wonder if he'll go back to her out of familiarity when things get too hard and too emotional with me.

Being with Katia doesn't endanger the empire or put him on the receiving end of his father's wrath.

What did you think was going to happen? Mason warned you this wasn't the kind of world you came from, and you stayed anyway.

Every survival instinct I have tells me I can still leave and forge a life for myself away from this, but the thought of leaving Mason doesn't sit well with me.

It's unthinkable.

I can't bear the thought of being away from him, even if it means the path ahead is anything but smooth.

I swallow past the lump in my throat. "Maybe you're right, and maybe you're not. Either way, agreeing will make your job a little easier. At the very least, you can earn brownie points with Mason when you tell him I've snuck out."

"Fine," Katia says. "If it'll get me out of this conversation, let's go."

"What, just like that?"

Katia shoots me a withering look. "Do you want me to change my mind? Let's go."

With that, she steps to the side and makes a sweeping hand gesture. Together, we descend the stairs and past rows of closed doors, past the kitchen staff, and to a door in the back. She sticks her head out first, then motions to me.

Katia waves to some of the men posted on guard, and they barely spare me a glance.

When we get into a silver sedan, parked next to a row of other expensive-looking cars in the driveway, I hold my breath and stare at the gates. Slowly, they creak to life, and we drive through. Katia keeps both eyes on the road and ignores me as the world outside rushes past in a blur of shapes and colors. At the traffic light, she taps her fingers against her thighs impatiently.

I press my face against the glass and try to calm my racing heart.

I know Katia isn't doing this out of kindness.

If anything, she's probably hoping I get kidnapped again, so she can be rid of me, but I'm still thankful to her for agreeing.

I've never gone this long without seeing my dad, and not being able to talk to him drives me crazy.

Regardless of how things are between us, I need him to know that I love him.

A lump rises in my throat as I focus on the car next to us and see an older man with salt-and-pepper hair tapping the wheel. He turns to the little girl next to him, and the two exchange a smile full of love and mischief. My heart aches as I look away and blink back the tears.

Katia huffs. "Get a grip. There are people out there who don't have families."

"I know."

She shoots me a look. "You have no idea how lucky you are."

I swallow past the lump in my throat and shove my hair out of my eyes. "I liked it better when you were threatening to kick my ass."

Katia scoffs. "Yeah, well, I'm only giving you this advice because if you start crying, I'll have to throw you out of the car."

I cross my arms over my chest and give her a scowl.

The traffic light turns green. She presses down on the gas, and the car lurches forward with a screech. Katia says nothing as we take a series of turns, venturing deeper into the city.

Eventually, the tall metal buildings give way to two story Victorians with manicured lawns and gravel driveways. Katia stops in front of my parents' house. She turns off the engine and turns to face me with a frown. Her eyes sweep over my face, and the gleam in her eyes leaves a bad taste in my mouth. I stiffen and wait for the next blow, but it never comes.

"Don't make me drag your dead body out of there," Katia says with a dismissive wave. "I don't want to get blood on the leather seats."

I shove the door open and glance down both sides of the empty street. "I'll try not to bleed out."

"Just don't do it in the car," Katia fires back before looking away from me.

She's scanning the area for threats, and although I know it's irrational and ridiculous to be grateful to her, I'm still glad she's around.

Asking Katia to teach me to shoot is out of the question when she'd probably be happy to watch me shoot myself.

Anything to keep her hands clean and get you out of the way. You need to keep a close eye on her.

I force myself to place one foot in front of the other until I'm standing outside the small gate at the front lawn. The lock gives way with a rickety sound as I push it open and keep moving. Suddenly, I see myself taking the same path on my way home from school, pigtails brushing my shoulders. Then, I see myself on my first trip home from college, huffing and panting as I drag a laundry bag behind me.

At the top of the stairs, I pause and inhale.

It feels like another lifetime.

I'm still lost in the memory of how it felt to come home anytime when the door swings open, revealing my father with a thin sheen of sweat on his forehead. The blood drains from his face when he sees me, and his mouth falls open. His mouth moves a few times, a muscle working in his jaw, but no sound comes out.

After what feels like forever, he lowers the book he's holding.

"It's good to see you, Dad."

"What are you doing here?"

51

"I tried calling you, but you weren't picking up."

He stares at me a moment longer before looking past me. "Your bodyguard looks like she'd rather be sharpening her knives."

"That's pretty accurate except for the part where she's my bodyguard. She's more like... never mind."

I don't know how to explain Katia.

He gives me another indecipherable look. "We were told you were safe, but you shouldn't be here."

I ignore the twinge in my chest and move toward him. "Told by whom? You know what, never mind. It doesn't matter. I've been trying to get in touch with you for days. We shouldn't talk outside. Can we go inside?"

Wordlessly, he spins and hurries inside.

I follow him, pausing to secure the lock in place. In the study, bright afternoon light is pouring in, jazz music is playing through the laptop, and books are in piles scattered all over the floor. He reaches for a towel draped over the back of his brown leather armchair and wipes his face.

I finish scanning the room. "I know that things got ugly the last time we were here, and I don't care what kind of deal you had to cut to save yourself and the house. I know it was because—"

"Deal?"

I take a deep breath. "I know you made a deal with the men who held you hostage. They told you to lure me here, and in exchange, they'd get you out of the deal with Mason. Right?"

His eyebrows knit together, but his face gives nothing else away. "I don't know what you're talking about."

"It's okay, Dad. I'm not mad. I know you probably felt like it was the only thing to do. Maybe they told you they'd release me or something when they were done..."

"Release you? What the hell are you talking about?"

I pause. "You couldn't have known how dangerous it was going to be, so even though I'm angry and hurt…it's not why I'm here. Things are… different now. I'm doing my best to protect you, but it might take some time."

He holds a hand up and frowns. "Hold on a second. I don't know what you think you know, but I didn't make any deal with those… *monsters* who broke in. Noah dropped by to check on me when they ambushed us. They told me to call you; that's it."

I stare at him for a long moment.

I want to believe he's telling me the truth.

My father takes my hands in his. "Sweetheart, I know I was hard on you before…it was a lot to take in, but whatever you're involved in and whoever you're messed up with, we can figure it out together. I've been looking into hiring us security, and I've got a friend in France who's willing to host us for a few months."

I search his face. "What are you talking about?"

He squeezes my hand and drops his voice. "It's not safe here anymore. I can see that now. I think the house is being watched, but it doesn't matter. Noah's put me in touch with a security firm his dad recommends. I'm sure they can take care of things while we get our affairs in order. You don't need to do this anymore."

One by one, I pry my fingers away, and my stomach clenches. "I can't leave."

"Whatever he has on you, he won't be able to do anything about it when you're on another continent."

I open my mouth and snap it shut again. "He probably has allies everywhere, but that's not the point. It's not… it's not about the deal I made anymore, Dad."

His eyes tighten around the edges. "He's got his hooks in you, doesn't he? Noah told me about him. What does he have on you, London?"

I clear my throat. "He doesn't have anything on me."

He frowns. "I don't know what kind of mess you've gotten yourself into, but we can figure this out."

"I know you want to help me, but I don't want you to," I reply. "I'm telling you the truth. I know it's hard to understand, and I'm sorry you got dragged into all this. I never wanted it to come to this."

My father frowns and opens his mouth.

He's interrupted by the sound of a loud bang, and I throw myself at him before I know what's happening. We crash against his mahogany desk, knocking a few things to the ground. My heart is pounding as I cover his body with mine and squeeze my eyes shut. When the door to the study bursts open, fear snakes its way up my back and settles around my chest.

The arms around my waist don't slacken. "It's me."

I squirm against Katia's hold, my heart still racing. "What are you doing? Let me go."

She releases me abruptly, and I turn to my dad. He's scrambling to his feet, blood dripping from a gash on the side of his head. There's an acid taste in my mouth as I lead him to the armchair by the fireplace. When I can't find anything to use, I rip off a piece of my shirt and press the fabric against his head to staunch the bleeding.

The metallic smell of blood fills my nostrils.

"How long do we have before they get in here? Can you get us out the back?"

Katia is by the window, studying the world outside. "I already checked the perimeter. There's nothing out there."

I press the fabric harder against my dad's wound, and he winces. "What do you mean there's nothing out there?"

Katia lets the curtain slide back into place and whirls to face me. "Looks like it was an old car."

I'm on my feet. "You want to bet our lives on that?"

Katia levels me with a look. "I've been doing this for a long time, Barbie, so I'd watch my mouth if I were you. Since Mason doesn't know we're here, it would be unfortunate if you were to have an accident on the way back."

I ignore the chill racing up my spine. "If you were going to do something, you would've done it already."

Katia takes a menacing step in my direction. "Are you sure about that?"

My stomach lurches, but I steel myself. "We need to get my dad to a hospital. He needs to get checked out."

"We need to get back to the estate in case it wasn't a car," Katia hisses, sparing him a quick look. "It's just a scratch, and a hospital will attract too much attention."

"I'm not leaving until I'm sure he's safe."

Katia throws her head back and spouts something in a language I don't recognize. She lowers her head and looks at me. "He's got ten minutes to pack, and then we'll drop him off at the nearest friend's house. If he's not ready by then, I am dragging you back whether you like it or not."

"We'll be ready."

Katia looks at my father and then back at me. "Clock's ticking, Barbie."

With one last glance at my father, she strides out of the room. For a long moment, I can't breathe, and my mind is racing out of control. Upstairs, in the master bedroom, my father stands in the doorway, pressing the torn piece of cloth to the side of his head.

"What are you doing?"

I throw his suitcase onto the bed and move to the closet. Blindly, I throw clothes into it. "Didn't you hear what Katia said? We have to get you out of here because it's not safe."

"It's my house," he replies. "I'm not going anywhere. Whoever is trying to come after me, I can handle it."

"No, you can't, Dad. I'm not saying this to be cruel, but you're either walking out of here, or I'll make Katia drag you out."

His eyes bulge. "You wouldn't."

"I don't think you want to test me."

I don't care if it humiliates him because at least he'll be alive to hate me.

My father presses his mouth into a thin white line. "I don't like the person you're becoming."

"I know, but I'm keeping us alive."

I spend the next few minutes throwing a few more things into the suitcase. Finally, I drag the suitcase down the stairs. My father trudges down the stairs behind me, carrying an old box with him. Wordlessly, he brushes past me and toward the front door.

Katia is waiting for us on the porch.

She yanks the bag out of my hand, and I fish out my keys. I cast one last look around the darkened house, years of memories playing out in my mind's eye. My chest is tight with emotion as I slam the door shut and turn the lock. After giving it a firm tug, I hurry down the stairs and try not to sprint to the car.

In the rearview mirror, I sneak glances at my dad, who has his hands folded in his lap and a strained look on his face. Katia maneuvers the car with one hand on the steering wheel, and the other on the dagger at her waist. Once we reach our destination, she swerves and turns into a dark alley.

I barely have time to hug my dad before she hauls him out.

I'm halfway out of the car when Katia emerges from the shadows and gets into the driver's side. I wait until she's far enough away before I take a deep breath. "You're going to tell me that I should keep my distance for a while."

Katia doesn't look at me. "You already know you should, but you insisted on going anyway."

"If I want you to help me see someone, a friend, will you help me do that?"

Katia shoots me a withering look. "What about this day has made you feel like I'm willing to do things for you? I'm supposed to protect you, not run errands and arrange secret meetings, Blondie."

I curl my hands into fists. "Miss Deveroux can help make arrangements for my family. I'm not going to let them fend for themselves. She works at the club, so she's got to be trustworthy, and she helped me when I first started working—"

Katia holds a hand up. "I don't need the history. I know who she is."

"So, you'll help me?"

Katia grips the steering wheel tighter and swerves suddenly, knocking me back against the seat. Before I can reply, she presses down on the gas, and the tires screech in response, the seatbelt digging painfully into my chest. I glance in my side mirror and see a few black unmarked SUVs gaining on us.

"It wasn't an engine banging, was it?"

"Lucky for you, I don't feel like dying this way," Katia says in a low voice. "Hang on tight."

She winds down an unpredictable path, but each time I think we've lost them, they appear on our tail until we're on a bridge. Suddenly, they break off and drive on either side of us. Katia curses and presses down harder on the gas pedal, but it doesn't help.

The two vehicles slam into us, and the impact sends shock waves through my system.

I can barely see past the spots dancing in my field of vision, and when they hit us again, I taste blood in my mouth.

Katia tries to muscle her way out, but the car skids out of control.

We're pushed off the bridge and free-falling through the skies. Fear slams into me as I squeeze my eyes shut and send up a quick prayer. We crash against the water, and the breath is knocked out of me. I fumble with my seatbelt, managing to wrench it off. The assassin next to me is still wrestling with hers, panic etched onto her face.

Water rushes into the car from all sides.

I inhale a deep mouthful of air before my head submerges.

Darkness envelops me as my lungs grow tight, and my last thought is of Mason and the war he's going to wage on my behalf.

I gasp and sputter as I kick for the surface, my eyes still burning.

With trembling fingers, I shove my hair from my eyes and spot a figure bobbing to the surface nearby. My muscles ache as I swim toward Katia and place an arm around her shoulders. I'm grunting and panting as I drag her to the shore. We barely make it as my muscles give out, and I collapse next to her.

I hear sirens in the distance as I stare up at the dying evening light.

My lungs are on fire as I lay there, trying to muster up the energy to move, and vaguely aware of Katia dry-heaving next to me.

Please don't let this be for nothing. I don't want to die here. I have to get back to Mason.

CHAPTER FIVE

Mason

"We're not there yet."

Jack Payne glances at me from the corner of the room. He sips from the glass in his hand, his face giving nothing away. "You've risked everything we've worked for, and now, you refuse to do what needs to be done where your siblings are involved."

I school my features into neutrality. "Oliver and Olivia are better off where they are."

Being far away has its advantages.

I always have eyes and ears on them, but there's a difference between keeping an eye on things from a distance and bringing them back into the circle.

Oliver, especially, isn't cut out for this kind of life, and I'll be damned if I go back on my promise to my mother.

"I'm doubling security on our warehouses, and I'll call in a few favors to make sure they're both safe. I've got this under control," I say.

"Like you had the security issue under control?" my father shoots back.

I curl my hands into fists and swallow back the retort.

I should've anticipated the ramifications of going after London and exposing what she means to me, but I didn't care at the time.

Now, it's coming back to bite me in the ass.

It's not like you didn't try to fight your feelings for her, but you saw how pointless it was. You can't turn your back on her now.

Everyone has targets on their back because of me, and although I can't escape the guilt and disgust that swirl through me at the realization, I know there's no room for anything but cold precision.

Except everything is snowballing out of control far faster than I anticipated.

The Fitzpatricks and Everetts might not have planned our self-destruction, but they put the dominoes in place, and now, they just have to sit back and watch everything crumble.

For the umpteenth time, I wonder how long they've been planning it all.

If it wasn't for the deal I made with London to work at my club to pay off her dad's debts, and spare his diner, I'm sure they would've found another way to screw us over, and I'm waiting to have enough evidence to bury them.

"… with the Thayers," Jack finishes. "You'll need to be present, of course."

I straighten my back. "I thought the Thayers were one of the lesser families we have an alliance with."

Jack steps away from the window. "They are, but we can't afford to be picky about allies now. Thatcher Thayer and I have already been in touch, and you'll be present at the next meeting."

I nod.

"There's talk of strengthening our alliance, and I get the feeling the old man is talking about forming something a lot more secure."

"We can offer them shares in our more prominent businesses."

Jack crosses over to me. His eyes drift to the scar above my eye. "You've been spending too much time at the club, boy. Not all deals are business-related."

I stare at him. "You're talking about marriage."

His dark eyes watch me over the rim of the glass, and he purses his lips. "It's good to see you haven't forgotten everything I've taught you. Yes, the Thayers have wanted to ally themselves with one of the bigger families, and right now, our interests are aligned."

"I will not marry a Thayer."

Jack cocks his head. "No? Perhaps I'll offer up Oliver's hand instead."

"He has nothing to do with this," I reply a little too quickly.

"No, but for the good of the family, maybe your brother will do what needs to be done."

Someone coughs in the background, and I glance over at Mathew, who has been standing so still that I almost forgot he was there.

"What about Mathew?"

My twin shoots me a withering look.

"I have other plans for him," Jack replies. "You, on the other hand, have a mess to clean up, and I won't always be around to give you solutions."

"I will not marry a Thayer," I repeat.

Even though I know it's the smart move.

Anyone who isn't London holds no interest for me, and if it means having to find other ways to secure an alliance, I'll figure something out.

"Marry the Thayer and keep your plaything on the side." Jack's voice is sharp and cold. "You know it's the best way to clean up your mess."

"I will not marry someone I can't be faithful to. Even I have standards, and I'm pretty sure screwing with a Thayer after marriage won't help matters."

Jack sets his glass on a table. "Mathew, do you want to remind your brother of what's at stake?"

Mathew rolls up his sleeves. "With pleasure."

"This is between me and him," I say without looking at Mathew. "Unless you want to reset your shoulder again, back the fuck off."

Mathew advances on me, the gleam in his eyes growing more pronounced in the dim light of the room. "Unlike you, I know how to take orders."

I ignore him and look to my father, who is behind my desk, pouring himself another drink. "This is fucking ridiculous. Stop him before he hurts himself."

Jack rummages through the mini fridge behind him and adds a few ice cubes to the glass. Slowly, he brings the glass to his lips and looks at me. "For years, you had me convinced that you were the right choice. Meanwhile, your brother has been by my side every step of the way, and he isn't afraid to get his hands dirty."

"While he's been by your side, I've been the one expanding the empire and making us more money than any of us know what to do with."

Mathew lunges at me. I easily sidestep him, and he skids to a halt. Then he spins and levels me with a look of hatred. I move away again, but this time, Mathew throws out a curled fist, missing me by a few inches.

I have him pinned against the wall before he finishes growling. "You're never going to be like me, Mathew, so you might as well give up."

Mathew and I both know our father has been pitting us against each other since we were old enough to hold guns, solely for his amusement. Long ago, I tried to convince myself it was to toughen us up, but I've long since accepted the fact that our father is just a piece of work.

Why am I letting either of them get under my skin?

I haven't spent the past few years building my tolerance to their bullshit just to falter now.

I release Mathew and take a few steps back. "I am not doing this."

Mathew spits at the ground at my feet and bares his teeth at me. "She's made you weak. The old you would've done more than pin me to the wall, and you know it."

I flash my brother a warning look. "That can still be arranged."

He takes another swipe at me and misses, and I punch him in the side.

Mathew's eyes narrow into slits. When he launches himself at me again, I pin him to the floor.

Carlisle bursts into the room as Mathew bucks and thrashes to throw me off. "I'm sorry to interrupt, but there's something you need to know."

Jack heaves a sigh and sets his glass down. "Doesn't anyone in this place know anything about manners? I can see my son isn't the only one who's going to be taught a lesson."

I look at Carlisle. "This had better be good."

"Katia and London are missing."

I'm on my feet in front of Carlisle before I know what I'm doing. "What do you mean they're missing?"

Carlisle clears his throat. "It seems they snuck off the property. We're not sure where yet, but we have reason to believe it was to see London's father—"

I let out a litany of curse words.

"—unfortunately, they were run off a bridge on the way back," Carlisle finishes.

The blood roars in my ears as fear and disbelief settle in my chest. "What the fuck did you just say?"

"The car crashed into the water."

I shove Carlisle against the wall, my vision turning red. "How the hell did they make it off the estate?"

I want to pummel whoever's responsible for this mess, but this has Katia written all over it.

My assassin is the only person capable of coming and going as she pleases.

Maybe my father was right, and I've given her too much leeway.

In all the years I've known her, I've never seen Katia waver, and I admire London for pulling off the impossible. I wrench the door open and stride out, ignoring my father and brother calling out to me.

There's a loud cacophony of voices and a blur of faces and colors as

I stride out the front door, my only thought of London and her safety. A moment later, a black car pulls up outside the main door, and I jump into the back. I'm barking out orders, but nothing I say makes any sense. Carlisle sits in the passenger seat, and I hear something about a search party, but I'm not listening.

All I can picture is London's face frozen in terror as water fills the space around her.

I'm going to wring Katia's neck.

How in the hell did she let this happen?

With a growl, I press the button for the partition between us, silencing the rest of Carlisle's sentence. I clench and unclench my hands as a headache builds and pounds in the back of my skull. When I squeeze my eyes shut again, it's not London's face I see in my mind. Instead, I see my mother's pale face lying on a king-sized bed.

I imagine a window open in the master bedroom, and a warm breeze wafting in while tiny particles of light dance on hardwood floors. Then I hear my mother's voice, and I feel her small and cool fingers close around mine, her bright eyes begging me to save Oliver. I swallow, and I can still see the desperation and fear written in her eyes.

I blink again, and my mother's face turns to London's, and even though her mouth is moving, no words are being formed.

With a little more force than necessary, I pour myself a generous amount of whiskey and take a long sip. I glance out the window and take another sip, hoping it'll chase away my guilt and confusion.

I have to keep my promise to my mother, but I have no idea how to do that without endangering London.

How am I supposed to navigate this mess?

With a scowl, I shove the car door open without waiting for the car to stop. Carlisle falls into step behind me as I peer over the side of the bridge and into the rushing water. A tow truck nearby is pulling the car from the wreckage. There's a bitter taste in my mouth as I make my way under the bridge, my heart sputtering when I spot the trail of blood.

I stop breathing as I kneel on the bank in front of the water and study the scene. Slowly, I rise to my feet when I spot two pairs of footsteps, and the air whooshes back into my lungs. A heartbeat later, I turn to face Carlisle.

London isn't dead. She can't be.

"Spread out and find them," I say calmly. "Bring me whoever is responsible for this. I'm going to nail their goddamn balls to the wall."

Carlisle doesn't say anything.

"What the fuck are you waiting for?"

It takes every ounce of self-control I have not to take my anger out on everyone around me. I examine the blood stains and keep myself from imagining the worst. My men are still searching the area when Carlisle returns, dragging someone by their neck. The man's hands are bound behind his back, and there's a bag draped over his head.

I pull it off, and other than a few scrapes and bruises, our prisoner is intact.

As his eyes meet mine, I punch him in the stomach. Carlisle yanks his head back, and tears spring to the man's eyes, but he says nothing. I punch him over and over, the crunch like music to my ears. On the fifth punch, the man lets out a wheeze, and it clears some of the bloodlust darkening my vision. My knuckles are raw, and the man has blood streaming down the sides of his face, but it does nothing to quell my anger.

"He was found surveying the area nearby," Carlisle tells me, in a low voice. "He's one of the Fitzpatrick men. I've seen him a few times. There was a car too, but it drove off. Some of my men are chasing it now."

I turn back to the man and give him a cruel smile. "You can either talk now or later. It doesn't make a damn difference to me. I'm going to have my fun anyway."

The prisoner stares at me through his good eye, blood already caking on the side of his mouth. "I'm not going to say a damn thing."

"I was going to give you a quick death," I say, "but since you've offered nothing useful, I'm going to let my men have their fun with you once I'm done."

Carlisle hands me a pair of pliers. After pausing to peel off my jacket and hand it to one of the men, I kneel. Then I dig my nails into the man's cheeks, eliciting a howl of pain. He squirms and tries to scramble back, but Carlisle holds him firmly in place as I lift one of the man's fingers and study it. In the background, my right hand man makes a few phone calls then returns to whisper something in my ear.

"It's amazing how much pain a human can endure," I say as I stroke his finger. I wait for another moment and smile. "You can bring a man to the brink of death over and over, but you know what really drives the point home? Giving a man hope and then snatching it away. Say, for example, that little family you have tucked away in the suburbs. Good call, making sure they have a different last name."

The color drains from his face as he sucks in a harsh breath. "You're bluffing."

My smile grows wider. "You sure you want to take that chance? Your twins already hate you. Imagine their last thought being of how their father failed them."

His eyes tighten, and he yanks on his restraints. "They have nothing to do with this. Leave them alone."

I position the pliers over his fingernail and tug. "Don't they? You went after my family tonight, so it's only fair that I return the favor."

Thin beads of sweat roll down his face as I tug harder.

I keep my eyes fixed on his face as I yank out the fingernail, and he throws his head back, a hiss of pain slicing through the night air. When he tilts his head to look at me, I see fear and know I'm close to breaking him.

I'll do whatever needs to be done to bring London home.

"I will rip you apart and leave you bleeding," I tell him. "You'll beg me to end your life. If that doesn't work, your family will learn about consequences the hard way."

With that, I rise to my feet and motion to Carlisle.

He hands me a large leather bag, and I open it and peruse my options. Underneath the pale light of the moon, I know the prisoner is studying the tools and wondering how far he can take this before he breaks. I roll my shoulders and reach for a small, silver chainsaw.

I hold it up to the light and hear the man swallow. "Let's try this again, shall we?"

***

Carlisle and another man drag the man's inert body as I watch, the smell of blood filling my nostrils. Once they disappear, I return to scanning the area as my hope grows fainter. Little by little, my men clear out until only Carlisle and I are left.

I'm still reviewing my options as Carlisle drives us home for a debrief.

I'm not giving up, but I need some time to think where it's safe.

Leaving the estate means I'm exposed, and there's too many eyes and ears everywhere for me to do what needs to be done.

I'm going to find London, no matter how long it takes.

The wrought-iron gates open, and I do a double-take when I see London on the front steps, her hair matted, and her wet clothes clinging to her. She stands as the car stops. I also see Katia in the shadows with her left arm in a sling and a cut down the side of her face. She doesn't flinch when I give her a withering look before crushing London to me.

She's warm and solid and real, but it doesn't dull the roaring in my ears.

My chest aches as I linger for a moment longer, needing to make sure she doesn't disappear.

Relief and frustration pump steadily through me as I draw back to look at her, hungrily drinking her in.

Half of me wants to lock her away forever, and the other half wants to keep her chained to my side.

London is going to be the death of me, I'm sure of it.

"It's good to see you, too," London says. "I thought it would be better if I waited for you out here."

I tuck her into my side and turn to Katia. "I'll deal with you later."

"Don't take it out on her. I forced her—"

I silence London with one look. She snaps her mouth shut, and I half-drag, half-carry her into the house, past my irate-looking father and my disgruntled brother in the foyer. Upstairs, I throw the door to my master room open and motion to London. She reluctantly steps in and turns to face me.

The door clicks shut, and I say nothing as I peel off my jacket and throw it onto a chair. London stares at me, myriad emotions dancing across her face. After a long pause, she clears her throat.

"I know what you're going to say."

"Do you?"

She nods. "You're going to rip me a new one for sneaking off the estate when you told me not to, and for endangering Katia's life. But you knew I wanted to check on my dad, and that he wasn't answering his phone."

I remain silent.

"I got in touch with Noah and asked him to check in, but I wasn't sure he'd do it because of how we left things…"

"I see."

London drops her hands to her sides. "Don't look at me like that. I didn't have a choice. I tried to talk to you about this, but you wouldn't listen, and then you distracted me."

I raise an eyebrow. "So, you thought it would be a good idea to sneak out with Katia, knowing full well that my enemies are lurking around every corner? You're right. That was a far better option. How did that work out for you?"

London winces. "I figured I was as safe with Katia out there as I am in here. I didn't know they were going to run us off the bridge—"

"How did you make it back here?"

London blinks. "We hitchhiked. Well, I did most of the talking. Katia was a little out of it. She hit her head pretty hard. She should see a doctor."

I curl my hands into fists at my side. "So not only did you sneak out, but you also asked a stranger to bring you back? Did it not occur to you that it might've been a ploy to get past the Mason estate?"

I can't tell whether I want to shake some sense into her or hold her to me and never let go.

"Well, when you put it like that, I—"

"You, what? You had good intentions? You made sure they didn't drop you off at the front gate? Tell me, London, which part of the plan did you think through? Because from where I'm standing, the whole thing was fucking stupid and dangerous, and I should punish you right now for what you did."

London's eyes flash. "Okay, I know I screwed up, but what would you have done if you were me? You were off doing God knows what, and I had to make sure my family was safe. You didn't honestly expect me to sit around, did you? That's why you had Katia watching me."

I cover the distance between us and level London with a look that would've had my enemies cowering. "I thought you had enough goddamn sense to figure out that Katia was meant to protect you from... uncertainties within, not drag her off on a suicide mission. I should lock you up and take away the key."

London's mouth falls open. "You wouldn't."

I rake my hands through my hair and scowl. "Today is not the day to test me. Did anything else happen I need to know about?"

London looks away, a furrow appearing between her brows. When she looks back at me, her expression is pained.

IVY BLACK AND RAVEN SCOTT

"When we were at my dad's house, there was a sound like a gunshot. Katia told me it was an old car backfiring, but I don't think that was true."

I let out a stream of curse words. "Is there anyone else you'd like to announce your presence to? Why don't I just march you over to my enemies myself? Save us the time and hassle."

London scowls. "I made sure my dad is safe. You can be pissed all you want, but I'm not going to apologize for that."

"You will."

"I will not," London counters hotly. "It doesn't matter what you do."

This stubborn, infuriating woman is going to be the death of me.

"I want to renegotiate the terms of my contract."

I frown. "Excuse me?"

"I want to extend the terms of my contract in exchange for money to get my family to safety. You can do that, right? Arrange for them to start over somewhere safe."

I stare at her in disbelief. "The contract is no longer valid."

London's face falls. "I have nothing else to bargain with, but I'm sure I can pay you back. I just need to—"

"Shut the fuck up, London. This is no time to bring up the contract, and you don't need to barter for money."

London's eyebrows draw together. "I don't?"

"Take off your shirt."

London's eyes bulge, and she takes an involuntary step backward. "You can't be serious."

"Take off your shirt," I repeat. "Now."

Her fingers move to the buttons of her shirt. As it falls to the floor, I push her onto the bed. Then I lower myself onto the floor and reach for her mud-caked shoes. After throwing them over my shoulders, my hands move slowly to unfasten the button of her jeans. London's breath hitches in her throat as she stares at me.

Wordlessly, she tilts her hips and allows me to slide the jeans off the remainder of the way.

When she's in her bra and underwear, I stand up and step into the bathroom.

London gives me a confused look when I return and kneel in front of her to run a wet towel over her skin. A sigh falls from her lips as I take my time, cleaning every inch of her skin until she's covered in goosebumps. As I reach her stomach, she swallows, and her fingers move to the back of my head to thread themselves through my hair.

A tingle races up my spine as I place one arm on either side of her and wait for her to look at me.

"If you want money, all you have to do is ask. You're not under contract anymore."

"Oh."

I lean forward and brush my lips against hers. She sighs and melts against me. When she runs her tongue along my lower lip, I growl and plunge my tongue into her mouth. As we fall backward onto the bed, my hands move to her arms, pinning them over her head.

London whimpers when I stop kissing her, her eyes half-closed. "What are you doing?"

"Look at me," I say, in a whisper-soft voice.

London's eyes flutter open, and the hungry look she gives me almost makes me abandon all reason.

"You are not under contract," I repeat in a stronger voice. "You are here because you choose to be. I will give you money, but if you sneak out again, there will be consequences."

"Like what? You'll handcuff me to the bed?"

I hold both hands in a vise-like grip and rub myself against her. "That's not a bad idea. I know you're used to a different life and having independence. I'm not trying to take that away, but if you want to be a part of this world... *my* world, changes have to be made."

London nods slowly. "Okay."

I lower my head and pepper her neck with hot, open-mouthed kisses. She wriggles against me, and it sends another jolt of desire through me. "I am not going to apologize, either. I do what I have to do to keep you safe. If you wanted something different, you shouldn't have stayed."

London shakes her head. "I only want you."

I release her hands, stand up, and lean over the bed. After pulling out a pair of handcuffs, I let them dangle from my hands and look at her. "Good. Now, about that punishment."

London looks between my face and the handcuffs. "I thought you said that would happen if I snuck out again."

"I think a demonstration is in order, don't you?" I lean over the bed so our faces are inches apart. "You need to say the words, London, and surrender yourself to me."

Something moves in me as her eyes sweep over my face. "I do."

Nothing else matters as we fall backward, and I lose myself in her.

CHAPTER SIX

London

"We need to get you to a hospital." I glance out the window and into the darkness, and my stomach lurches again. "We can't stay here."

"No one will find us here," Katia hisses. "Outside, we're exposed."

I glance around the abandoned shack with its stacks of firewood on one side and a large sheet covering a dusty worktable. Then I swing back to Katia, who is holding out her hand and examining it.

Even in her weakened state, she could still kill me.

I wouldn't blame her if she tried after the mess I got us in.

How are we supposed to get back to safety?

"You need to push the arm back," she says. "You'll rotate and shove."

Bile rises in my throat. "I can't do that. I'm not a doctor. I'll only make it worse."

"I am not going to ask you again, Blondie," Katia snaps. "You're the reason we're in this mess. The least you can do is help me with the pain."

I kneel in front of her and frown. "Are you really going to guilt me into this?"

"Just do it." Katia whips a rag out of her pocket and bites down on it. Then, she holds out her arm and looks at me. My throat is dry as I gingerly take her arm and count to three. Then, I raise her arm and suck in a deep breath, abruptly shoving the arm back with a wince.

Katia spits the rag out and heaves a breath. Wordlessly, she rips off a piece of fabric and uses it to bind her arm to her side. Her eyes are a little tight and unfocused *as she looks at me. "How are you going to get us out of here?"*

I rake my fingers through my hair. "Me? I don't know how to do these things."

Katia rolls her eyes. "I have a burner phone in my boot. Miss Deveroux's number is programmed into it. Don't give me that look. You wanted her to help and prove she's trustworthy. Now's your chance."

I reach for the boot. "Won't that make things worse?"

Katia blinks. "Too late to worry about that now, Princess. We'll just have to grin and bear whatever Mason dishes out. Think you can handle that?"

I square my shoulders and dial Miss Deveroux's number.

She answers on the fourth ring.

It takes a few tries for me to force the words out of my mouth, and when I do, Miss Deveroux is quiet for so long that I think she hasn't heard me. Then, the line goes dead. The bitter taste of disappointment and frustration is in my mouth.

"She'll be here," Katia says. "It just might take her a while to sneak out unnoticed."

"You should save your strength," I say.

"I don't need you to tell me what to do," Katia growls. "I can end you where you stand."

I snort and bend over to shove the phone back into her boot. "I know you can."

Katia's eyes fly open, and for a moment, they're surprisingly clear. "You could've left me back there. You could leave me here right now."

I shrug and lower myself onto the hard floor next to her, considering my next words carefully. "I still could. You never know."

Katia smiles. "You're a terrible liar."

"It's good to know that you're grateful to me for saving your life," I grumble without looking at her. "Next time, I'll just leave you by the side of the road."

"There will be no next time."

A cold wind rattles against the window, and I glance up sharply. I rub my hands up and down my arms and try to ignore the lurch in my chest. "It must be nice to always be so sure of things."

Katia makes another, weaker sound. "You have to be... keeps from... getting killed."

I turn to look at her. "If you have a concussion, you shouldn't sleep."

Katia raises her middle finger at me. "I'll be fine."

"Mason will find us," I say. "He has to."

Even if I have to deal with his anger, it's better than the alternative.

I don't want to have to explain why I snuck out and allowed his favorite assassin to get concussed.

My mind spins with possibilities as I sit, listening to the wind whistle. Now and again, I think I hear footsteps outside the shed, and I freeze. A short while later, I move to the back of the room and use the pale moonlight to rummage through a box. When I find an old wool blanket that smells like wood shavings and dried water, I wrinkle my nose and carry it to Katia.

She stirs when I cover her, but says nothing.

Unable to sit any longer, I begin to pace the shack and wring my hands.

I have no idea how long we're there, but when I hear an engine outside and bright headlights cast shadows along the walls, I panic. My hands tremble as I reach for one of Katia's daggers and place myself between her and the door. The doorknob rattles, and a heartbeat later, the door flies open.

The dagger in my hand sails through the air and lodges itself in the wall next to the hooded figure.

As she pulls her hood down, I breathe a sigh of relief, and my knees nearly give out. "Thank God it's you."

Miss Deveroux glances from the dagger to my face. "It's a good thing you have terrible aim."

"She'll need to work on that."

We glance at Katia, who is trying to push herself up. I race to help her, and she pushes me away. Frowning, I try again and throw her arm over my shoulders. Miss Deveroux takes the other arm, and we carry Katia outside, where a drizzle has started.

I blink and see a black Cadillac parked haphazardly on the side of the road. Huffing, I hoist Katia higher and place one foot in front of the other. Miss Deveroux yanks on the back door, and together, we push Katia inside. She pitches forward and lets out a sigh as I hurry to the passenger side and climb in.

A blast of hot air hits me in the face.

Miss Deveroux gets in a moment later and clicks her seatbelt into place. She turns up the heat and places both hands on the wheel. "Sorry, I couldn't get here sooner. It was hard to sneak out."

I hold my hands up to the heating vents. "Thanks for coming."

"I couldn't say much because I wasn't sure who was listening," Miss Deveroux continues without looking at me. "Too many people to keep an eye on."

I nod. "I'm sure."

A moment later, she dims the headlights and starts the engine.

For a long while, all I can hear is the windshield wipers swishing. I focus on the rhythmic motion while warmth returns to my body. Eventually, we merge onto a main road, and a few other cars are honking. Miss Deveroux says nothing. I realize we're approaching the club.

Everything is a blur as Miss Deveroux leaves the Cadillac in an empty parking spot and gets out of the car.

She ushers us in through the back door of the club after handing us two hoodies.

Then, we're in her office, where she examines Katia closely.

Then, we sneak out the back door and she marches us to the estate, where the guards see Katia and let us through. Katia and Miss Deveroux share a look before she ducks in through a back door. I wait until I'm sure she's gone before I turn to the older woman, words failing me.

"Seems like a lot has happened since we last saw each other."

I chuckle. "You have no idea."

Miss Deveroux's eyes are wide and concerned as she studies me. "Just be careful. In this world, not everything is what it seems."

"I knew you'd come."

Miss Deveroux gives me a small smile. "I'd better get back before someone notices I've been gone too long. Wouldn't want word about this getting out any more than it already has."

My chest tightens, and my stomach dips. "You'll be careful, right?"

"I always am. I'll see you soon."

She disappears into the shadows, and I stand in the doorway, not knowing what to do next. When Katia returns, having changed her clothes, she pulls me inside. We're halfway up the stairs when there's a buzz through the house. I draw my arm back and make a beeline for the front door. Katia is hot on my heels as I stumble out and sink onto the stairs.

Everything feels right when I find Mason in the darkness, and he races toward me.

My heart jolts as I sit up in bed, covered in sweat. I run a hand over my face before placing it over my chest. I take several deep breaths and wait for my eyes to adjust.

I'm not in the abandoned shack.

Katia isn't going to bleed out on my watch.

Mason has no idea that Miss Deveroux rescued us, and I want to keep it that way.

I know I can trust Mason with my life, but I'm not sure of the lengths he'll go to in order to protect his image, including silencing a valued employee.

I won't let Miss Deveroux be punished on my account when her only crime is coming to our rescue.

Still, guilt courses through me as I turn to look at Mason.

I try to forget the dream as I fall back onto the mattress and pull the covers up to my chest. Then I stare at the ceiling and count backward from fifty. Halfway there, I feel Mason stir, and I flip onto my side to look at him. His eyes dart open. He looks at me for a minute before unfurling an arm and pulling me closer to him.

I let his familiar smell wash over me.

"Why aren't you sleeping?"

"I was," I whisper. "Why aren't you?"

"I felt you tossing and turning. What can I do to help?"

I reach out a hand and trace his features, stopping at the scar over his eye. "I'm fine; don't worry."

Mason kisses the inside of my palm and exhales. "I will always worry about you. Sometimes, I wonder if…"

"If I'm going to run off?"

Mason searches my face. "It wouldn't be hard. I won't try to stop you."

"I am not going anywhere." I let my fingers move from his eye down the slope of his nose and pause at his lips. "It's not what I thought it would be, but I don't scare easily."

"I know you don't."

"About earlier…"

Mason takes my hand in his and kisses each finger. "I forgive you for sneaking off."

I raise an eyebrow. "I wasn't going to apologize. Well, not for that part. I'm sorry I dragged Katia into it."

"She's survived worse."

"She was just trying to help," I add. "She shouldn't be punished on my account."

Mason's expression turns serious as he moves back to look at me. "I'm grateful she was there to help you, but she should've never let you go in the first place. Katia knows that better than anyone."

"But…"

"There are things you shouldn't question, London, especially around other people. Katia knew what would happen when she agreed to your plan. What happens next is on her."

"But you can't—"

Mason presses a hand to my lips, and his expression darkens. "I can, and I will. In my world, mistakes must be punished. Consequences are how we keep people in line."

I push his finger away. "Katia is loyal to you. She would never disobey you."

Mason gives me a pointed look.

"Not without good reason," I stutter. "Are you going to punish me, too?"

Mason's eyes sweep over me, his face giving nothing away. "Would you like me to?"

"I…" A flush creeps up my neck and cheeks, and anticipation courses through me. "I'm not sure, but I guess it's only fair since I'm the reason we got run off a bridge."

I have no idea why I'm asking when I know it's not important.

Not with everything else going on, but I'm also aware of the fact that control is important to Mason.

He needs to have some semblance of it, and while a part of me doesn't relish the idea, I also know it's important to give him some leeway.

Mason shakes his head. "That isn't your fault. I'm going to make sure whoever is responsible for this pays. We've already sent them a message."

A chill races up my spine, erasing all of my earlier wanton thoughts. "How?"

"Don't ask questions you don't want answers to," Mason warns. "It's nothing for you to concern yourself with."

I hate that he's shutting me out, but I'm also not sure I want to know.

My eyes sweep over his face. "What about my dad?"

"What about him?"

"He needs protection. If they found me there, who knows what they'll do next? There's also my mom. She lives in another state, but they could find her if they wanted to."

Mason doesn't say anything.

"I know you're spread thin as it is, but they're my family," I continue. "I can't just leave them."

"I don't expect you to. As long as you don't ask me to protect Noah."

I frown. "Do you think they'd go after him, too? He is a part of my life—"

"*Was*," Mason corrects before pushing himself up and on top of me. He pins my arms over my head and kisses my jaw. "I'd rather not discuss him while we're in bed."

I moan when he begins to pepper my neck with kisses. "Mason…"

He stops kissing my neck and looks at me. "I'll see what can be done about your parents, but I draw the line at your ex."

My stomach dips, and another surge of guilt courses through me. "Is that part of my punishment for sneaking off, or is that because you don't like Noah?"

Mason rubs himself against me, and I whimper. "He doesn't deserve to be protected."

"But I…" I trail off when he presses his mouth to mine, silencing the rest of my thoughts. His kiss is slow and sensual at first, as if we have all the time in the world. I enjoy the feeling of his taut body pressed against mine as a fire starts in the pit of my belly. Mason still has me pinned against the mattress when he uses one hand to stroke me over the fabric of my cotton pants.

Desire pumps through me.

His hand darts underneath the waistband of my pants, and he splays his fingers over my underwear. Then, the kiss turns hungry. Suddenly, he's no longer asking for permission. I link my legs around his waist and nudge him closer, and his touch turns urgent and demanding.

My heart pounds in my ears as one finger darts between my wet folds.

I wrench my lips away and throw my head back in a moan.

Mason pushes another finger in, and I tug my hands against him. "I want to touch you."

Mason presses his mouth to my ear, sending a ripple of goosebumps across my skin. "Right now, we're doing this my way."

I squirm again. "But—"

"Stop thinking and just enjoy yourself."

He uses his free hand to pull the rest of my underwear down.

A draft of cold air kisses my flushed skin, and a minute later, his fingers are moving again. Abruptly, he releases my arms, and one falls to my side while the other reaches for the nape of his neck. Mason shifts out of reach and leans over the bed to rummage through the drawer. I blink and make out the vague outline of a handcuff.

There's a loud clicking sound as the cool metal closes around my wrists.

Mason secures my arms on either side of the bedpost and leans back. "This is a good look on you."

My throat is dry as I swallow. "Is it?"

Mason nods, and his eyes move over me, leaving a trail of heat in his wake. "At my mercy. I can do whatever I want to you, London."

My pulse skitters, and I nod. "Yes."

Mason stands up and kicks off his pants. Then, he hooks one thumb around his boxers, revealing his proud erection. I tug against my restraints when Mason climbs back onto the bed and crawls toward me.

His smile is a flash of white in the darkness before he nudges my legs apart.

His breath is tantalizing and hot against my skin, and I lower my head to look at him as he settles between my legs. Mason's tongue darts out, and I arch my back, desire burning me from the inside out. His tongue begins to dart back and forth, licking a steady path that sends waves of pleasure through me. I squeeze my eyes shut and focus on how his mouth and fingers feel, how every inch of him is pressed against me, and how nothing else matters.

The world outside our door ceases to exist.

When a hand darts to drape over my stomach, I feel myself hurtling toward the edge. Beads of sweat form on my back and forehead, and my breathing turns shallow. I bite down on my bottom lip hard enough to draw blood. Mason glances up at me, and the feral look on his face is almost enough to make me explode.

His eyes stay on me as he licks me again, and I come undone.

My entire body shakes and writhes as I ride out my high, his name a chant on my lips. Mason's tongue continues to sweep. Abruptly, he stops, and I stare at him through hooded lashes. He props himself up on his elbows and crushes his lips against mine.

Then, he stands, and I have a moment to admire his sculpted body before he turns his back to me. He rummages through the drawer again and pulls out a silk blindfold. My heart jumps into my throat as he leans over.

"Always so eager."

"Only for you." My voice is hoarse with desire. "You're the only one who can make me feel this way."

His touch is feather light as he leans forward, the overpowering smell of him washing over me. His fingers work quickly as the blindfold falls over my eyes, and the rest of the world melts away. I tense as I tilt my head and listen for his voice.

My lips part as I feel his hands on my arms and then behind my back.

A heartbeat later, he unhooks my bra, and my breasts spill forward. He rubs his stubble against my chest, and I try to cross my legs. Mason growls and keeps a hand on my thighs. Slowly, he takes one nipple in his mouth and rolls it between his teeth. When he moves onto the other nipple, I tug on my restraints and gasp.

I need Mason to quench the fire inside of me.

My nipples are as hard as diamonds as he moves away, and I whimper. I hear his breathing deepen, and my stomach flip-flops. Mason kisses me and kicks my legs apart. He nips my lower lip and then thrusts into me in one quick move as I cry out.

"That's it." Mason's voice floats around me. "I want to hear you beg for me."

"Mason," I plead, in between gasps of air. "I... oh, oh."

He eases out and slams back into me. "You, what? Say it, London."

I buck against him, my heart galloping steadily at this point. "I... yes, just like that."

Mason's chuckle sends another wave through me. "You like it rough, don't you?"

He circles his hips and slides out of me. I lift my back off the mattress and lick my lips. Mason slams into me again, and waves of pleasure build within me. His fingers dig into my waist as he steadily eases in and out of me. My chest is tight as I listen to the sound of his heavy breathing and wonder how much longer I can hold out.

His fingers move to the back of my neck, and when he whips the blindfold off, my vision is blurry. I blink, and Mason is poised over me, his skin slick with sweat. He throws one of my legs over his shoulder and thrusts in. My mouth forms a surprised O as he throws my other leg over his shoulders, and it feels like I'm floating.

How does he know exactly how to drive me to the edge of ecstasy and back?

Mason's rhythm changes, turning frenzied. His breathing comes in short, quick puffs as he pounds into me. Then he lowers my legs, and I link them around his waist. I try to remember to breathe as Mason reaches over me and unlocks the handcuffs. I rake my nails down his back, and he hisses.

He laces his fingers through mine and pins my hands on either side of me.

Pressure continues to build as we buck against each other, the bed dipping and creaking with each movement.

All at once, I'm falling, gasping, and writhing with pleasure as I come undone beneath him.

A few moments later, Mason's release comes in short, quick spurts. He throws his head back and shouts when he's done. My vision swims in and out of focus. Slowly, Mason eases out of me and collapses onto the mattress next to me. I turn to face him, and he drapes an arm around me.

I exhale as I snuggle into his side and wait for my heart to stop racing.

Mason presses a kiss to the side of my head.

I awake the next morning to a thin steam in the room and the smell of soap. I pull the sheets up as I sit up and rub the sleep from my eyes. I notice an envelope on the pillow next to me. My eyes widen as I see the amount of cash inside.

I leave the envelope on the nightstand and stand up, but Mason is nowhere to be found.

Katia is waiting outside the door when I emerge with damp hair and fresh clothes a while later.

"I want to hire protection for my dad," I tell her. "Maybe my mom, too."

Katia doesn't say anything.

"Also, maybe we should look into more protection for me, so you're not overwhelmed," I continue. "I'm sure you have better things to do than watch me all the time."

Katia scoffs. "I do, but you'd better get used to having me around."

I sigh. "Okay, how about having someone else around for my peace of mind?"

Katia raises an eyebrow. "You're smart not to trust me, Barbie."

"You could also train me," I add, after a brief pause. "I think it's important that I learn how to hold my own."

Katia bursts into laughter. "You have no idea what you're asking for, do you?"

It's a free pass for Katia to kick me around, and I hate that she's enjoying this so much.

Mason handing me an envelope full of cash is his way of helping, and while it stings to realize he doesn't want to be more involved, I know he's got a lot on his mind.

He's giving you the space to make decisions and trusting you to make the right ones.

First, I need to make sure my parents are safe.

And then I need to find a way to help stop the war, but I have no idea what I'm meant to bring to the table.

I spend the rest of the morning reviewing security options vetted by Mason, with Katia hovering over me and a sense of impending doom in the back of my mind.

Chapter Seven

Mason

"The meeting should've been somewhere else." Jack's eyes dart around the brightly lit room. "You'd better hope this goes well."

I reach for my drink and take a sip. "It will."

I've spent the past few days making sure every detail is tended to.

The Thayers won't be able to refuse us.

A moment later, the door to the room opens, and Carlisle steps in first. He gives me a nod before melting into the shadows. Then a tall man with strands of silver in his hair and a goatee steps in, a hand immediately going to the button of his expensive Armani suit.

Two more men step in, with similar buzz cuts and bulging muscles that fill out their clothes.

Finally, a woman with midnight black hair and striking green eyes is revealed, and her face gives nothing away as she looks around. She hikes her purse up on her shoulders and wrinkles her nose at something.

My father steps out from behind the table. "Thatcher. I hope they've given you the welcome you deserve."

Thatcher Thayer straightens his back. "Your welcoming committee needs a little work, Jack, but I'm willing to overlook that."

Jack takes his hand and offers him a firm shake. "I'll make sure to look into the details later."

"A glass of your finest whiskey is a good way to apologize," Thayer replies. "And how about something to eat?"

I signal to Carlisle, who steps forward. "We have an excellent menu—"

Thayer holds up his hand. "My chef is here with me tonight. He's already familiarizing himself with the kitchen."

I clear my throat. "Of course."

I already hate that we're licking this man's boots, but I can't afford to complain.

Given the rumors that are spreading, we need every ally we can get because Michael Fitzpatrick was right.

That disastrous meeting is already causing fissures far beyond anything we could've imagined.

I can't underestimate the importance of finding powerful allies, even shallow and egocentric ones like Thatcher Thayer.

It's just one more pill I have to swallow.

Thatcher glances around the room. "You should have asked me to help you with the décor. This place needs an overhaul."

Jack laughs, and it sounds forced. "Of course. How ridiculous of us not to have thought of you first."

Thatcher waves away his comment. "That's quite right. Most people don't think of these things, but I was talking to the Kardashians at this premier the other day, and..."

I tune him out and study his men intently.

The two of them stand near the door, their dark eyes scanning the room. I want to be offended that Thayer felt the need to bring security, but I also can't blame him, given all the uncertainty.

Most of which you caused, remember? You're meant to be figuring out a way to clean up your mess, not nursing your ego.

Half an hour later, Thatcher is in the middle of another story about a fashion show he helped curate, and my head is pounding. During the few times my father has tried to steer the conversation in another direction, Thayer finds a way to make it about himself or his family.

At the one-hour mark, I walk over to the drink cart in the corner.

Thatcher has an apron tied around his neck and is holding a lobster tail in one hand and gesturing with the other. I pour a generous amount of bourbon and raise the glass to my lips. I'm halfway through the drink and debating whether or not this alliance is worth the headache when Thayer's daughter walks up to me.

She gestures to the cart, and I set down my drink.

I hand her a drink, and she adds a few ice cubes and tilts it in my direction. "You'll have to excuse my father. He loves talking about his… conquests."

I make a noise in the back of my throat. "Perhaps business matters should be left to someone else."

She laughs. "That's what I keep saying, but some of the families we're in business with are a bit more traditional."

"There are ways around that."

She takes a sip of her drink. "So I'm told, but we're not here to discuss that, are we?"

I eye her over the rim of my glass.

"I know your father has discussed an alliance," Elise Thayer continues. "I'd like to further discuss the particulars."

I glance at my father, who has a pained expression on his face as he listens to Thatcher discuss another gala. "Shouldn't your father be the one having this discussion?"

Elise doesn't reply.

"I'm listening."

"You need allies for the upcoming war—"

"*Potential* war," I correct. "Nothing is set in stone."

If all goes according to plan, we'll avoid a war, but I know better than to leave us unprepared.

Like it or not, the Thatchers are the only viable option we have.

I know they're already being propositioned by the enemy, who is circling and looking for ways to cut us off.

Rumors about the meeting have already spread.

We can't stay ahead of the damage, but I am doing everything I can to minimize it.

For the first time in decades, the Paynes are on shaky footing. I want to kick myself for not having seen this coming, but I know I've been played. I had gotten too complacent, and our enemies saw an opening.

I'd be impressed if I weren't livid.

"Then a potential partnership is all the more important, don't you think?" Elise turns to face me. "You and I can be useful to one another."

I study her intently. "Can we?"

Elise smiles. "I know you're a man who likes to have fun, Mason Payne, and that's what I'm looking for."

An image of London flashes to mind, and it takes me too long to brush it off.

Elise touches my arm and laughs. "I'm not proposing marriage or even anything real. Just a mutually beneficial partnership."

I raise an eyebrow. "Why?"

Elise moves her drink to her lips, and her eyes move over my face. "I have my reasons. I see no reason why we can't both get what we want."

I grunt noncommittally.

"Non-exclusive, of course," Elise adds quickly. "I don't care what you do in your spare time."

I down the rest of my drink and stare at her. "You want us to put on a show for everyone?"

Elise sets down her drink and shrugs. "It's not all that different from what we do every day, but we will have to make a few public appearances to sell it."

"For the cameras, you mean?"

Elise steps closer to me and drops her voice. "For everyone, including our families."

"What's in it for you?"

Elise pats my hand. "I think every relationship has to have secrets, don't you? It keeps things interesting."

"If you're trying to screw me over…"

Elise arches a brow at me. "Why would I try to do that when there's a potential war coming? I know better than to make an enemy of the Paynes."

Her offer is intriguing, but I know better than to bite.

I need to know what her angle is because there's no way she's just agreeing to this without a caveat.

Elise Thayer's endgame is the same as mine, but it doesn't mean we can work together.

I don't like being kept in the dark.

Still, I know better than to outright refuse her.

I have enough problems as it is without having to worry about offending the Thayers, too.

Isn't that what you wanted? The appearance of an alliance without the hassle? It's better than you could've hoped for, and you'd be an idiot to not consider it.

London isn't going to like this.

It's one thing to have an understanding between the families, but it's quite another to have the press fawning over us and splashing pictures all over the news.

It's not the kind of publicity I like or want, but Elise Thayer is a public figure.

She's been on the cover of several lifestyle and fashion magazines. The press is obsessed with her, and as much as I hate to admit it, selling our relationship means flaunting it in public.

And it's the only option I have.

"I can live with being your beard," I murmur close to her ear. "So long as you don't fuck with me. If you do, you'll find out why I have a reputation."

Elise turns her head so there's an inch of space between us, a strange glimmer in her eyes. "Noted."

I tuck a lock of hair behind her ear. "Any other terms you'd like to discuss?"

"What you do and who you do it with is none of my concern, but be discreet," Elise says quietly. "I'll offer you the same courtesy in return."

My eyes move over her face again. "That sounds reasonable."

Elise pats my hand. "I look forward to our partnership."

I look away from her and see our fathers looking at us. "As do I."

I spent the ride home trying to come up with a way to break the news to London. As we pull up to the estate, my father leaves the car and makes a beeline for an empty room that has been temporarily converted into his study. I follow in his wake. My phone pings, and I stare at the date.

Suddenly, my father's impatience and surly mood make sense.

"I can take care of anything else business-related for today." I step into the room and let the door click shut behind me. "Is there anything I can get you?"

He wheels to face me. "You and Elise seem to be getting along."

I nod.

Jack sits behind his desk and drums his fingers against the desk. "Thayer and I will discuss a few more of the particulars of our alliance. We'll need to offer a bigger portion than we initially thought."

"I can take care of the details."

He narrows his eyes. "I will not be sidelined. One battle doesn't mean you've won the war, boy."

I meet his gaze unflinchingly. "I know what today is."

To his credit, his careful mask doesn't slip. "Today is the day we secured an alliance with the Thayers."

"It's Mom's birthday," I add. "I can set up a call with Olivia and

Oliver, and I'm sure Mathew is lurking somewhere—"

"Get out," Jack interrupts.

"You can't just ignore what today is, of all days. I know you miss her—"

Jack crosses over to me in a few strides and twists my arm behind my back. "If you value your life, you will not finish that thought."

I offer no resistance as he pushes me toward the door. "She deserves to be remembered. You know that."

"I don't need her birthday to remember her." His voice is deceptively soft. Then, he slams the door shut in my face.

Why did I think today would be different?

I can't remember the last time any of us talked about her together or even lit a candle for her.

Without her, other than the blood running through our veins, we have nothing in common.

I've spent more time than I'd like to admit making my peace with it.

"Ah, the prodigal son returns. How did you fuck up this time? Did you pull a gun out on Thayer?"

I clench my hands into fists and turn to face Mathew, who has an infuriating grin on his face. "Not today."

Mathew moves closer to me. "You know, it's good that Dad is finally realizing what a fuck up you are. I've been trying to tell him for years, so you're doing me a favor."

My eyes narrow into slits. "I suggest you shut the fuck up before I rip your tongue out."

"What's the matter, did your plaything realize she chose the wrong Payne brother? Don't worry, I'll show her what a real man is like."

I slam him against the nearest wall and bare my teeth. "One of these days, you're going to push too far."

Mathew smiles. "It's not far enough as far as I'm concerned. When the women in your life realize what they're missing, they'll come to me.

Even your new little friend. I've heard Elise Thayer is a wild little thing."

I grab Mathew by his neck and push my face against his. "Do you know what today is?"

Mathew trails off and raises an eyebrow. "Why the fuck should I care?"

I push myself off him. "Yeah, you're right. Why should you care that it's Mom's birthday?"

Mathew's expression changes. "Oh."

I clear my throat. "Exactly. Today of all days, we shouldn't be fighting."

"Mom hated it when we fought. Remember that birthday when we were ten, Olivia was eight, and Oliver was five? When we tried to make her a cake?"

I pause. "I remember you almost setting the house on fire."

Mathew snorts. "You remember wrong. I was putting out the fire. It was your idea not to grease the pan."

"That's not how I remember it," I reply.

"You and I remember a lot of things differently."

I open my mouth to protest and slam it shut again. Then I exhale. "Yeah, I guess we do."

I don't want to argue with Mathew during one of the rare moments when we're not at each other's throats.

This entire day feels wrong.

It's not how we're supposed to be honoring our mother, but short of dragging everyone into the same room, there's nothing I can do.

Like every year, everyone will honor her in the way they see fit.

"I did copy you a lot when we were growing up," Mathew murmurs. "I thought if I did, Mom would like me better."

I give him an incredulous look. "What are you talking about? Mom loved all of us equally."

Mathew makes a noncommittal sound in the back of his throat. "You were her favorite, but I was determined to take that away from you."

I stare at Mathew as I figure out what to say.

It's one of the few moments I feel he's being honest.

Mathew retreated into himself after her death. When he finally re-emerged, he wasn't the same.

For years, I've only ever seen him as cold, cruel, and calculating, but I've never given myself a chance to wonder why or how he got there.

You're not the only one who had to change after Mom's death. He loved her too, remember?

Suddenly, I'm not looking at the brother who's been waiting on the sidelines to catch me screwing up.

I'm seeing the little brother who used to follow me around the house and stare at me with those big eyes.

"Mathew—"

"Anyway, there's no point in getting emotional about it. It's just another day."

I frown. "You sound like Dad."

"At least one of us does," Mathew replies. "Someone has to protect the Payne family legacy. I bet it tears you up knowing it won't be you. Enjoy it while you can, brother."

Without waiting for a response, he turns and strides off.

I press two fingers to my temple and rub in slow, circular motions. I'm halfway to the stairs when I see Katia and Carlisle standing in a corner, gesturing wildly. As Katia hears me approach, she turns to face me.

Carlisle says something to her, and she looks away.

In the room, I retrieve a bottle of bourbon from the bottom drawer and pry it open. When London emerges from the bathroom, I'm swigging straight from the bottle. She finishes towel-drying her hair and pads over to me, barefoot and smelling like spring blossoms. Wordlessly, she takes my hand in hers and tugs me onto the bed.

I take another long swig of the drink and look away. "Did you find a security team you like?"

London sighs. "There are a few promising ones, but I have to check with my dad."

I turn to her. "The less contact you have, the better."

Her insistence frustrates me. "You're not going to let that go, are you?"

"I won't."

I unlace our fingers and run them over my face. "I'll get some burners. Have you spoken to your mom?"

"I haven't been able to get a hold of her."

My mouth tastes like ash when I swallow. "It's probably just a coincidence."

I know better than London does how efficient and expedient my enemies can be.

Now that they know how valuable London is, there's no doubt in my mind that they're hunting down her family.

If they haven't found them already.

London reaches for my hand again and waits for me to look at her. "Are you okay?"

I blink. "Why?"

"You were muttering in your sleep last night…something about it being your mom's birthday?" London inches closer and squeezes my hand. "I don't know what you guys do to honor her—"

"We don't do anything." The words come out harsher than intended. "There's no room for sentimentality in my world."

London moves closer and presses a warm hand to my cheek. "Right now, it's just the two of us. There's no one else in the room."

My stomach dips. "She would've hated this. What we've become."

London presses her forehead to mine. "I'm sure she knows you're doing what you have to do. At least you're keeping Olivia and Oliver safe."

I release a harsh breath. "Not if my dad has a say in it. He's trying to force them both to come back, and knowing my dad, it's going to take a hell of a lot to deter him."

London climbs onto my lap and links her hands at the nape of my neck. "You'll figure something out. You always do."

I lean back to look at her, and my stomach stirs strangely when she lifts her eyes. "You sound surer than I feel."

London beams at me. "I figure one of us has to be. We can take turns."

I move her hands to my lips for a kiss. "Sounds reasonable."

London looks into my eyes, and her expression turns serious. "From what you've told me, I can tell your mom was an amazing woman, and I know you want to honor your promises, but I'm sure she knew how hard some of them were going to be. She wouldn't blame you for not being able to keep your word."

I don't say anything.

London's expression is soft and open. "I don't know what you'd like to do to honor her, but I can come with you."

I scooch backward onto the bed, keeping an arm wrapped around her. Then I tuck her into my side and lie down. "This is fine."

London drapes an arm over my stomach, and I can feel her eyes on me, wide and searching. "Do you want to tell me about her?"

I press a kiss to the side of London's face. "I don't know where to start."

"Anywhere you like."

Silence stretches between us.

London props herself up on her elbow. "What kind of food did she like?"

"Fried chicken."

London smiles. "She had good taste."

"I thought so, too. When we were younger, she used to insist that we have a ten-minute dance party every day before bed."

London's smile widens. "That sounds amazing."

"It was, and every birthday, she'd make us a cake. Each year, she'd try to be more outrageous than the last…"

The words pour out of me in a rush.

Half an hour later, London's eyes are growing heavy. I wait until her eyes drift shut before I pull the covers up to her chin. Then, I kiss her forehead and sneak out of the room.

Katia is waiting for me outside the study.

She follows me inside and shuts the door behind her. "We're no closer to finding out who orchestrated the car crash."

I stare daggers at her. "That's disappointing. Maybe I should look into finding a new assassin."

Katia stiffens. "I know I showed a lapse in judgment, but I figured she'd be safer if I were with her."

"You almost got her killed."

A muscle works in Katia's jaw. "I know."

"Find out who was behind the attack. I want them bound, gagged, and in front of me."

Katia presses her lips together and nods.

I step behind my desk and wave her away. "I have work to do. Next time, you'd better have good news for me."

CHAPTER EIGHT

London

I stare at the tiny particles of light dancing on the hardwood floors. Slowly, I raise the cup to my lips.

Katia is standing near the window, half-turned away from me.

She turns when I approach, and her dark eyes survey me quickly. "Coffee break is over. Time to go."

I frown. "Can't I go for a walk or something? The weather is nice."

Katia purses her lips. "Not now."

I open my mouth to protest, and Katia's arm darts out. She pulls me behind her, and a second later, Jack Payne walks into the kitchen. He opens a cupboard and takes out a mug. When he sees us, his expression tightens. I hold myself still as his face darkens.

A chill races up my spine as he studies me, and Katia shifts so she's almost obscuring me.

Without looking away, Jack pours himself a coffee. "Such a waste."

Katia stiffens. "Is there anything I can do for you, sir?"

Jack arches a brow in her direction. "You're busy playing babysitter. When you're done wasting your time, come and find me."

In one quick gulp, he downs his drink.

He casts another look over his shoulder, but I remain rooted to the spot until his footsteps recede. Once they do, my shoulders sag, and I exhale. My legs still feel unsteady as Katia moves away and closes her fingers around my wrist. I don't protest as she drags me out of the living room and toward the stairs.

Katia glances from the unmade bed to me.

Finally, she releases my wrist and scowls.

I step into the room and turn to face her, but she's melted into the shadows. Reluctantly, I let the door click shut and turn back around, the silence of the room closing in around me. Frowning, I cross over to the nightstand and yank the first drawer open.

Before I can talk myself out of it, I use the burner to dial my father's number.

It rings a few times before disconnecting.

"Goddamn it, Dad," I mumble, with a scowl. "Why aren't you picking up?"

My heart is pounding uneasily as I try him a few more times.

By the fourth try, sweat is pouring down my back and neck, and I can't shake the dread.

I cross over to the window, push the curtain aside, and fling the windows open. Early afternoon light warms the bridge of my nose, and the rest of my face, and I inhale deeply. Then I close my eyes and clench my hands into fists.

A loud bang pierces through the silence, and my stomach drops.

I look down at the phone.

My mother answers on the fifth ring, her voice subdued and uncertain. "Hello?"

"Mom? Thank God. I've been trying to reach you for a while. Are you okay?"

"London, is that you?"

Some of the tightness in my chest eases. "Yeah, it's me. Have you heard from Dad at all? We got into this fight—"

"He told me all about it. What have you gotten yourself into,

London?"

"I know what it looks like, and I'm sorry the two of you got dragged into my mess, but I'm—"

"Your father thinks you orchestrated the kidnapping just to make him forget the fact that you spent months lying about where you are."

A laugh falls from my lips before I can stop it. "What?"

"He thinks it's an elaborate scheme to get him to forgive you. Honestly, London, I don't know what to think."

I grip the phone tightly and begin to pace. "How about giving me the benefit of the doubt, Mom? You haven't even heard my side."

There's a voice in the background, and it takes me a minute to place it.

I stop pacing. "That's Dad, isn't it? I can hear him."

"I wanted to surprise you with a visit, and when I stopped by the house, I thought it was strange that your dad wasn't there—"

"You didn't go into the house, did you?"

"I was only there for a minute," she interrupts. "I called your father, and we agreed to meet up because he's worried about you."

I exhale sharply. "I'm fine. It's you two I'm worried about."

"Are you fine? Based on everything your father told me, you seem far from fine, London. Who is this guy you're involved with, and how could you lie to your father like that? After everything he's done for you."

"After everything he's done for me?" I pull the phone away from my ear in disbelief. Then I press it to my ear again and count backward from five. "What about everything I've done for him? I only lied to save him because of that ridiculous loan he took out. I had to… I made a deal to work off his debt. I did this for him."

What other choice did I have when they threatened to take the diner away?

Entering into a contract with Mason to pay off my father's debt was one thing.

I had agreed to work at Mercy, an exclusive underground club that operated in the shadows, because I saw no other way out.

It's not like I planned to fall in love with Mason and stay.

I don't expect my parents to understand, and I certainly don't think my father will own up to the role he played in any of this.

Even if he willingly entered into an understanding with Mason's lackey.

I'm not waiting for either of them to roll out the welcome mat, but they can at least stop acting like I'm out to hurt them.

Knowing that neither of my parents believes me hurts.

"Yes, he told me about the loan, but don't you think there was a better way to resolve the whole thing?"

"I'm all ears, Mom. I'm not going to apologize for doing what I needed to do to save Dad. And I didn't plan a fake kidnapping just to get back in his good graces. You know me. You know I wouldn't do that."

Mason's enemies were a step ahead, and targeting my father and ex to get to me had been the plan all along.

It was why they'd taken me in the first place.

I still woke up in a cold sweat at night, imagining myself in the silent room with iron bars on the windows and a guard posted outside. A small part of me still can't believe that Mason swooped in to rescue me.

My mother sighs. "I don't know what's happening, London, but it doesn't feel like we know who you are these days. You are not the woman we raised."

I suck in a harsh breath, and my ears start ringing. "I'm still me, Mom."

"You need to take a long and hard look in the mirror, London. The woman we raised wouldn't have made these choices or jeopardized her future. Don't even get me started on what you did to poor Noah. He wanted a life with you, and he treated you well."

There's a lump in my throat as I swallow.

In a daze, I listen to my mom outline all of the ways I've failed, and I realize she's not wrong.

This isn't the life we talked about, the one I dreamed about and worked toward for years.

In the blink of an eye, I turned my back on everything I've known, and I can't even tell my parents why.

Even if Mason and I hadn't agreed it was for the best, neither of them would understand.

As far as they're concerned, Mason is to blame, sent to tempt me and lead me astray, and nothing I say or do will make them believe otherwise.

By the end of her tirade, a heavy ache settles into my bones. I perch on the edge of the bed and listen to my father ranting in the background, and tears prick my eyes. Once she's done, I bow my head and try to keep the tears at bay.

Crying won't change what my parents think of me, and it won't make what I did to Noah any better.

Mason is right.

Emotions are a nuisance, and they have no room in this life. My new life.

"Fine, Mom. I'm a major fuckup," I interrupt. I stand up and curl my free hand into a fist. "But it doesn't change that I did what I did for the right reasons, and I didn't call to have you list all the ways I've disappointed you. I know you can't understand my decisions, but I at least expect you to make your peace with them."

"London—"

"We'll talk about it later when we're all calmer," I continue. "Just please stay safe. Both of you."

Without waiting for a response, I hang up and squeeze my eyes shut.

A heartbeat later, I cross over to the door and wrench it open.

Katia falls into step beside me as I take the stairs two at a time, needing to drown out the roaring in my ears. I find Mason's office and give a quick rap on the door before throwing it open. Mason is sitting behind his desk, the first few buttons of his shirt undone, and a drink in hand. He motions to Katia, who disappears and pulls the door shut behind her.

Slowly, he stands up, and his eyes sweep over me. "You look like you want to kill someone."

I cover the distance between us, wind my fingers through his hair, and kiss him.

Mason growls and yanks me toward him, the low thrumming in my ears drowning out everything else. I nip his lower lip, and he makes another sound that goes straight to my core. Abruptly, he hoists me up, and I wrap my legs around his waist. Then he carries me over to the armchair and sets me down.

His eyes are dark with hunger when he pulls back to look at me. "What's going on?"

"I don't want to talk," I tell him, pausing to pull my shirt over my head. "I don't want to think. I just want to feel."

Mason raises an eyebrow. "You might want to think this through."

I unhook my bra and let my breasts spill forward, and Mason raises an eyebrow. "No, I told you, I don't want to think. I just want you. Right here. Right now."

Mason purses his lips together. "Not like this."

I frown. "What are you talking about?"

Mason's fingers move to the buttons of his shirt. In a few quick moves, the shirt falls to the floor with a flutter. Wordlessly, he walks backward, his eyes never leaving my face. Then he turns the lock with a click.

"I realize we should've had this conversation a little earlier, but I was thinking of other things at the time."

I give him a blank look. "I don't know what you're talking about."

Why isn't he kissing me?

Why isn't he drowning out the vicious voice in the back of my head reminding me of all the ways I've failed?

Why does he have to choose now, of all times, to have a conversation?

"Boundaries. A safe word," Mason says. "If we're going to keep doing this, you need to feel safe."

I stand up and clear my throat. "I do. I trust you. I'm here, aren't I?"

Mason's eyes drift over me, leaving a trail of heat in his wake. "I want to keep that trust because even if you do… the dynamics are different now."

I blink. "Okay."

This isn't how I pictured standing half-naked in Mason's study.

I'm supposed to be bent over a desk or a chair, all thoughts of being a failure being driven from my head with each thrust, kiss, and touch.

I don't know why he's choosing now to be considerate, but I'm still touched.

I know it isn't easy for Mason to let people in, to relinquish some control, and to see it firsthand makes me fall for him a little more.

I love seeing snippets of the kind and thoughtful man behind the mask, the kind few other people get to see.

Maybe you haven't screwed up so badly after all.

Mason crosses over to me and stops an inch away. "I'm going to fuck you, London. Make no mistake about that, but when we do, I want you to completely give yourself over to me."

"I'm doing that now," I argue, my fingers moving to trace his chest. I stop at the waistband of his pants and look up. "What do you need me to say?"

Mason pulls me against him. "I don't need you to say anything. You need to know you can say no. You can refuse things."

I search his face. "You're serious about this?"

Mason quirks an eyebrow. "Why wouldn't I be?"

I sigh and link my fingers behind his neck. "Okay, I'll tell you if there's something I'm not comfortable doing."

"And if it's too much."

"And it's too much," I repeat, pausing to brush my lips against his. "Okay?"

"I want this to be different," Mason adds, in a lower voice. His eyes are soft now and boring into me with such intensity that it's making my pulse quicken. "I know you're used to a different kind of relationship."

I link my fingers over his neck. "I'm here. I don't want to be anywhere else. I don't want anyone else."

Mason searches my face and cups the back of my neck. "I don't know how to do the romance, flowers and feelings part of all this."

One half of my lips turn up into a smile, and butterflies settle in the center of my stomach. "You're trying though."

Mason blows out a breath. "I am."

"I don't care about the optics, Mason. The fact that you're trying it's… everything."

Mason gives me a half smile that sends a swarm of butterflies straight to my stomach. "Good."

Fuck me.

What is it about this man that makes me want to lose myself in him till nothing else exists?

Even now, with my parents' words still reverberating inside of my head, all I can think about is him, and how much I want to curl up against him.

I don't want any space, physical or otherwise, between us.

"This is enough," I murmur, pausing to use my hand to make a sweeping hand gesture. My chest is tight with emotion as I sort through my next words carefully. "*You* are enough."

Mason claims my mouth with his, and the energy between us shifts and crackles.

In one quick move, Mason has me pressed between him and the desk, the smooth wood digging into my back. He draws back to look at me and tucks a lock of hair behind my ear. "I'm sure you're going to realize how fucked up this all is…."

"Not a chance." I breathed. "I'm not going anywhere."

"In that case…"

Suddenly, his mouth is on mine again, hot and demanding.

He nips my bottom lip, and his tongue darts in, plunging and sweeping. My breath hitches in my throat as he rubs himself against me. Then he uses one arm to pin my arms over my head as the other pinches my nipples. A thick fog of desire settles over me as I squirm against him.

Mason pulls back abruptly. "Take the rest of your clothes off and sit on the desk."

The blood is roaring in my ears as I do as I'm told.

Mason rummages through a drawer and pulls out a pair of handcuffs and a whip. He waits until I'm sitting on the desk to cuff me to either side of the desk, leaving me naked and exposed. I lick my dry lips and watch him through hooded eyes as he circles me, his bare chest glistening underneath fluorescent lights. Slowly, he circles back to the front and stops in front of me. Then he runs the whip along the inside of my thighs, causing goosebumps to break out.

"Remember your safe word." Mason's voice drops to a husky timbre that gives me chills. "We'll take it slow."

I nod, and he moves the whip back. It makes a low cracking sound before it connects with my legs, sending a jolt of pleasure and pain through me. The molten pressure in my belly pools as he strikes again, against my other leg.

"God, you have no idea how fucking sexy you are right now." Mason's voice is barely above a whisper. He crushes his mouth against mine and runs his tongue along my lower lip. Before I can open my mouth, he undoes my handcuffs, and my hands fall to his shoulders. I rake my fingers down his back, and he growls, sending another wave of desire through me.

Nothing else matters outside this moment.

We are the only two people who exist.

Mason wrenches his lips away and kisses a path down my neck. He takes one nipple between his teeth and tugs. I sink my nails into his hips and throw my head back. He moves onto the other nipple, and I moan, the sound echoing back to me in the stillness of the room. Suddenly, Mason hoists me up and spins me around.

He binds my hands and pushes me forward so that I'm bent over the desk.

My pulse skitters and anticipation washes over me.

His breath is hot against my ear. "You will only submit to me, London. No one else can make you feel this way."

My throat is tight as I nod. "Yes."

A heartbeat later, I hear a crack, and the whip connects with the bare skin of my behind. I jerk in surprise and bite back a moan. Mason growls and uses the whip again, and it sends shock waves through me. I fix my stare on the cream-colored wall behind his desk and try to remember how to breathe when I feel him licking a path down the curve of my back.

I shiver when a hand darts between my wet folds.

Breathless, I arch my back and grind against him. "That feels amazing."

Mason tugs on my lobe and exhales. "Enjoy yourself, London. Open yourself to every sensation."

He pushes another finger and begins to swipe.

I squeeze my eyes shut and marvel at every little nerve end in my body, attuned to him.

His heavy breathing alone is almost enough to make me unravel.

Circling my hips, I grind against his fingers, and he moves them furiously.

Spots dance in my vision as my release washes over me. I'm still shaking and gasping for air when Mason spins me around. When I realize he's naked, I let my eyes sweep over him, taking in every inch of taut and smooth skin. He runs the whip down the slope of my chest and pauses at my belly.

After securing the handcuffs again, he retrieves a pair of ties and binds my feet.

His eyes don't leave my face as he lowers himself in front of me, so he's eye level with my center. Mason wastes no time in letting his tongue dart out to lick my wet folds. I gasp and writhe, but something about being tied down and at his every whim is intoxicating.

I like knowing he holds the key to my pleasure.

Mason replaces his mouth with his fingers and rises to his feet.

He waits until I'm looking at him, panting and covered in sweat, before he thrusts into me. I buck against him and whimper. Mason eases out and thrusts back into me, harder this time, and I think I'm about to erupt into a million pieces at his feet. Then, he places his arms on either side of me and begins to move in slow, practiced strokes. I meet each thrust with one of my own until the desk creaks beneath the weight.

Mason's moans intermingle with mine.

He alternates between kissing my neck and tugging on my nipples until they're as hard as pebbles. I squeeze my eyes shut and focus on the pressure building within me, rising to a powerful wave threatening to consume both of us. Another wave of pleasure rips through me, and I cry out, my body spasming for so long that it feels like I am looking down on myself.

As my vision clears, I realize Mason has released my binds and laid me on the carpet in front of the fireplace. He hovers over me, a soft gleam in his eyes as I look at him. Slowly, he kisses every inch of my glistening skin until he reaches my lips. Tears well up behind my eyes at the tenderness of his touch, and the softness of his gaze. I spread my legs and link them around his hips. Mason shudders against me.

We move slower now like we're discovering each other for the first time.

I want to stay like this forever.

Mason frames my face in his hands.

Something low and pleasant unfurls in the center of my stomach, and I hold onto it as we move against each other.

He buries his face in my neck, and the smell of his soap and expensive cologne settles around me.

I run my fingers down his back and offer his ass a firm squeeze.

He says something unintelligible, and his rhythm changes, turning frantic.

A few moments later, he throws his head back and shouts, his release tearing through him. I hold him against me and study the smooth lines of his face as his mask slips, allowing me a rare view of the man underneath. All too soon, Mason stops shaking and holds himself still. With an exhale, he rolls off me and collapses onto the carpet next to me.

I tuck myself into his side as he drapes an arm over my shoulders.

His breathing quiets as we lie there for a long moment, neither of us saying anything.

Slowly, I prop myself up on my elbows. "I asked Katia to get someone to train me in the gym downstairs."

Mason smiles lazily. "I know."

"I know you know, but let's just pretend for a minute that we're a normal couple, and I'm telling you about my day."

Mason pauses and nods. "Do me a favor and kick their asses."

I laugh and rise to my feet. "I'll try, but I'm still learning."

Mason twists his head to look at me, and the half-smile on his lips makes my stomach do odd little somersaults. "Don't underestimate yourself. You're a lot stronger and more resourceful than you give yourself credit for."

"Am I?"

Mason's expression turns serious. "Absolutely."

I sigh. "Tell that to my parents. They definitely don't seem to share your feelings. In fact, I'm pretty sure they think I'm the biggest screw up in the world."

Mason frowns. "Screw them."

An involuntary laugh falls from my lips. "I know I should think that. I know I did what I could with the hand I was dealt, but I just…"

Mason laces his fingers through mine and squeezes.

I exhale. "There's a part of me that's always going to want their approval, you know. Even now when they're being unfair."

"I understand. I've been chasing my father's approval my whole life."

I hold my breath as I cock my head to the side and study him. "How's that going for you?"

Mason offers me another rueful smile. "Could be better."

I release another shaky breath and press my forehead to Mason's. "He doesn't deserve you."

Mason uses his other hand to cup the back of my neck, sending a shiver up my spine. "They don't deserve you either."

For a long moment, neither of us says anything.

I close my eyes and listen to the sound of his quiet breathing, and a strange sense of calm settles over me. Then, slowly, Mason draws back and brushes his lips against mine. I melt against him as I frame his face in my hands. When he pulls away again, I reach for his hand and bring my head to rest against the crook of his neck.

"I don't want to go."

"I don't want you to go."

Mason clears his throat and stands, and I get a brief view of him in all his naked glory before he turns his back on me. "Katia's friend isn't going to take it easy on you."

"I'm counting on it."

Mason bends down to reach for his boxers and snaps them on. "Am I going to regret this?"

I hug him from behind and kiss his shoulders. "Probably. So maybe you should come watch."

"As tempting as that is, I have work to finish," Mason replies, a laugh in his voice. "Maybe when I'm done."

He kisses me before moving to retrieve my clothes from the floor.

Before I finish getting dressed, Carlisle knocks on the door.

Mason adjusts the last of his buttons and unlocks the door, flashing me a heated look before throwing the door open. I wait a while longer and then head to the basement, where bright sunlight filters in through the open windows, and Katia is standing on a mat with her hands on her hips.

"You're late."

I stop at the foot of the stairs. "Only a minute."

"Our enemies won't wait for you to be ready," Katia warns. "Do you want my help or not?"

I move toward her. "I do."

I know I'm outmatched by years of experience and training, but I'll be damned if I ever feel helpless again.

Katia steps to the side, revealing a tall and dark-haired woman with bright eyes and a scowl. I hold out my hand, and she tugs me forward and slams me against the mat hard enough to knock the wind from me. When my breath returns, I find them both staring down at me.

Suddenly, I'm wondering if I've bitten off more than I can chew.

CHAPTER NINE

Mason

"I'm already attending one event with her this week." I pause to adjust my tie. In the full-length mirror, I see my father in the background, hunched over the phone, and his fingers flying over the keyboard.

"One event isn't enough. I want anyone who's someone to hear about our alliance with the Thayers."

"As long as the Fitzpatricks and Everetts get wind of what's happening, we're good to go."

I don't care about anyone else, but I know my father does.

He's always wanted to be in the spotlight, and now that his prime has passed, I'm the next best thing.

As far as he's concerned, I've caused enough damage already, and aligning myself with Elise Thayer is the least I can do to atone for my sins.

I know it's not enough to make up for the damage I've caused. It's why I've spent the past few nights visiting every warehouse we own, and why my days are spent monitoring our operations.

It feels like he's forcing me to attend to the mundane day-to-day operations to teach me a lesson.

You're lucky if that's all he does. You've seen the way he looks at London. The fact that he hasn't gotten rid of her yet doesn't mean he's accepted it.

If anything, I know he's waiting for me to do it myself.

My father has been unusually quiet since the disastrous meeting with the other mob families, and it's put me on edge.

A quiet Jack Payne is never a good thing.

And I hate not being able to uncover what he's doing in the shadows.

It's still better than what he could be doing. Sidelining you and taking the lead isn't the worst thing in the world, and you know it.

"It's not enough," Jack announces. "Not nearly good enough. Everyone needs to hear about this."

I spin around to face him. "As long as you and I are clear that it's not going to go further than an engagement."

The truth about my arrangement with Elise is on the tip of my tongue, but if there's one thing my years with my father have taught me, it's that he doesn't like being duped. He'll like it even less if he knows it's coming from me, and I can't afford to have that kind of scrutiny.

Elise and I might be putting on a show, but I've given her my word.

Jack lowers the phone. "In time, Elise will be able to persuade you otherwise. The Thayer heir has a good head on her shoulders. I'm sure she'll make a good case for herself."

I scoff but keep my mouth shut.

He advances on me, dark eyes glittering now. "You will be the doting fiancé tonight. I want you to sell your relationship to the world."

I don't need reminding of what's at stake. "I'm aware."

His hands move to my tie. After he adjusts it, he surveys me again, and it takes every ounce of self-control I have not to wipe the grin off his face.

The arrogant bastard thinks he's won.

I hate letting him think he's got the upper hand.

Be smart about this. What good will it do to have him know? Other than the fact that he'll be breathing down your neck. And that's assuming Elise doesn't pull the plug.

We don't need more enemies.

"You will do whatever the fuck Elise tells you to do," Jack adds. "I don't care what it is you need to do to sell it."

I nod tightly. "I know what I have to do."

He offers me another meaningful look before turning his back on me. Carlisle is waiting for us outside the office. He falls into step beside me, bringing me up to speed. At the end of the hallway, I turn right and spot a flash of movement.

When I turn to it, my stomach lurches as I notice London leaning over the counter, with Katia standing opposite her. Katia draws herself up to her full height, and London swallows as her eyes land on me. She stands up straighter and squares her shoulders as her eyes dart back and forth between my father and me. I ignore Jack.

Once he disappears, I cover the distance between us. "What are you doing here?"

"Even prisoners are allowed some free time now and again," London says. "Another work meeting?"

I clear my throat. "Nothing I'll enjoy."

London raises an eyebrow. "You should've gone for a cheaper suit."

I frown. "Appearances matter. You know that. Since we'll be out, you can go for a walk around the estate. Katia can accompany you."

London purses her lips. "I want to go see my parents."

I run a hand over my face. "We've already discussed—"

London holds up a hand. "I know how dangerous it is, so I'm coming to you first. Don't make me regret it."

"What happened last time won't happen again. You know I've made sure of it."

London clenches her hands into fists. "I thought you said I wasn't a prisoner?"

"You're not. Think of it as being a visitor to a foreign country. Certain steps and measures need to be taken to keep you safe, and some areas are strictly off-limits."

London's eyes flash. "My parents can't be off limits forever. I am not a helpless child. I've been training—"

I interrupt her with a humorless laugh. "You think that a couple of weeks of training is enough to prepare you for what's out there? Don't be naïve."

I am not going to let her put herself in danger.

Not after how close she came to dying last time.

And I don't fucking care if she hates me for it.

London's expression darkens. "And if I'm underprepared, whose fault will that be?"

I place my arms around her and pull her to me. She stiffens. "I don't want to argue with you about this."

London searches my face. "I don't want to argue either."

I give her a quick and rough kiss, and she melts against me, threading her fingers through my hair. My pulse quickens when she runs another hand down my back and stops at my behind. One arm remains wrapped around her waist, and the other darts under her shirt, finding her bra quickly.

London's breath hitches as I squeeze. "That's not fair."

"I don't play fair," I murmur into her mouth. Slowly, I press hot, open-mouthed kisses down her neck, and my nails dig into her waist. "Don't push it, London. I'm already giving you a lot of leeway, given the kind of danger you're in. This is nothing compared to what it could be."

London leans back to look at me, and her expression falls. "So, I should be thankful it isn't worse?"

I cup her face in my hands. "Yes."

London squirms against me, and I release her. "I don't accept that."

"You don't have to. I don't need you to accept everything I do. I'll still do what I have to in order to keep you alive."

She can hate me all she wants, but in time, London will come to terms with the fact that it's in her best interest.

All that matters is keeping her alive and safe.

"I'm not a child."

I scowl. "I have somewhere else to be. We'll talk about this later."

London's mouth falls open. "But—"

"Later," I interrupt, more forcefully. "There's food in the fridge, and you can order anything you want."

Without waiting for a response, I leave the room.

In the foyer, I glance over my shoulder and meet Katia's gaze.

Abruptly, I look away and reach for my scarf. After securing it around my neck, I shove my arms into my coat. A gust of cold wind rushes past as I step outside and frown at the car parked at the foot of the stairs. Inside, my father already has a drink in his hand and is saying something into the phone. He levels me with a withering look when I jump in and pull the door shut behind me.

The car ride to the movie premiere is a blur.

We pull up, and I see that Elise is dressed in a midnight-blue dress, with her hair pulled up into an elegant updo. I exit the car, hold my arm out to her, and pull her closer. There's a flash behind me as I kiss her cheek, and my stomach clenches. Elise tucks her arm into the crook of my elbow and leans forward, her floral perfume washing over me.

"You're cutting it close, aren't you?"

I maintain my charm. "I'm here, aren't I?"

Elise pretends to adjust my tie. "Don't talk to any reporters unless I'm there. And try not to look so stiff."

I stop to tuck her hair behind her ear. "I'm not a circus performer."

I loathe having every part of my life picked apart.

Unfortunately, I know it's part of ensuring the Thayers remain our allies, and while I hate the hundreds of prying eyes on us and the din of conversation rising and falling around us, I'm committed to seeing this through.

There are more and more camera flashes, and I do my best to ignore them.

Questions are shouted at us from every direction, but I tune it all out.

Elise's fingers dig into my elbow as she tugs me forward, her rehearsed smile never slipping.

On the red carpet, she pauses every so often to wave someone over, and I play my part dutifully.

I imagine London by my side the entire time.

When I place my arm around Elise's waist and kiss her ear, I picture London in the figure-hugging dress with a slit down the side. All the faces blend into each other, and the voices recede to the background as my headache grows.

I keep an image of London at the forefront of my mind.

She gets me through the last of the introductions, and we duck inside.

In the theater, hundreds of pairs of eyes are on us, so I lace my fingers through Elise's. I spot our fathers sitting together, with Thatcher grinning from ear to ear. Jack's eyes assess us as I move Elise's hand to my lips and kiss each knuckle. She giggles and places her head in the crook of my neck.

"It'll be over soon."

I nod and don't reply.

The rest of the evening is a blur of faces and voices I can't be bothered to pay attention to.

After posing for a few more pictures outside, Elise gets into the car with me, and her shoulders sag. Once the partition is up, she leaves a few inches of space between us and pours herself a drink. I stare out the window at the world rushing outside. The car pulls up on the other side of the city, outside a brick townhouse in an affluent residential area where a red Tesla is parked out front.

Elise blows me a kiss over her shoulder on the way out. "Don't be late next time."

"I wouldn't dream of it."

London is fast asleep when I return to the estate, peel off my clothes, and leave them in a pile on the floor. By the pale light of the moon, I tiptoe over to her, pull back the covers, and exhale. As I curl myself around her, London stirs and moves an arm over my head. I wrap my arms around her waist and nuzzle her neck.

"How was your work thing?"

"Fucking long," I murmur, my fingers splaying themselves across her stomach. "I thought of you the whole time."

London whimpers. "I don't like fighting with you."

"I can think of much better ways to spend our time."

***

By week's end, I'm sure I'd rather sit through one of my father's lectures than attend another event with Elise by my side. The past few weeks have been a series of events from fashion shows to galas to movie premieres, all with the same group of people and the same inane chatter. To her credit, Elise doesn't falter, and I have a begrudging respect for her.

By the second week, there's a pit in my stomach at the number of pictures floating around, and the knowledge that London is a tabloid story away from uncovering the truth. I want to come clean to her, but I know it won't do us any good.

London won't understand.

How could she?

She's never had to lie to protect an empire.

How do you think she's going to feel about you spending so much time with another woman? London is considerate, but even she has her limits.

It's exhausting having to come up with reasons to leave the house.

I almost want it to catch up to me. At the end of the second week, I dress for another movie premiere. As usual, my father is lurking in the background. In the hallway, I see London in a pair of yoga pants with a thin sheen of sweat on her forehead, and I consider how much trouble I'll be in if I skip the event.

What's one more movie premiere?

When I catch the murderous gleam in my father's eyes, I give London a tight smile and force myself downstairs where Elise and her father are waiting. Elise spends the entire car ride there texting on her phone. As we arrive, Elise puts her phone away and turns to me with the same practiced smile I've grown accustomed to.

"We need to be photographed at your club."

I climb out of the car and hold out my hand for her. "No."

Elise tucks her hand into my elbow. "You know it will be suspicious if we aren't."

I match her stride and ignore the clamor of voices around us. "If you knew about my club, you would know I'm doing you a favor."

Elise pushes herself up on tiptoe and brushes her lips against my cheek. "I told you that I want to have fun."

I lower my eyes to hers. "Fine, but we do it on my terms."

I hate that she's right and considering how much of her world I've been exposed to, it's high time she sees mine.

As long as I figure out a way to make sure London doesn't get wind of any of it.

"I'm glad you're finally coming out to play," Elise says. "It took you long enough."

I wink. "Be careful what you wish for."

Being on the outskirts suits us just fine because the last thing Elise wants is to dance too close to the flames.

She throws her head back and laughs, attracting the attention of a few photographers standing behind the railing. "You underestimate me, Payne. That's fine. I love a good challenge."

I wrap my fingers around her wrist. "Don't—"

A loud banging sound somewhere to my right interrupts me. A heartbeat later, there's another loud sound, and my heart stops. Suddenly, the group of security guards nearby rushes toward us and forms a protective circle. I step in front of Elise, my hand moving to the gun at my waist.

Elise's eyes widen when I pull out the weapon. "You can't let anybody see that."

"That's the least of our problems right now." We all move together toward the car. "Unless you want to get blood stains on that expensive dress, I'd suggest you shut the hell up and let me do what I do best."

People race past us in either direction, panic on their faces.

I keep both hands on my gun as a cacophony of voices moves around us, and my eyes sharpen into focus.

A scream slices through the air, but I don't turn to it.

The security team rushes into a black sedan, and I barely have a chance to glance over my shoulder at the inert form of a woman bleeding out on the ground before the door slams shut. The car screeches away a few moments later, and I reach for my phone.

Elise is sitting as far away from me as possible, the free hand at her side trembling. Her other hand is reaching for the decanter of alcohol. After pouring herself a generous amount, she opens the mini fridge, and the soft light illuminates how pale she looks.

I spend the entire ride on the phone barking out orders and fuming.

How in the hell did they find us?

And who were they targeting?

The gates to the Mason estate open as a security guard waves us through. We pull up the gravel pathway, and my father and Thatcher Thayer are waiting for us at the bottom of the stairs. I get out of the car first and hold my hand out to Elise. No one says anything as we stride into the house, and the door slams shut behind us.

Then, everyone begins to speak at once.

I release Elise's arm and sigh. "I already have men combing the scene for the shooter."

"We won't let him get away," Jack says. "I can assure you both that this is an isolated incident. I'm sure it has nothing to do with our alliance."

Thatcher scowls. "Our family has been going to premieres and galas for decades, and there has never been an incident like this. Weeks after our alliance, my daughter almost gets shot."

"She didn't," I offer. "I told you I would keep your daughter safe."

Thatcher glares at me. "That's only if you don't get shot either, and I don't know how you'll avoid that when you came so close tonight."

I rip off my tie and throw it on the floor. "I can handle myself."

"Even when he was little, he was able to hold his own."

I glance past Thatcher's shoulder and do a double-take when I spot Olivia's blonde hair and bright green eyes. She crosses over to me, and I remain rooted to the spot as she wraps her arms around me and pulls me in for a hug. Then she draws back to smile at me, but all I see are the circles under her eyes.

Goddamn it.

What is the hell is my sister doing here?

It takes every ounce of self-control I have not to turn on my father and wrap my fingers around his throat.

"Liv, this is Elise." I shoot my father a pointed look that he ignores. "Elise this is my sister, Olivia. Liv is in town on business."

Olivia holds her hand out and gives Elise a quick shake. "It's nice to meet you."

"How's Paris, Liv? You showing them how a Payne gets things done?"

Olivia laughs. "You know I am."

"Good. I hope you're settling in okay. You can ask Mrs. Rodriguez for anything you need."

Olivia rolls her eyes. "I remember how things work. I haven't been gone that long."

As far as I'm concerned, she hasn't been gone long enough, and I have to push back against the rage bubbling up inside of me.

I'm not surprised that Jack went behind my back, but I'm terrified of what it means.

Our father has threatened to bring Oliver and Olivia into the fold for years.

I've lost count of how many times he's demanded they join the family business.

With Olivia here, it's only a matter of time before Oliver follows.

Fear and guilt settle in my stomach.

At least if they're nearby, you can keep an eye on them. No need to waste precious resources to keep tabs on them.

Except I know having them in the thick of things won't end well for any of us.

Being back has already taken a toll on Olivia. I can see it in the way she keeps shifting and the tense set of her shoulders.

I wonder how much our father has told her.

"Back to the matter at hand," Jack interrupts. "I've just received word that someone has been apprehended. He's being brought to the estate as we speak."

Thatcher gives a tight nod. "I want to be present when he's being questioned, but I'll have to change."

"I'll make sure clothes are provided for both of you." Jack's eyes dart between Thatcher and Elise. "And anything else either of you needs."

I spot the top of London's head just as it disappears behind the island in the kitchen. I press two fingers to my temples and glance over at Olivia. She's studying our father and clenching and unclenching her hands into fists. I wait until the right moment, then sneak off to find London crouched behind the counter in the kitchen.

Her eyes widen when she sees me, but she says nothing.

I'd be impressed if I wasn't so pissed. I close my fingers around her wrist and tug her behind me, toward the back stairs.

Once we're in my room, I release her wrist and let the door click shut. "Are you trying to get yourself killed? Do you have any idea what would've happened if I hadn't been the one to spot you spying in the kitchen?"

London stiffens and rubs her wrist. "I wasn't spying, and you're deflecting from what matters."

I raise an eyebrow and lean against the wall. "Enlighten me."

"I heard everything," London hisses. "I can't believe you would lie to me like that."

"It is business."

London's expression tightens. "Bullshit. You were out with that woman, and you were at some kind of event."

"And?"

London bristles. "Don't stand there and make me feel like I'm crazy. She's the reason you've been getting home later the past few weeks."

"Yes."

London sucks in a harsh breath. "I heard an alliance mentioned. She's part of it, isn't she?"

I move to stand directly in front of her. "Ask me what you want to know, London."

She searches my face.

She doesn't say anything for a long moment, and I see the gears turning in her mind as she studies me.

Finally, she takes an uncertain step back. "The alliance between the two of you, it's not just about business, is it?"

"Ask the goddamn question."

London clenches her hands into fists. "It's personal. Your father brokered some kind of deal in exchange for her family's help."

"Yes."

London inhales sharply. "How personal is it?"

"Do you really want to know?"

She gives me a small nod.

"We're pretending to be engaged. Thatcher has been trying to ally himself with one of the powerful families for years, and we need the numbers and resources."

London presses her lips into a thin, white line.

I move closer and wait for her to look at me. "You know there's nothing between us. You know there's no one else."

London's face gives nothing away. "Do I? I only know what you tell me."

I frown. "Do you have any idea what I've risked for you? And keeping you here when my father is a breath away, waiting for me to fuck up..."

"If I'm such a liability, why are you keeping me around?"

I bark out a laugh. "Goddamn feelings. My father was right about them being a hassle."

London stares at me in disbelief.

"Elise Thayer and I are not involved in any way that counts," I say slowly. "It's a mutually beneficial arrangement championed by our families."

"Why didn't you tell me?"

Silence stretches between us.

London runs a hand through her hair. "What did you think I was going to do? Did you think I would cause a scene or go to the press or something?"

"No."

"Bullshit. You were worried about my reaction. You're the one who insisted we be honest with each other and not keep secrets."

"You knew who you were getting involved with."

London points a finger at me. "Don't you fucking do that. Don't act like this is my fault when you're the one who doesn't know how to be in a relationship. So, there are parts of your job that I won't like and things you have to do. I can wrap my head around that."

"Including the fact that I have to drape myself over another woman in public?"

London winces. "I'm not crazy about it, but I know there's a lot about this—*your*—world that I don't know. What I don't appreciate is being lied to."

"I didn't lie to you."

London purses her lips. "You kept it from me, and that's just as bad."

"If you're looking for full transparency, this won't work," I tell her evenly. "Even if you think you can handle it, you can't. I'm not patronizing you; it is a fact. Do not expect me to find you at night and share every detail of how my day went. I didn't tell you because I didn't think it was necessary. You have enough on your plate, and I didn't want to upset you."

My headache is pounding now, making me more impatient than usual.

I know I'm supposed to ease her into things, but I don't have time to when we're in the middle of a goddamn war.

"I don't expect you to tell me everything," London whispers. "But at least the things that matter. You should've told me."

"She doesn't matter."

Why can't I make London see that?

The cameras, the pictures, the whole charade...none of it means anything.

"Elise Thayer is a means to an end," I add, after a lengthy pause. "You have nothing to worry about."

"I need some space." She turns away from me. "I think we should sleep in separate rooms tonight."

Her words feel like a dagger through the heart, and I'm tempted to ignore them.

But I know it won't do me any good.

I'm wading in unfamiliar waters, and the last thing I want to do is to sink because I don't know how to be in a relationship.

For now, we'll do things London's way.

I draw myself up to my full height. "Don't try and sneak downstairs again, or I'll punish you myself."

Without waiting for a response, I storm downstairs. At the foot of the stairs, I spot Elise, who has a drink in one hand and a cigarette in the other. My fingers move to the first few buttons of my shirt, and I make quick work of them. Then, I snatch the drink out of her hand and watch Elise through a thin plume of smoke.

"Trouble in paradise?"

"Don't," I warn between sips. "You and I are *not* friends."

This arrangement has caused enough trouble for one night.

The last thing I need is for London to catch us whispering.

Elise drags in another breath and blows it out. "We could be, you know. I see no reason why our arrangement can't be beneficial on all levels."

I level Elise with a blank look. "Did my father put you up to this?"

Elise takes the drink from my hand and downs it. "Nobody puts me up to anything."

"Mind your own damn business then," I snap back.

A short while later, Elise disappears, and I stalk off toward the basement. Mathew's voice drifts upstairs, and I hear him mention my name and London's. Then it goes quiet, and I head downstairs, pausing at the bottom to roll up my sleeves.

A dark-haired man is tied to a chair in the center of the basement, a single light bulb dangling over his head. Blood is caked to the sides of his face and his nose, and he's breathing heavily. As I step closer, the prisoner watches me through his swollen eye. I yank him back by his hair and wait until he's done hissing and looks at me.

"I can make this quick," I tell him, "or we can keep doing this. Your choice."

He says nothing.

A heartbeat later, he doubles over when I punch him in the side. I see Thayer in the background, his nose wrinkled in disgust. My father is standing next to him, his knuckles bloodied and bruised.

I recognize the murderous glint in my father's eyes.

It's going to be a long night, but the man brought it on himself.

He knew we'd retaliate.

Hours later, my blood is still pumping when I go upstairs and step into the guest bathroom. After running my fingers under warm water, I turn the past few hours over in my mind. In the kitchen, I retrieve an ice pack and press it against my hand. On my way upstairs, I hear a few hushed whispers coming from my study.

Frowning, I move in that direction, and Olivia steps out with Carlisle on her heels.

I melt into the shadows and watch them gesture furiously.

Carlisle looks up and spots me, and some of the color drains from his face. Olivia wheels around and scowls. I stride toward them and give Carlisle a meaningful look that has him hurrying off. Once he's out of earshot, I turn back to Olivia and ignore the knots in my stomach.

"What the hell are you doing?"

"Don't you have anything better to do than spy on me?"

"Livvy—"

"Don't." She holds up a hand. "I know what you're going to say. I'm not stupid. I'm being careful."

I blow out a breath. "That's what you said last time."

There's too much shit going on for me to add worrying about Olivia to my list.

Having her here is supposed to make things easier.

Fucking hell.

When did Olivia start keeping secrets from me?

Probably around the time you started hiring a team to take shifts, keeping an eye on her in Paris.

"I'm here," Olivia says. "That should be enough."

"Be careful around Carlisle."

Olivia raises an eyebrow. "Shouldn't you be keeping an eye on London? Don't look so surprised that I know about her. You know how

Mathew likes to run his mouth, especially if it involves one of your screw-ups."

I huff and say nothing.

Olivia takes a step in my direction and lowers her voice. "You know that Dad is waiting for the slightest whiff of trouble to get rid of her?"

"I don't need you to fucking remind me of what's at stake," I snap back.

A few moments later, after retrieving a bottle from my study, I storm upstairs. The door to my room creaks open. London is on her back, hair splayed behind her, and her fingers linked together. Her chest rises and falls evenly, and she doesn't stir when I slowly let the door click shut behind me.

I reach for the dresser chair and brace it against the door.

Then, I use my teeth to pry open the bottle and take a long swig.

London stirs.

I watch her through hooded eyes as she flips onto her side and curls against the pillow. Then, she releases a deep breath and goes still again.

I know I'm supposed to give her space, but I can't leave her defenseless.

All it'll take is one look at us coming out of different bedrooms for my father to sink his hooks into her.

I'm not going to let him touch her, even if it means spending the night in an uncomfortable chair watching over her as she fumes at me in her sleep.

I can handle her being upset and confused and even pissed.

But I can't handle the thought of anyone harming her.

Halfway through the drink, I stand up and walk over to the bed.

After retrieving a pillow, I prop it up against the dresser and slide against it. A few sips later, I'm cursing my father's name and wondering if this was his plan all along.

He wouldn't have risked a shooting to expose the arrangement to

London, but somewhere in his warped mind, he thinks Elise is a better fit.

What if the alliance is a ruse meant to push us together?

What if he's trying to dangle Elise as a better prospect?

She comes from the same world, so it makes sense.

I frown at London's sleeping form and try to picture Elise instead.

I know that being with someone level-headed and experienced like Elise is better in the long run, but that doesn't change how I feel about London.

I've already risked everything for her once, and I don't regret it.

As my eyelids grow heavy and I fight sleep, my thoughts drift to my father, and the lengths he's willing to go to secure his empire.

I wonder how long it will be before he throws me to the wolves.

CHAPTER TEN

London

"Again," Katia orders without glancing up from her blade. "That was pathetic, and you know it."

I grunt and throw another punch, causing the boxing bag to swing a little.

"Harder," Katia instructs. I feel her eyes on me, but I ignore her. "Just because Nadia isn't around doesn't mean I'll take it easy on you, Princess."

I know Katia is taunting me by dangling the promise of her colleague, but she's right.

I want her to be the one handing my ass back to me.

Nadia is skilled, almost as good as Katia, but without an axe to grind with me.

Although I've only pieced together a few snippets of the assassin's friend, what I have learned is enough to make me realize how insane it all is.

Having a former Russian spy as my trainer isn't what I had in mind, especially not someone who specializes in blank stares and grunts.

Knowing Katia, you can't be all that surprised that this is who she chose. You told her you wanted someone good and discreet.

I picture the two of them sharpening blades together in the wilderness somewhere, and it fills me with unease.

All it takes is one wrong move for Katia to sic her friend on me.

Suddenly, going to Katia for help doesn't seem like the inspired idea it was, not when Nadia is even more temperamental than her friend.

I pause to wipe away the thin sheen of sweat. "This is you taking it easy on me?"

Katia scoffs. "If I wanted to, I'd have you curled up on the floor trying to breathe through the pain, and there would be more than a few bruises on you."

I ignore the lurch in my stomach and lift my arms. "Noted."

I'm not in the mood for Katia—or anyone else—today.

All I can think about is Elise fucking Thayer, and how she looked tucked into Mason's side with her dark eyes roaming over him intently.

I throw a few more punches and wince when pinpricks of pain race up and down my arms. "Why aren't you fighting me?"

Katia leans back and crosses her ankles. "It wouldn't be a fight, and I've got better things to do."

"Yeah, like look at your blade," I spread my legs shoulder-width apart and pause. Then, I square my shoulders and throw one punch after the other until my hands ache and my lungs are burning. My breath comes out in short puffs as I lift a leg and do a side kick that barely moves the punching bag.

Growling, I use my other leg to kick and grimace when I nearly fall backward.

A twinge in my lower back has me shifting from one foot to the other and bracing my hands on either side of me. I inhale deeply and wait for the ringing in my ears to quiet. Slowly, I glance over at Katia, who is leaning against the wall and watching me.

"What?"

"Anger motivates you."

I scowl and turn away from her. "No, it doesn't."

Katia strolls over to me. "It wasn't a question, Princess. It was a statement. Something has you riled up."

I bite back the retort.

Am I that obvious?

Or am I not hiding my feelings as well as I'd like?

Katia stops a few inches away from me. "Don't favor one leg. Make sure you're transferring your weight often, and don't come in hard at the beginning. It's about how well you hit, not how often."

I rear back, landing a punch squarely to the bag. "Fine."

Katia chuckles. "Who knew it was so easy to get under your skin? Let me guess. It was seeing the Thayer heir yesterday, wasn't it? There's been rumors about her and Mason for years, you know."

"Shut up." I pause to swat away an errant lock of hair. "You don't know what you're talking about."

Katia inches closer. "Don't I? I mean, I can't blame you. She's fucking gorgeous, and she comes from money."

I throw my leg out, and Katia catches it in midair. "Let go."

Katia tightens her grip. "She's also from his world, so it makes sense for them to be thrown together."

I squirm and try to pull back my leg. "Just because it makes sense on paper doesn't mean it'll work in the real world."

I'm living proof of that.

I walked away from Noah, a nice and stable guy I could've had a normal relationship with, for a man like Mason.

Even my parents think I've gone insane, but I won't let any of it get to me.

Not the frustration, not the fear, and definitely not the jealousy.

So what if Mason has a past?

It will keep being flaunted in your face, even if you don't go looking for it. It's everywhere.

Another image of Elise and Mason with their heads bent together flashes to mind before I shove it away.

Katia releases my leg. "Good. Channel that anger and put it to good use."

"I know what you're trying to do." I throw another punch that Katia intercepts. "If you're not going to help, get out of my way."

Katia releases my arm and rolls her shoulders. "Alright, Princess. Let's see how quick of a study you are."

She peels off her jacket.

Her expression is one of schooled boredom as she points at me.

I inhale and, on the count of five, I charge her.

Katia sidesteps me easily, and I sail past her, skidding to a halt a few feet away. When I wheel around, red-hot anger pumps through me.

She's toying with me, and I hate her for it.

I charge again, but this time, I feign right and land a punch to her right. Without missing a beat, Katia pivots and kicks out her leg. The breath leaves my body as I crash to the floor and pain blossoms behind my eyelids.

Everything hurts.

But it still won't drive away the images haunting me.

I hate that Elise is everything I'm not and that she gets to be with Mason in public while I have to hide away like some dirty little secret.

You know it's not up to Mason. It's just business.

When I open my eyes, Katia is looming over me, her expression blank. "Get up."

On trembling legs, I push myself up and exhale. "You're losing your touch. Is that all you got?"

Katia throws her head back and laughs. "You really are pathetic."

I launch at Katia's middle. She stops laughing when I wrap both arms around her waist and pull. She shoves me back, and I stagger, the whistling in my ears growing.

Suddenly, all I'm picturing is Katia in Mason's study.

All I see are her long fingers tracing a path down his bare back. I taste bile as I imagine her throwing her head back and moaning as Mason thrusts in and out of her. I shove the image away and launch myself at Katia again.

"Enough." Katia throws out a hand to stop me. "You need to learn your limits."

I growl, my breath coming out in short puffs. "You don't get to tell me when I've had enough. And stop holding back."

Katia's eyes bore into me. "No."

"Come on, isn't this what you wanted? Now's your chance. You can hit me right now, and Mason wouldn't be able to do a thing."

I try for her middle again, but it's no use.

I'm never going to beat her.

But I don't care.

I want to feel anything other than despair and helplessness clawing their way inside of me, making me want to rip my hair out.

What good is it going to do me anyway?

You're never going to compare to any of them. Not even Miss Deveroux who had the skill and discretion needed to land Mason, and Katia knows how to give him what he wants in the bedroom. What do you have to offer, other than a headache, and throwing their alliance into an uproar?

I don't realize that I'm attacking Katia until she wraps her arms around me to hold me still.

The blood is still roaring in my ears, but I can't stop.

Finally, Katia releases me.

When her fist connects with my face, I feel a sickening crunch and stumble backward. Then, I taste blood in my mouth and feel it ooze from my nose. Wordlessly, she crosses over to me and hands me a towel.

I press it against my nose and wince. "I knew you wanted to do that."

Katia shrugs. "You asked for it. I'll get you an ice pack. Don't move."

As she leaves, I sink into the nearest chair, my anger gone, replaced by a deep sense of shame and frustration. I tilt my head back and inhale mouthfuls of air. When Katia returns, she's got a clean towel in one hand

and an ice pack in the other. Hissing, I force myself to my feet and let the blood-soaked towel fall to the floor.

"It's not broken." Katia hands me the new towel. "But it's going to hurt like hell in a bit."

I snatch the towel from her hand. "Whatever."

For a long while, neither of us says anything as I wait for my breathing to return to normal.

Every inch of my body aches as Katia leads us out of the basement and follows at a safe distance until I reach Mason's room. A first-aid kit is waiting for me inside, but I storm past it and into the bathroom.

I hop into the shower, stand under the head, and try not to imagine Mason with anyone else.

Steam fills the room as I secure a towel around my chest and pad out of the bathroom.

After wadding up strips of cotton, I shove them up my nose and breathe through my mouth.

Gingerly, I change into a clean pair of yoga pants and a cotton shirt.

I take a few sips of water and reach for the laptop on the dresser.

Grimacing, I ignore my mangled reflection on the screen and drum my fingers on the desk. The laptop boots up, and I wait impatiently for a search webpage to load. I type in Elise Thayer's name. Her image pops up, and regret floods my veins.

Katia is right.

She's got movie-star looks and style to match.

And her net worth is more than I'll make in ten lifetimes.

The more I scroll, the worse I feel until I have a pounding headache. An hour later, I push my chair back and stand up. I shove my arms into a hoodie and pull the hood down, so it conceals half my face.

Katia doesn't say anything when I emerge.

At the bottom of the stairs, I turn to face her, ignoring the pain blossoming in my face. "I'm going to the club."

"There's a table in the back you can use."

In silence, she leads me from the manor and into the late afternoon air. A warm breeze drifts past us as we cross the lawn that separates the estate from the business complex. I try not to think about the fact that none of Mason's men stop us as we stride past.

Slowly, Katia leads me around the back of the building, and she punches in a code that opens a door. My eyes widen as we step inside, and the smell of alcohol and perfume hits me. Katia leads us down hallways until low, rhythmic music fills the air.

The hallway opens into the main part of the club, and it takes a minute for my eyes to adjust.

As it does, I glance around at the low light and the few clients scattered around.

Katia clears a path to a table on the top floor that overlooks the club.

I sink onto the couch, and she disappears.

She returns with Miss Deveroux and a tray with a bottle of wine and bowls of food.

Katia gives me a long, measured look and disappears again. Miss Deveroux glances between the two of us and then perches on the edge of a seat. She reaches for a handful of peanuts, her crunching snapping me out of my reverie. Then, she clears her throat and leans back.

"I haven't said anything about your involvement; don't worry. Mason thinks we were picked up by a random stranger."

Miss Deveroux pops open the bottle and pours a generous amount into two glasses. "Do I need to ask about the bruises?"

I grimace and take the glass from her outstretched hand. "I pushed Katia too far when she was training me."

Miss Deveroux makes a face and takes a small sip of her drink. "I'd ask what you did to deserve winding up with her as your instructor, but I don't think you'd tell me."

I lean back against the couch and grimace. "She's the best."

Miss Deveroux's eyes move over me. "You can still change your mind, you know. About leaving, I mean. It's not too late."

I ignore the lurch in my stomach. "I'm not changing my mind."

I'll do what I need to do to survive.

"I can talk to her—"

I shake my head. "No, I don't want you getting more involved than you have to. I know how Mason would see it."

Miss Deveroux takes a sip of her drink. "I know there isn't much I can do, but I'm here."

Slowly, I pull my hood back and turn to face Miss Deveroux. Her mouth falls open as she leans forward to inspect my face. She lifts a hand and drops it. Then she opens her mouth again, but before she can say anything, there's a loud banging sound.

Fear settles in the pit of my stomach and coils its way around my chest.

There's another loud banging sound, and I reach for Miss Deveroux's hand to pull her down. She flips over the table, sending glasses and bowls in every direction. My heart pounds as I sit there, calming my racing heart. Katia appears next to us and pulls me to my feet. She whips out a gun and motions to us.

My stomach lurches as we follow her downstairs and past the chaos.

Men with bulging muscles race past us in either direction. I swallow hard when I see a few inert forms on the floor and smell the unmistakable odor of blood. Miss Deveroux reaches for my hand, and I squeeze it. Katia leads us down a dark hallway to a storage room in the back.

She punches a code and pushes me in. "I'll be back."

Miss Deveroux hurries in after me, and a second later, the door hisses shut behind us.

I have no idea how long we sat there, waiting for Katia to return.

When the door opens again, relief floods my veins, and I stumble to my feet. I'm surprised to see Mathew standing on the other side of the

137

door with a gun in his hand. He takes in Miss Deveroux before turning back to me. Then, he holds out his hand.

"Katia sent me to get you."

"Where is she?"

"You can ask her when you see her."

"I don't believe you," I tell him. "I don't trust you."

Mathew huffs and shifts from one foot to the other. "I don't know what bullshit Mason filled your head with, but we don't have time for this."

"Make time."

Mathew takes a step in my direction, and my heart skips a beat. "Fucking move before I make you."

"You won't touch me."

Mathew's eyes narrow further. "My brother needs to teach you your place."

"I don't think so."

"I know you're being cautious," Mathew sighs, "but you have nothing to worry about, London. I'm not going to hurt you."

Something about the gleam in his eyes doesn't sit well with me.

It's eerie seeing Mathew flip the charm on and off, and I realize with a cold certainty that I can never underestimate him.

"I'm going to wait for Katia," I tell Mathew. "I'm sure she'll be back for me."

I wonder if Mathew has done something to her.

She's a trained assassin. I doubt Mathew could get the jump on her. But maybe they struck some kind of deal so she can look the other way while he takes care of you.

I ignore the lurch in my chest when Mathew steps toward me. "I don't have time for this. We're going right now."

I steel myself as Mathew's hand darts out and closes around my wrist.

"I'm doing you this courtesy because you're a Payne. Now get your hands off her before I slice your fingers off one by one."

Mathew drops his hand and wheels around, some of the bravado fading as Katia strolls toward us.

Relief floods my system as she stops a few feet away, and her gaze flicks over to me. "The coast is clear."

Katia and Miss Deveroux exchange a glance, and Miss Deveroux gives my hand a squeeze on her way out of the room. Katia and Mathew are staring each other down.

Mathew blinks first, taking several steps backward. "You're wasted on my brother, Katia. All you have to do is come to me willingly."

Katia motions to me, and I fall into step beside her. She levels Mathew with a cold look. "We have things to do."

I feel Mathew's eyes on my back as we head back to the basement of the estate.

Katia hands me a water bottle, and I realize my hands are shaking. I force myself to my feet, take several deep breaths, and unscrew the lid. Then I tilt my head back and down the bottle, but it doesn't chase away the dryness in my throat or the tightness in my chest.

"You could've gone with Mathew."

I toss the water bottle into the nearest trash can and turn to her. "Was I supposed to?"

"He's a Payne."

"He gives me the creeps," I reply. "Besides, I get the feeling he's not someone you can trust."

Katia blinks. "Did Mason tell you that?"

"He warned me about Mathew, but he didn't tell me much else. I'm not going to push him. He'll tell me when he's ready."

Katia frowns. "And you're okay with being kept in the dark?"

"I choose to believe that Mason will open up to me when he can. If there are things he can't share with me because they're not his secrets to tell, that's fine, too."

Katia's eyes move over me. "That way of thinking will get you killed."

I shrug. "Maybe, maybe not."

Katia mulls that over. "You can choose something different, you know. Some people aren't lucky enough to have that option."

I tilt my head to the side and study her. "I know."

"You weren't born into this life, and you're not well-suited for it like other people are. You don't even have the stomach for violence, and yet, you choose to stay."

"Yes."

Katia faces me again, and there's a furrow between her brows. "No one should willingly choose this life, Princess. Maybe you're not as smart as I thought."

I study the assassin before me, and with a start, I realize what she's trying to tell me.

Katia isn't jealous of me because I'm with Mason, or at least that's not the only reason.

She's annoyed because I can walk away from all this, and I'm choosing to stay.

Suddenly, I find myself wondering about the deadly woman in front of me and the kind of life she's had thrust upon her.

"No one ever asked you if you wanted this life, did they?"

Katia's expression darkens. "A Patrova is meant to serve. Our opinions don't matter."

"They should." A surge of pity rises within me. "You deserve to have a say in your life."

Katia's eyes narrow. "And yet, it seems that even with options, some people continue to make the wrong decisions by falling for the wrong people."

"Katia—"

The door to the basement flies open, and Katia jumps to attention between me and the threat. I glance over her shoulder at the dark-haired man with bright eyes and a frown.

"It's good to see you, Katia."

She stiffens. "I can't say the same for you."

The man's gaze moves to me, lingering a bit too long for my comfort. "You must be the famous London I've heard so much about."

"Who are you?"

"I can see Mason hasn't bothered with the family tree. I'm Oliver Payne."

Fuck.

If Mason's younger brother is here, things have gotten much, much worse.

CHAPTER ELEVEN

Mason

I slam my hands against the desk hard enough to make it rattle. "We're not done discussing this."

Jack glances up from his chair by the fireplace and eyes me over the rim of the glass. "Throwing a tantrum is beneath a Payne. Surely, you have better things to do."

I curl my hands into fists and step out from behind the desk. "We had a deal. Olivia and Oliver were supposed to stay out of this."

And with everything else happening, I don't have time or patience to wonder about what new game my father is playing.

I have no idea what the Fitzpatricks and Everetts hoped to gain with their little demonstration at the club last night, but I do know that it's pissed me off.

Even more so because we can't seem to find out who fired the shot.

At least no one is dead. A few injured employees is nothing in the grand scheme of things.

Having to spend all morning in my study, pouring over the evidence has left me in a bad mood.

I should be out there looking for the little shit myself.

I need something to do otherwise I'm going to do something stupid, like open fire on my enemies at every location until they hand Michael and

Lance over.

Stupid little fucks.

What did they think was going to happen when they attacked the club?

They did it because they can. They're growing bolder and bolder, and now you have a slew of clients with concerns you don't know how to answer.

"Deals change." Jack nonchalantly moves the glass to his lips for a sip. I fold my arms over my chest and glare at him. "Your brother and sister belong in the heart of the empire, not off chasing ridiculous daydreams. It's time for them to grow up."

I stop in front of my father and let my eyes sweep over him. "We had an agreement. They're of no use to you."

I haven't spent the past few years honing myself into a weapon just to fail.

Olivia and Oliver aren't supposed to be anywhere near this. If my father was anyone else, I'd already have put a bullet in his head.

So much for reaching an understanding.

He hasn't spent the past couple of weeks sidelining me just to teach me a lesson. Rather than wait for me to clean up my mess, he's gone over my head and done what he thinks is best. As usual, he's been operating in the darkness and moving pieces into play, and I've been too busy focusing on the imminent threat to notice.

How had I forgotten how cunning and manipulative my father is?

My siblings aren't here for any other reason other than to pull my focus.

He's testing me with another one of his mind games.

Goddamn prick.

Why couldn't he just leave them alone?

Olivia has always toed the line of our world, with one foot on either side for years, but the minute she wanted to get away, I helped her.

Oliver has never shown a bit of interest in anything we do.

If anything, he's regarded it with disgust and horror.

How in the hell had my father lured him back?

My father rises to his feet. "Shouldn't you be attending some event with the Thayer girl?"

"Elise and I are meeting there, and we're not done talking about this."

Someone knocks on the door, and I turn to it, anger and frustration pounding through me. When Carlisle pokes his head in, I cross over to him and glance over my shoulder.

"I'll find you later."

Jack scoffs and sits down, crossing his legs. "No, we're done here. You have another mess to clean up."

I stare at him for a few more seconds and say nothing.

In the car, I dial Oliver's number.

It goes to voicemail after the sixth ring, and I resist the urge to throw the phone against the window. I drum my fingers against my chest and go over each possible scenario before discarding it. A short while later, we pull outside the docks, and Carlisle opens the door for me. I fasten the top button of my jacket and take quick, even strides.

Lance Fitzpatrick is waiting for me on the far end of the docks, his profile outlined in the dying light of the afternoon sun.

Carlisle returns to my side after a quick sweep and gives me a quick nod.

"Are your men satisfied?"

"Hardly, but I'm sure they'll have their fun soon enough," I reply, coming to a halt a few feet away. "And here I thought you were the brains of the operation. Only a fucking idiot would've agreed to this."

Lance's eyes tighten in anger. "You didn't leave me much of a choice. What kind of man threatens another man's brother?"

"A man who knows what needs to be done." I draw back my jacket to reveal my gun. "If you don't have the stomach for it, you're in the wrong line of work."

"You know it's not that simple," Lance says.

I raise an eyebrow. "Is that why Everett keeps you around? Because you like to wax poetic? That's fucking pathetic, but I guess I shouldn't expect more from either of you."

"You like to hear yourself talk, don't you? I'm here, that should tell you all you need to know."

I move toward Lance and chuckle when he winces. "Yeah, how did you convince them to let you off your leash?"

Lance doesn't reply.

I chuckle. "Everett doesn't know you're here, does he? Oh, this is better than I thought. I have to be there when he finds out."

"Fuck you."

I laugh harder. "Well, I'm not easily surprised, but congratulations. Not that it matters much. They'll probably gut you like a fish for going behind their back."

Lance straightens his back. "I'm doing what needs to be done."

"Trouble in paradise? What a shame."

I haven't heard whispers about problems between the two allied families, but since Lance is there, I have to assume they're at odds.

It doesn't leave me a lot to work with, but I see my window of opportunity.

"Since you're here, I'm going to do you the courtesy of amending the initial offer," I continue. "Thirty percent of our shares from the business we conduct using the docks."

Lance stifles a laugh. "You didn't honestly think it was going to be that simple, did you?"

"Thirty-five percent."

Lance rolls his shoulders. "We want half of the profit you get from the banks and forty percent of the business you conduct through the docks.'

"What makes you think I'll agree to that?"

"We know about your alliance with the Thayers," Lance says. "What

145

a desperate move. You don't have a lot of options."

"The Paynes always have options," I spit back. "I know business isn't great. Got yourself into some serious debt, have you?"

Lance's expression shifts and hardens. "Since when do the Paynes resort to spying?"

"I call it keeping an eye on our interests."

"Stay the fuck out of our business, Payne. You're already on thin ice with the other families. I doubt you want more trouble on your plate."

I take my gun out and hold it up to the light. "Do you know how long it takes a man to bleed out?"

"Your scare tactics don't work anymore. I know you wouldn't have called this meeting if you didn't need a truce."

I remove the safety from the gun with painstaking patience. "I always say it's important to be well prepared. You should've done your part, Fitzpatrick."

He doesn't flinch when I point the gun at him. "You shouldn't have underestimated me."

In the distance, I hear the screech of tires and the wail of sirens.

Carlisle shifts closer to me, and a ripple of unease moves through the men.

Abruptly, I reach for Lance and twist his arm behind his back. He doesn't say anything as we step forward, and I scan the docks carefully, my heart hammering as a slew of cars pulls up.

Michael Everett gets out first, and I zero in on him.

"If you don't make sure they clear a path for us, I'll tell my man to put a bullet through your brother's head and dump his body in the water," I warn. "I'll make your sister watch, of course. After that, I'll have my fun with her."

"I don't believe you," he replies.

"I'm getting out of here either way, so it's up to you if you want his mangled remains to be found or not. Clock's ticking."

Lance goes quiet, and I wonder if I've pushed too far.

Michael approaches us, and his steps falter when he sees the gun pressed to Lance's temple.

"This feels like old times," I mention. "As much as I'd love to continue this trip down memory lane, I have somewhere to be."

Michael blocks my path. "You're not going anywhere."

Behind him, I see Carlisle and two of my men creep up. In a few quick moves, they take down the closest of Michael's men, giving us an advantage. Suddenly, Michael spins around and starts shooting.

I release Lance and dive behind the nearest dumpster as bullets sail through the air.

The smell of gunpowder and sweat hangs heavy in the air as all hell breaks loose.

I peek out and fire off a few rounds, smiling when one of them lands in Michael's side. He howls, and his eyes widen. He fires back at me, missing my ear by an inch. Adrenaline pumps through me as I drop back behind the dumpster and check my gun.

Carlisle's left eye is bleeding, and he's covered in sweat when he finds me.

Back to back, we hurry across the docks and over a few inert bodies.

The car materializes out of the smoke, but I also hear Michael just behind us. I wheel to face him and aim for his head. I curse as the bullet sails past him and lodges into the man behind him. Michael's face is dark with fury as he reaches for the gun and aims.

Carlisle steps in front of me a minute too late.

Pain shoots up my leg, and I see my blood dripping onto the ground. I blink, touch the wound, and rub my fingers together. The gun in my hand falls to the ground with a clatter, but I quickly reach for the dagger tucked into my sock. It sails through the air and hits Michael squarely in the chest.

His mouth forms a surprised O as he crumples to the ground.

I don't have time to gloat as more men pour in from the shadows and smoke.

Carlisle and I throw ourselves into the back of the car, and the wheels screech as we drive off to the Payne estate.

My father is waiting at the top of the stairs when we return, a scowl on his face.

I ignore Katia and Carlisle and make a beeline for the study, where Doctor Ackles is waiting for me. I pour two drinks and hand him one. London materializes in the doorway as I sit down and roll up the hem of my pants. Another sharp pain races through me as I grit my teeth and focus on a spot over the doctor's shoulders.

Doctor Ackles says nothing as he cleans the wound.

Katia pours me another drink, and I finish it in one gulp.

I'm used to the pain, but it doesn't mean it doesn't piss me off.

You should be out there, making sure Everett's lying in a ditch somewhere, painfully bleeding out.

I shift as Doctor Ackles leans over me, his eyebrows knitted together in concentration. The smell of disinfectant fills the air, and I see a flash of silver. Carlisle shifts closer to me, and I grip my armchair with both hands, forcing myself to count backward from ten.

Pain blossoms behind my eyelids.

I bite back the howl as Doctor Ackles pinches the skin of my leg and spots dance in my field of vision. A heartbeat later, he drops the bullet into a bowl with a loud clank. Sweat breaks out across my forehead and back as I lean away.

Doctor Ackles's fingers are warm and steady against my skin as I feel the needle weave through it. I don't realize how hard I'm gritting my teeth until I hear London's quiet gasp and see her standing behind my father with Katia at her side. I look at Katia, who tries to take London's arm and steer her away, but London's eyes flash as she inches away.

Always so stubborn.

I don't know if I want to kiss her or throw her into my room and lock the door.

Once Doctor Ackles is done, my father strides toward me and peers at the wound. With a scoff, he leads the doctor away, with Mathew following close behind. Carlisle retrieves the bowl and first-aid kit and hurries off, too. Katia glances between me and London before spinning on her heel and stalking off. Slowly, London shuts the door behind her.

"Do you need me to get you anything?" she asks.

"What part of keeping yourself out of trouble don't you understand?" I snap.

"I heard them talking about trouble at the docks, and I knew something had happened. I had to check on you."

I cover the distance between us and frown. "You should've stayed upstairs."

London lifts her chin. "I already told you I'm not going to cower and hide. How many times are we going to have this argument?"

"As many times as it takes for you to get the fucking point. Every time you're anywhere near my father, you're endangering your life. Just because he hasn't retaliated doesn't mean he's not planning something."

"I'm aware of that. I know he's difficult—"

I snort. "Difficult isn't a word I would use to describe Jack Payne. Asshole. Bastard. Those are words I'd use, and right now, there are too many things for me to worry about without adding endangering your life to the mix."

"I am not a liability," London replies. "Katia has been training me. You won't have to worry about that soon enough."

"You honestly believe that, don't you?"

London let her hands fall to her sides. "You need someone strong by your side. I can be that."

"I don't care about that," I shoot back.

"I know that having someone like Elise makes more sense—"

I raise an eyebrow. "This is about you being jealous? Of Elise fucking

149

Thayer?"

"You're telling me that you haven't thought about it? How much easier it would be to have her by your side properly?"

I pull her to me. "I'm only going to say this one more time. I'm not interested in Elise Thayer. She means fuck all to me."

Myriad emotions dance across London's face before she adopts a neutral expression. "She could if you let her."

I let out a low, incredulous laugh. "You're starting to sound like my father."

"I know her family has connections. She could probably figure out a way to end the war. I've been looking her up."

Ice races up my spine and spreads through my veins. "You've what?"

"I know how to cover my tracks online." The words pour out of London's mouth in a rush. "No one will know how to trace me here, but I had to know what I was up against."

I press my lips together and say nothing.

"She's gorgeous and smart, with the right kind of connections. On paper, she makes so much sense, but on the ground, too. And her family is one of the oldest families in the city—"

"I see you fell down the rabbit hole," I grumble. "Tell me, did your research show you why the Thayers don't have an exclusive alliance with any of the families?"

London stares at me.

"It's because they don't have enough clout to be important," I tell her. "Or they didn't, until we allied ourselves with them."

London's eyes move over my face. "What about your siblings? I overheard your sister the other day. She's got a connection to one of the families, doesn't she? You could use that."

I release London. "What did she say?"

London frowns. "I wasn't paying attention to the specifics—"

I growl. "Think long and hard."

London sighs. "Why don't you just ask her?"

I know Olivia isn't going to bring me into the loop.

Not if she's planning what I think she is.

I will not let her derail her life like this, not even if it means bringing an end to the war.

She's worked too hard for too long to let things go sideways.

London's expression softens as she reaches for me. "You should talk to her. I'm sure this whole thing can be sorted out."

I stiffen as London takes my hand and tries to lace her fingers through mine. "Talking isn't going to resolve anything."

Not if Olivia has already set the wheels in motion.

Fucking hell.

How am I supposed to be everywhere at once?

I can't keep tabs on my father, our enemies, and my siblings.

"You haven't even tried," London protests. "I'm sure if you hear her out, the two of you can figure out a way together."

I yank my fingers back. "Olivia didn't get herself out just to get sucked back in. I will not let her do this."

"You can't control everyone around you," London says. "I know it comes from a good place, but people need to be able to make their own decisions."

"Are we still talking about Olivia?"

London doesn't say anything.

Olivia, I can deal with, but I can't stand the look on London's face.

It reminds me too much of the look my mother wore around my father, the kind that I later learned was one of hope, yearning, and heartbreak.

How far into my world can I drag London without shattering her?

How much of her will remain when all is said and done?

How many times will they go after her and her family before the horror of what she's agreed to settles around her?

You can still send her away. You can still do the right thing.

But as I stand across from her, hungrily drinking her in, I know I won't.

I'm too selfish to do the right thing and too far gone to be the man she deserves.

Several more moments pass in silence before I turn my back on London. I step behind my desk and ignore my throbbing leg. When I lower myself onto the leather chair, she crosses over to me and braces one arm on either side of the mahogany desk.

"I'm not going anywhere," London says quietly. "You trying to push or scare me away won't work. No one made me stay."

I eye her. "It's not like I've made it easy for you to leave, with a target on your back."

"You'd find a way to keep me safe if I wanted to leave."

I sigh. "I already told you that I'm not a hero, London. I am not the man who will do the right or selfless thing."

"I don't need you to be."

I drum my fingers against the desk. "I have business that needs tending to. Send Katia in on your way out."

London leans back and stares at me for a long, tense moment.

Eventually, she moves to the door and steps past Katia.

"Bring me Olivia."

Katia nods.

When Katia returns with my irate-looking sister, I push the chair back and stand up. Then I give Katia a meaningful look, and she exits the study, letting the door click shut behind her. Olivia shoves her hair out of her eyes and scowls.

"I'm not a lap dog you can summon."

"Whatever you're planning, you will put an end to it." I pause to give her a long, measured look. "I know you're not stupid enough to think it will work."

Olivia's eyes flash. "I might not have climbed the ranks, but I still remember a thing or two about how this works."

"No, you don't. What you're doing is going to get us all killed."

"It won't—"

"*Back the fuck off, Olivia,*" I snap. "I don't care what the hell you think you're doing, but I don't need one more problem to deal with. I already have enough on my plate."

"Did you ever think that there might be another way to do this?"

I cover the distance between us. "You will *not* use your history with Michael Everett to get their attention."

Olivia's eyes sweep over my face. "Who told you?"

"It doesn't matter. This ends right now," I repeat. "Do *not* go behind my back, Olivia."

"Don't try and scare me, Mason. I'm not one of your lackeys."

"If you were, you'd be in the basement right now, begging for your life." I ignore the pounding in my ears. "The only reason this hasn't blown up in your face is because you're a Payne. Don't make the mistake of thinking that makes you invincible. Pull the fucking plug, or I'll do it for you."

When our father steps into the study a short while later, we're still staring at each other. He gives Olivia a pointed look, and she stalks out with her head held high. The door barely closes before Jack advances on me, a dangerous glint in his eyes. I roll up my sleeves and look directly at him.

"Go ahead."

Jack stops in front of me and frowns. "You're not going to deny that you went behind my back and orchestrated a meeting when I explicitly told you not to?"

I square my shoulders. "No."

He and I both know the truth, and I'm not going to walk back anything about my meeting with Fitzpatrick, not when it's shed some light on a few things.

Our enemies aren't as united as they'd like us to think.

All I have to do is strike them where it hurts the most, and the rest will fall into place.

Provided London and Olivia don't stir shit up in the meantime. You need to make sure a close watch is being kept on those two.

CHAPTER TWELVE

London

I sigh and let the curtain swish back into place.

Slowly, I wander over to the burner phone on the nightstand and pick it up. The screen is blank, and there's a bad taste in my mouth as I put it down and ignore the knots in my stomach. With a frown, I walk back to the door and press my ear to the wood.

It's unusually quiet today.

Even Katia is nowhere to be seen, although I'm sure the assassin is just blending in nearby.

I hold my breath as I tug on the doorknob, and the door creaks open to reveal Katia polishing a dagger.

"You're pathetic," she says.

I open the door the rest of the way and frown at her. "Excuse me?"

"You heard me. I know you two got into an argument yesterday. Pretty sure the whole house knows, and without Mason, you are a sitting duck."

"No, I'm not."

Mason and I had exchanged a few terse words about the argument, but it still lingered between us.

I had no idea how to make it better.

But maybe ignoring it was a good place to start.

Katia's eyes sweep over me, stopping at my bare feet. "You've had a good run, Blondie. If it makes you feel better, you lasted a lot longer than any of us thought you would."

I stiffen. "I am not going anywhere."

All couples have fights, and Mason and I are no different.

I will not let one disagreement ruin what we have and what we're trying to build.

Katia scoffs and slowly sheathes her dagger. "It's only a matter of time. You could do yourself a favor and get it over with. Have some self-respect."

I force myself to count backward from five. "Does this kind of thing usually work for you? You enjoy intimidating anyone Mason takes an interest in, don't you?"

Katia shrugs. "You keep telling yourself that you're different, but you aren't. Sooner or later, his father will take away his shiny new toy, and when he does, you'll wish you were dead."

I tilt my head and study her. "It really bothers you that he chose me, doesn't it? You think you're a better fit for him because you're from his world."

"I am a better fit—" Katia begins.

I interrupt before she can go any further. "And yet, even when there was no one else around, he still didn't choose you. You're never going to mean more to him. You're convenient because you're there."

Katia's expression darkens. "I should've left you in that club."

"I'm sorry he didn't choose you," I reply in a quieter voice. "It must be hard for you, watching all of this."

I have no idea why I'm trying to find common ground, but I have enough enemies within these walls, and I don't feel like adding Katia to the mix.

Having Mason parade me around when she's held onto the hope that it would be her must sting.

I remind her of what she can't have, and whatever anger and resentment she feels toward me is justified.

I can't imagine being in her shoes.

I know I shouldn't push my luck with her when she could easily attack me and make it look like an accident, but I don't care.

I'm tired of being thought of as helpless and weak.

If you're going to survive this, you're going to need thicker skin, and you need to get over the fact that Mason has a past. You do, too.

Granted, my past isn't standing across from me, looking like they'd like to put a bullet in my head, but I won't hold Mason responsible for what came before me.

The only way for us to make it through is to stick together.

Unless his father finds a way to get rid of you first.

Before Katia can respond, a radio crackles at her waist. She takes a few steps back and barks out something in a language I don't recognize. Then she levels me with a withering look and turns her back on me. I remain in the hallway for a while longer before forcing myself to move.

At the foot of the stairs, I spot Mason heading toward me.

Once he reaches me, I realize two things at once.

The first is that he's giving me the same small, gentle smile that makes my heart flutter.

The second is that he has a black eye.

With a frown, I take his hand, and he allows me to tug him back into the room. As soon as the door shuts, I lead him to the bed and wait for him to sit down. Wordlessly, I duck into the bathroom and blink against the fluorescent lights. A moment later, I'm rifling through the medicine cabinet.

Mason fills the doorway. "What are you doing?"

"You need a better first-aid kit," I respond without looking at him. "Or your own hospital or something."

Mason snorts. "We already have an on-call doctor. This was me

157

blowing off some steam and it's just a black eye."

I turn to face him and raise an eyebrow. "And I got run off a bridge a few days ago."

Mason's smile vanishes, and he straightens his back. "That's different. You could've died."

"Infections can kill, too." Without waiting for his reply, I stalk past him and back into the room. Mason follows me and sits on the chair I pull out for him.

"You can't compare a car crash to an infection."

I take a piece of cotton out of the box and douse it with disinfectant. "You shouldn't keep things from me either, but here we are."

Mason exhales and lets his arms fall to his sides. "You're right. I shouldn't have lied about Elise. I didn't think you'd understand."

I kneel in front of him and press the cotton to the small cut over his eye. "You should get some ice for that."

Mason grunts quietly.

I stop cleaning and swallow past the lump in my throat. "Does this have anything to do with what went wrong yesterday?"

Mason presses his mouth into a thin line.

For a long time, he says nothing, and then he slowly nods.

I withdraw my hand and look at him. "Was it your dad?"

Mason doesn't say anything.

I release a shaky breath. "He's working hard to make sure all other dads look a lot better in comparison. Suddenly getting grounded for sneaking out doesn't seem so bad."

"He won't be getting any Father of the Year mugs."

I return to cleaning the wound. "Is he ever going to stop punishing you?"

Mason shrugs. "Maybe. I can take it."

"You don't have to." My touch grows softer. "I don't know how things work in your world, but I'm pretty sure being the head of the family gives you some leverage."

"I'm the head of the business, not the family," Mason corrects gruffly. "But he's still Jack Payne, and no matter what I do, I'm always going to come up short."

My throat is suddenly dry. "I'm sorry."

"Thank you."

I stop cleaning and let my eyes sweep over him, from his smooth, arched brows, down the slope of his nose, and over his sharp jaw. He's giving me an odd look.

"What?"

"You're not responsible for other people's mistakes, London," Mason says quietly. "It's not up to you to save the people you love, especially if they don't want to be saved."

"I was going to tell you the same thing."

Mason makes a noncommittal sound in the back of his throat.

I reach for his hand and lace my fingers through his. "I know we're not a normal couple. I know violence is a part of your world, but you can talk to me about these things."

Mason searches my face.

Suddenly, I'm not looking at the man who's clawed his way to the top of an empire. I'm not looking at the man who has watched the life leave other men's eyes.

I'm not even looking at the man who offered to let me take my father's place because he wanted me. I'm looking at a little boy who desperately wants his father's approval, and it makes my heart feel impossibly tight.

Poor Mason.

I can't imagine what it must have been like to grow up with a father like Jack Payne always looking over your shoulder and waiting to punish you.

What kind of father does that to his children?

A sudden burst of anger courses through me as I stand up and throw

159

the cotton into the trash can by the door. Mason stands up and walks over to me. His touch is soft as he tucks a lock of hair behind my ears.

"I can handle my father," Mason repeats. "No matter what he does to me, do not go after him."

I nod.

Mason wraps an arm around my waist. "Good. There's only enough room for one reckless person in this relationship."

I raise an eyebrow. "We can't take turns?"

"Absolutely not."

I frown. "We'll see."

Mason shakes his head. "I have some work to do. And I've got some important people visiting."

"You want me out of the way?"

"It's safer for you there."

I raise an eyebrow. "Even after the shooting?"

Mason's expression tightens. "Yes."

I blink. "I don't understand."

Mason blows out a breath. "My father isn't at the club, and it's safer than visiting your parents…"

"Is this you trying to compromise?"

Mason frowns. "Take the win before I change my mind. Katia will take you."

I don't know how I'm supposed to respond.

All I know is that there is a warm buttery feeling in the center of my stomach because I know how hard this is for him.

Maybe there's some wriggle room after all.

I pause, a small smile hovering on the edge of my lips. "Okay. I appreciate this."

Mason grunts then his mouth is scorching against mine.

Before I can deepen the kiss, he wrenches himself away and walks out. I touch two fingers to my lips and wait for my heart to stop pounding.

Katia is waiting by the door when I come out a short while later. In silence, she leads me down a series of hallways that end at the back door.

The late afternoon sun is on my back, but the warmth does nothing to ward off the chill in my bones.

Miss Deveroux lets us in through a back door, her usual kohl-rimmed eyes flicking to me and moving to Katia. Then she motions to us, and we follow her in, and my eyes water from the thin plume of smoke and the stench of hard liquor. The dimly lit hallway spills out onto the main floor, and it takes a minute for my eyes to adjust.

My eyes dart all around, taking in the circular booths with well-dressed men and women in skimpy clothing who are draped all over the men. Now and again, one of these men is led past, and I don't miss the hungry glint in their eyes. Katia's glare helps them steer clear of us.

I'm becoming oddly attached to having her nearby, even if she knows how to get under my skin.

She knows how to do that because you let her and because a part of you wonders if what she says is true.

I try to shake the thought as Miss Deveroux steps behind the bar and tilts her head. Katia pushes me in front of her, and we find an empty table in the back. Once I sit down, Katia disappears into the crowd, and I sit there alone, listening to the rhythmic music pumping through the speakers.

Is this my life now? A series of dimly lit rooms and danger around every corner?

I'm not sure why Mason thought letting me come here was a good idea.

All being back here does is make my skin crawl and remind me of the endless months when I tried to keep my head down and focus on the job.

Already, it feels like a lifetime ago.

I'm not even sure I'd recognize that version of me.

I'm not sure I'd want to.

I lean back against the booth, scanning the area intently but not registering anything until Katia walks back with two drinks in hand. She hands me a sweet-looking drink with an umbrella and sets the other one down. Her posture is erect, and she keeps one hand at her side, close to where I know she keeps her dagger. I see a flash of movement, and we turn toward it.

Several bulky-looking men emerge, half-dragging, half-carrying a light-haired man between them.

A shudder ripples through me as they stride past. "I don't think I'll ever get used to that."

Katia doesn't look at me when she replies. "I'll be nearby."

I sit up straighter. "Aren't you going to sit?"

Katia raises an eyebrow. "I'm not here to socialize, and definitely not with you."

I gesture to the other drink. "Isn't that for you?"

Katia says nothing.

"I'll be keeping a close eye out," she adds. "Enjoy your little break."

Without waiting for a response, she melts into the shadows. I wait for a few moments before curling my fingers around the glass. Slowly, I lift it to my lips and take a small sip. The fruity drink is a little too sweet for my taste, but it dulls some of the roaring in my ears.

I take a few more sips, and the hairs on the back of my neck rise.

Frowning, I scan the floor, realizing that a figure on the far side of the room is watching me. I squint, but I can't make out his features. I ignore the sliver of unease that races up my spine and turn my attention back to the drink. The roar in my ears turns into a quiet thrumming sound, and the edges of my vision blur as I lean back and sigh. Then, I set out my finished drink and lean across the table for the other one.

Out of nowhere, a hand darts out and closes around the glass.

I lick my dry lips. "That's my...."

The rest of the sentence dies on my lips as I blink, and I realize who I'm talking to.

Shit.

The pleasant buzz begins to clear when Noah's friend Steven leans forward and pulls his lips back into a sneer. "Well, isn't this a pleasant surprise?"

My stomach is in knots. "I can't say the same."

Steven chuckles and brings the drink to his nose to sniff it. "You can afford to ask them for the expensive stuff now, or at least that's what I heard."

I square my shoulders and give him a blank look. "I have no idea what you're talking about."

Where the fuck is Katia, and why isn't she dragging him back by the collar of his shirt?

Steven chuckles, and the sound sends another wave of unease through me.

I rise to my feet, and a figure steps out of the shadows, blocking the other side of the booth. I glance back at Steven, and he's sitting with his arm draped over the back of the booth.

"What the hell are you doing?"

"Word on the street is that you're off limits," he continues. "Something about fucking someone big."

I offer him the dirtiest look I can muster. "That's none of your damn business."

"I always did wonder what that mouth of yours would feel like. You were wasted on Noah, you know. He doesn't know how to please a woman."

I scoff. "And you do? Did you honestly think that ratting me out to Noah was going to get you anywhere?"

Steven shrugs. "I can show you one hell of a good time, baby. And I bet you like it rough."

"Not interested," I reply coolly. "This conversation is over."

Steven's hand darts out and closes around my wrist, and his eyes flash.

"It's over when I say it's over."

I look from the hand around my wrist to his face and back again. "Let go."

He leans in so I can smell the alcohol on his breath. "Not until I get what I want. I want you on your knees, London. You got away last time, but this time, you're not going to get so lucky. Let's see how far you can take it, huh?"

Without warning, he tugs, and I lose my balance and fall against him.

I throw my head back. His arms, which were closing around me, lose their grip, and Steven makes a muffled sound in his chest. Then I throw my full weight back, and we crash to the floor, a pinprick of pain racing up my leg. My heart pounds.

Slowly, he rises to his feet and rolls his shoulders. "I knew you'd be fun."

I get up from the floor and orient myself immediately, standing with my legs hip-width apart.

With a growl, he launches at me, and I stay still. Once he's close enough, I punch him squarely in the jaw. Another slice of pain shoots up my arm, but I ignore it. He growls and tries to pull me against him. I squirm and buck so that we fall backward against the table. His grip loosens, and I kick out my leg, forcing him to the floor.

He glances at me, dazed.

I drop down to dig my knee into his chest. "You've always been an asshole. I just didn't think you were stupid, too."

He tries to stand, but I don't let him.

Adrenaline pumps steadily through me as I wait until he meets my gaze. "Nothing to say?"

"You'll pay for this, you bitch," Steven warns. "You have no idea what kind of power I have here."

I remove my knee as he scrambles to his feet. "I don't give a shit."

All at once, the same bulky men I saw drag a man off earlier appear around us. They form a half-circle but don't look at us. He stands up straighter and glances at them. "Well, it's about time."

"I apologize for the inconvenience, Mr. Montrose." Jack Payne appears from the shadows, his expression blank. "Tonight is on us."

The man nods and gives me a feral smile. "This isn't over."

Then, Jack Payne turns to me, and it takes every ounce of self-control I have not to react.

My every instinct is screaming to run.

His dark eyes sweep over me, tight and emotionless pools of black until they land on my face. With a flick of his wrist, he dismisses the men until we're alone, and I wish he hadn't. I know the men won't lift a finger to stop him, but having them nearby made me feel better.

Fuck.

Is he the reason Katia didn't interfere?

What did he do to her?

"I tolerate your presence, but only because my son has made it clear that he'll burn everything down for you," Jack tells me, each word dripping with ice and disdain. "You've already caused a lot of trouble, and now I find you here, assaulting one of our best patrons."

I swallow and clench my hands. "I wasn't assaulting him. He forced himself on me."

The look Jack gives me is one of malice. "I didn't tell you to speak. You will learn to do as you're told, and if my son is incapable of teaching you that lesson, I will."

Fear blossoms in my chest.

He takes a small step in my direction, and I remind myself not to move or even breathe. "I know everything there is to know about you, London. I know where you went to school, and I know about your pathetic attempt to protect your parents."

I don't look away.

"Sooner or later, my son will grow tired of you. In the meantime, I won't allow you to cause any more disruptions to the business," Jack says. "There are plenty of ways your parents can be dealt with."

Without waiting for a response, he takes out his phone and holds it up to me.

It takes a full minute for me to realize what I'm watching, and when I do, I grow cold all over.

"All it takes is one word from me," Jack says, in a low voice. "My man will even make it look like an accident."

I try and fail to swallow.

Jack presses something on his phone, and the image shifts, and I find myself staring at an unfamiliar building, overlooking the water. My heart twists on itself when he swipes through and shows me another picture, this one of Mathew on the other side of the street, and half-hidden in the shadows.

"Your mom almost slipped under the radar," Jack continues, in the same tone of voice. "It's a good thing she decided to come visit her darling daughter. I have special plans for her."

"Stay away from my parents." The words are out of me before I can stop them, and I want to kick myself.

Jack lowers the phone, and his expression darkens. "Whatever power you think you have is an illusion. Do I make myself clear?"

I glance from the phone to his face and back again, a sliver of fear settling in the center of my stomach.

I will not give him the satisfaction of seeing me balk, even when I want to hightail it out of there.

He might not like me, but if I run away, it will only make things worse.

Breathe. Just breathe. If he wanted to do something to them, he already would have.

Katia materializes by my side, her face pinched in concern.

"I'm glad we had a chance to chat," Jack says. "I'll hold you to our understanding, London."

Once he leaves, the air rushes back into my lungs, and my knees buckle.

Katia holds me upright and takes me to Miss Deveroux's office.

There, she leaves the door propped open and helps me sink onto the couch. Wordlessly, she hands me a drink, and her eyes widen when I down it in one gulp.

"Where were you?"

"I thought you could handle yourself with Noah's friend, but when I saw who interfered, I tried to step in, but his men wouldn't let me."

I grip the glass tighter, my heart still hammering wildly. "Okay."

How far is Jack Payne willing to go?

Is it already too late for my parents?

"What did he tell you?"

I exhale sharply. "Nothing I didn't already know. I'm ready to go back now."

Katia sets my empty glass down and checks the hallway before I step outside.

In a daze, I follow her back to the estate, replaying the scene in my head. When I blink, I'm back in Mason's room, and the ringing in my ears is back. The door shuts behind me, and I race into the bathroom. I barely make it to the toilet before the contents of my lunch rise, and I empty my stomach.

My eyes are watery, and my stomach lurches when I'm done.

You knew your parents would be at risk.

But it didn't dawn on me how selfish my decision was until I stood in front of Jack, desperate to get away.

My stomach is still roiling when Mason finds me standing by the window, looking out at the moonlit estate a while later. He draws me to him and murmurs something in my ear, and I sink against him, inhaling his familiar smell.

You can do this. You can find a way to get your family out and keep them safe. You have to.

CHAPTER THIRTEEN

Mason

I flip onto my side and reach across the bed for London, needing to feel her warm body against mine. When my fingers find cold sheets instead of London's familiar curves, my eyes fly open. My heart is pounding as I sit up in bed and glance around, but I don't see her anywhere. I move into the bathroom and flick on the lights, giving my eyes a minute to adjust.

Where the hell is she?

A brief image of London tied up somewhere in the house and at my father's mercy flashes through my mind, and it makes my stomach clench. I shove the thought away and reach for the nearest shirt to pull over my head. I'm halfway out the door when I double back for my gun. In the hallway, I creep forward and quiet my breathing.

The house is eerily still.

I tiptoe down the stairs slowly, gripping the gun tightly.

At the bottom, I flatten myself against the nearest wall and listen.

I don't like how quiet it is.

After sending Carlisle a text, I venture deeper into the house, stopping at my study and my father's makeshift office before I peer out the window. The estate is bathed in the soft glow of the moon, and a few moments later, I see the guards exchange shifts. I let the curtain slide back into place and retreat into the shadows.

I shouldn't have fallen asleep.

I should've stayed up to keep an eye on London, especially when she refused to tell me what happened with my father.

I didn't like hearing it from Katia, especially given the strain between us, but I know how intimidating Jack Payne is.

You were also afraid that if you pushed her, she'd realize how close she came to danger and run.

It's not lost on me that London is far from prepared to deal with my world, and how one small incident could tip her over the edge.

It took every ounce of self-control I had, coupled with the ashen look on London's face, for me not to race out of the room and hunt my father down.

He's toying with me—with us—and I almost wish he'd go the more direct route.

I hate not knowing what he's got in store.

Focus. Find London. Make sure she's safe, and worry about your father later.

After scouring the house, I meet Carlisle at the back door. I taste bile in the back of my throat as I return inside and pause in front of the door leading to the basement. When I press my ear to the door and hear a low grunt and a hiss, I almost rip the door off its hinges. My eyes are wild and unfocused as I reach the bottom of the stairs with my gun out.

There's a single light bulb on, and Katia is leaning against the wall on one side of the room. Her black hair is in its usual braid, and her eyes are pinched in annoyance. In the middle of the room, London is standing in a pair of yoga pants, her shirt soaked with sweat, and her hair pulled into a high ponytail.

She lifts a leg and kicks the punching bag again and again.

Neither of them notices me as I lower my gun.

What the hell are they doing?

Katia looks amused. "Are you imagining that punching bag is me or Mason's father?"

"Both." London grunts, cocks her fist, and throws a punch. The chain that suspends the punching bag from the ceiling rattles. "I'm not picky right now."

Katia stops next to London. "That's not going to help you feel better."

London grabs the punching bag and levels Katia with a dirty look. "Are you volunteering to take its place?"

Katia shrugs. "You need a solution for your anger, not an outlet to help you repress."

"I wasn't aware you were a therapist, too."

London releases the punching bag, spins around, and lands a swift kick to the center. "I don't need your advice. What I need is… fuck. I don't know what I need."

"You want to feel like you're in control. Like no one can make you feel helpless again."

London snorts but doesn't reply.

"You also want to make sure your family is safe."

London glances at Katia. "Is this another lesson in weakness? Because I am not in the goddamn mood. I've tried to talk to them already, but they won't leave. I mean, hell, even Noah gets how serious this is and has hired extra security. I've tried to get him to talk to me, but I think I've burned that bridge."

"Sounds like that boy has common sense after all."

London scowls. "He's always had common sense."

"Debatable."

London's eyes flash as she moves to Katia and clenches her hands into fists. "You have no idea what you're talking about."

"You're right. I don't."

"I've dealt with a lot of assholes in my life, but Jack Payne…"

"He's not your run-of-the-mill asshole."

London turns her focus back to the punching bag as if she can summon my father there through sheer will. "I just stood there. He threatened my family, he's got people watching including Mathew, and I…I just fucking stood there like an idiot. I should've done something."

"It would've made things worse. Mathew isn't going to do anything."

London throws her hands up and begins throwing punches again, one after the other in quick succession. "He's already threatened me and my family. How much worse can it possibly get?"

"Threats are nothing in our world. You got off easy."

London stops punching and faces Katia again. "You don't like him much, do you?"

Katia doesn't say anything.

"What if we work together to take him down? We could recruit other people. I'm sure you're not the only one—"

Katia throws her head back and laughs, cutting London off. "Blondie, if you've got some kind of death wish, keep me out of it. We cannot go after Jack Payne."

"Why not?"

"Because you'll get yourselves killed," I add, emerging from the shadows. Two pairs of eyes turn to me, and London squares her shoulders while Katia looks away. I stop in the middle of the room and make a big show of putting away my gun. London's eyes flick from the weapon to my face and back again until she crosses her arms over her chest and exhales.

"What are you doing here, London?"

"Practicing."

"In the middle of the fucking night? I don't think so. Let's go."

"No."

I turn to Katia and frown. "You're supposed to be keeping her out of trouble. Clearly, I've overestimated your abilities."

Katia shifts from one foot to the other, but her face gives nothing away.

I know her well enough to know that she's keeping her anger under wraps and on a tight leash.

I've known her long enough to know that she takes pride in her abilities.

My words have found their mark.

I have no idea what London has that blinds Katia, but endangering her life once is inexcusable. Twice is asking for trouble, and she's lucky I have a war looming, or we'd be having a different conversation. As it is, I'm still mulling over the appropriate punishment to get my point across.

Katia knows it's coming, but she's smart enough to know it can't be stopped.

"It's not her fault," London argues hotly. "She's doing the best she can."

"I don't care what bond the two of you have forged, but stay out of it," I snap. "She knows what she's signed up for, and she knows who she works for. She also knows better than to interfere when it isn't her business. Or maybe you need reminding."

Katia stiffens. "No, I don't."

"There will be no more talk of taking my father on," I say. "I know neither of you is stupid enough to think these walls don't have ears."

"He has to be stopped," London protests. "You can't expect me to sit around while he puts a hit out on my family."

I turn to London. "You can, and you will. I already told you that I'd take care of it."

London blows out a breath. "But Mathew—"

I clench one of my hands into a fist and ignore the surge of irritation coursing through me. "I said I'm taking care of it. Katia, take London back up to her room and make sure she stays there."

"But—"

"Go." I level London with a pointed look. "Don't make me do something you won't like."

London raises her chin and stares at me. "We need to talk about this."

I glare at her. "I will fucking drag you out of here kicking and screaming if you don't leave."

Still, she hesitates.

"Or I can throw you over my shoulder," I add. "Your choice."

She strides past me with Katia following on her heels. I wait a few moments before leaving the basement, pausing to lock the door behind me.

I know London isn't happy with me, but I don't care.

She needs to fall in line before she causes any more damage, and I can't figure out how to get through to her.

You can find other ways to make your point.

Growling, I storm into my office and go straight to the small table with the glass decanter. I pour a drink and swirl the amber liquid around the glass as I consider my options. I'm itching to teach London a lesson, but I know I can't handle this in my usual way.

London isn't a problem to be dealt with.

No matter how frustrating she is, she's not doing it on purpose.

The last thing she needs is another reason to leave.

I'm halfway through my second glass when I realize that talking doesn't work.

So, what are you going to do? Lock her up and only allow her out for brief periods to eat and get fresh air? She'll resent you if you treat her like a prisoner.

I push back against the irritation and frown into my glass.

When I turn back around, a third drink in hand, Carlisle is darkening my doorway, a few fresh cuts on his face. He approaches my desk, stopping on the other side, and linking his hands behind his back. His eyes are gleaming.

"You finally have some news."

Carlisle nods. "Yes. You were right. The man we caught at the crash site… he's a contractor. The Fitzpatricks and Everetts hired him to stage the attack on London and Katia. Their goal wasn't to have the car crash. It was to send a message."

The glass cup in my hand shatters, sending shards in every direction.

I ignore the blood dripping down my hand and step out from behind the desk. "And why are you fucking telling me? I said I wanted whoever was responsible on their hands and knees in front of me."

Carlisle clears his throat. "They're not the only ones responsible."

I motion for him to continue.

"There's a contract killer for hire," Carlisle continues. "There's a bounty on London's head."

I stop in front of Carlisle and ignore the chill that races up my spine. "You have one minute to explain why the hell you didn't know about this."

"I don't know when it happened." Carlisle's words pour out in a rush. "I was investigating the Everett and Fitzpatrick involvement. I didn't know there was another player—"

I hold up my hand. "What the fuck are you talking about?"

A flash of something moves across Carlisle's face. "The bounty hunter wasn't hired by the Everetts or the Fitzpatricks."

"Who the hell hired him?"

Fucking hell.

"I'm still working on that. The trail has gone cold," Carlisle replies. "I've got men out there working on finding out who the killer is."

"There's only a handful of them," I say. "You should be out there yourself, not in here giving me excuses."

Carlisle presses his mouth together and doesn't say anything.

"Bring me a name, or it's your fucking balls I'll serve London," I warn. "Maybe I should've gone with one of your brothers after all."

A muscle works in Carlisle's jaw.

"Whatever the bounty is on London's head, triple the contract and offer the same amount for whoever brings me the name of the person behind this."

After nodding swiftly, Carlisle turns and leaves the room.

I reach for another glass and hurl it across the room. It explodes against the wall. I reach for another glass, and another, until it looks like a tornado has ripped through my study, leaving debris in its wake.

It doesn't quench my rage, but at least it gives me something to do.

I leave the study, taking the stairs two at a time until I reach my room. The bathroom is shrouded in a thin mist, and I can make out London's outline behind the shower curtain. She pokes her head out to look at me, and our eyes meet briefly before I stalk back out of the room.

I'm staring out the window when London emerges with a towel wrapped around her.

She pads over to me, and I turn to her.

When she steps into my arms, and I crush her to me, I realize that it isn't just anger building within me. All of the worry and fear I've been carrying around rises within me till it reaches a breaking point. I make a low noise in the back of my throat and hold her tighter.

I'm going to rip that bounty hunter apart with my bare hands if I have to.

He's not touching a hair on her head.

And I'll be damned if I let them or anyone else take London away from me.

London lets the towel drop to the floor and takes my hand to lead me to the bed. She pauses to pull on a pair of sweatpants and a sweatshirt, never once letting go of me. The bed dips and creaks as she pulls me down next to her. Then, she curls herself around me, and I drape an arm over her shoulders and exhale.

I recognize the vise-like grip around my heart.

It's been decades since I've felt it, not since I saw my mother struggling to breathe as the light faded from her eyes. I swore to myself I'd never feel that way again.

For the first time in a long time, I'm terrified, and I have no idea what to do next.

Or how to protect London from the fallout.

Fuck.

How much more danger am I going to put her in before I do what needs to be done?

CHAPTER FOURTEEN

London

"Get your fucking hands off her."

My eyes fly open, and it takes a few seconds for me to rub the sleep away. Frowning, I look at Mason and find him flat on his back, his hands clenched into fists, and his eyes squeezed shut. There's a thin sheen of sweat on his forehead and a pained expression on his face. He's breathing heavily.

I push myself up and reach for him. "Mason?"

"No." He thrashes, and one hand darts out. "This isn't happening."

I inch closer and touch his face. "Wake up. You're dreaming."

His head whips back and forth, and he says something else, but I can tell he's still in the throes of his nightmare. I throw the covers back and cradle his head in my hands. "Open your eyes."

My heart is pounding as I throw one leg over him, then the other, so I'm straddling him. I lace my fingers through his and press my forehead to his. "Come back to me."

Mason stills, and nothing happens for a long moment.

I move my mouth to his ear and inhale. "I'm here. Come back to me."

Mason's eyes fly open, wild and unfocused. His body is rigid until he sees me. Abruptly, he pries his fingers away and grips my hips. Something about the desperate gleam in his eyes makes my stomach clench further. I rock gently, and a low, startled sound falls from my lips when he raises his hips and rubs himself against me.

I exhale. "Tell me what you need."

In one quick move, Mason shifts, so I'm pinned beneath him. He lifts my arms over my head and lowers his mouth to mine. This kiss is different; it's tender and vulnerable, and it steals any last bit of resistance I have and drives sleep away. A rush of heat pools in the pit of my stomach as I sigh and lock my fingers behind his waist.

Mason growls and wrenches his lips away. "I need you."

"You have me," I murmur thickly. "I'm here."

Mason peppers my neck with hot, open-mouthed kisses that send waves of desire through me. "You're not going anywhere."

"I'm not going anywhere." My breath comes in short gasps as one hand holds mine tightly and the other traces a path down to my underwear. He spreads his fingers over me, and my pulse skitters.

"You're mine." Mason growls into my skin. "I won't let anybody take you away."

When he releases my hands, I thread my fingers through his hair and press my forehead to his. Slowly, I lift my other hand and place it on his chest, over his pounding heart. He releases a deep, shaky breath when I reach for his hand and place it over my chest.

A long moment passes in silence.

Mason's gaze softens as he drops his head and draws my bottom lip between his teeth.

I whimper when he shifts and settles between my legs.

"I'm yours," I say into the shell of his ear, another jolt going through me when he shivers. "We're together."

Mason moans into my mouth.

My fingers trace a path down his back, and I stop at his behind.

He pins my arm over my head and rubs himself against me.

I throw my head back and mewl.

Mason grins lustily. "You have no idea how fucking sexy you are when you make sounds like that."

I stare at him through hooded eyes as he pauses to lift my shirt and kiss a path along my ribcage. His touch is feather light as he reaches behind my back and pulls the shirt over my head. Once he tosses it over his shoulders, he gets up, and I catch a glimpse of his taut, muscled body, bathed in the soft glow of the moon, before he leaves his clothes in a pile on the floor.

My throat is dry, and a thick and heavy fog of desire settles over me as he lowers himself back onto the bed. Mason's legs come up around me, and he buries his face in my neck. I press a kiss to the side of his neck and link my fingers over his waist. When he angles himself and thrusts into me, I throw my head back and sigh.

Slowly, we begin to move against each other at a languid pace.

It's quiet, unhurried, and vulnerable, and I have to turn my head when tears prick my eyes. Emotion swells within me as Mason pushes my hair back and tilts my head to look at him. He covers my mouth with his, and I can almost taste the words he's holding back.

Everything between us builds into a deafening crescendo.

His hands drop to my waist, and he sinks his fingers there, eliciting a small moan.

Waves of pleasure build within me as I buck against him.

I don't recognize the sounds I'm making as I rake my nails down his back.

Mason drops a hand between us, and two fingers dart between my wet folds.

For a long moment, I forget how to breathe.

Suddenly, I'm falling, hurtling toward the edge of oblivion as my body writhes. Mason keeps me pressed to him as I ride out my high, his name a chant on my lips. Sweat breaks out over my forehead and slides down my back. I blink away the spots in my field of vision.

When I come back down, Mason is still moving inside of me.

He presses his mouth to my neck, his hot breath doing strange things to my insides. I drop my head into the crook of his neck and trace a path up to his head. When I move my fingers into his hair and tug, Mason growls. His mouth parts, and he sinks his teeth into my neck, sending waves of pain and pleasure ricocheting through me.

I look at him, and the depth of emotion in his eyes takes my breath away. To my surprise, Mason doesn't look away as he thrusts in and out of me at a slow, even pace, bringing me to the point of sweet and torturous pleasure. Our bodies fuse, and the walls between us crumble.

It's never been like this between us, vulnerable and intimate and personal.

Like we need each other to survive, to breathe.

I want to stay like this forever, moving together so I can't tell where he begins and I end.

My eyes well with emotion, but I don't look away.

He cups the back of my neck and bows his head. I link my feet behind his waist and savor every touch, rush of heat, and nerve in my body as it reacts to him. Mason's rhythm doesn't change as his hands move over my skin, leaving a trail of heat in his wake. Goosebumps break out across my skin, and another orgasm rips through me, leaving a hollow ache in my chest.

Mason's release comes shortly after, and I hold him to me as his body jerks, and he grunts.

Once he goes slack, his arms come up around me, and he pushes my hair back. Then he eases out of me, and a rush of cold air moves between us. With a sigh, Mason tugs me back, so I fall against him, our legs tangled. I place my head on his chest, over the pounding of his heart, and hold my breath.

He drapes an arm around my shoulders and drops a kiss to the top of my head.

I fight off sleep and struggle to keep my eyes open because I'm afraid that if we move, if we even say anything, the moment will end.

Sometime later, I stir and find the curtains open, allowing bright sunlight to pour in. I sit up, rub a hand over my eyes, and stifle a yawn. Then I turn and find a note on Mason's side of the bed, in his neat cursive handwriting. I hold the note with one hand and use the other to throw the covers off.

I will do whatever I need to keep you safe. You are mine.

In the bathroom, I splash water on my face and turn on the shower.

When I step back into the room, with a towel around my body, a thin mist follows me. A tray of food is waiting for me outside the door, and I take it without sparing Katia a glance. Once I'm done, I step back out, and Katia steps forward. She gestures to me, and I fall into step beside her.

"Where are we going?"

Katia notices the hickey on my neck, and her expression darkens. "We've been instructed to leave the house for a few hours."

I sigh. "I thought we were supposed to steer clear of the club after the shooting, and the run in with Jack."

"We are, but it's safer than other places."

Although I know Mason must hate it, the club is the lesser of all evils.

At least there he's got eyes and ears everywhere, and it's within walking distance.

No matter how bad things get, he can get me out, but I still don't like being kept in the dark.

I sigh. "Do we at least know why?"

"It's not my place to question orders," she says tersely. "Nor is it yours."

A kernel of guilt settles in my stomach, and I frown.

How much more trouble can Katia endure on my behalf?

There's a difference between keeping me safe within the Mason estate and protecting me from myself.

I know it's only a matter of time before Katia snaps, and I no longer have any leeway.

I'm on a tight leash, and I have no one to blame but myself.

I follow Katia down a familiar path and out the back door. Outside, we slow to a stroll, and Katia nods to a few of the guards along the way. Once we cross the path separating the estate from the club, Katia's strides lengthen, and her hands move to her sides. Her eyes dart around until we reach the back of the club, where Miss Deveroux is waiting for us, her features half-hidden in the shadows.

She leads us inside and up to the main part of the club.

Only a few people are milling around, and the music is turned down low.

Katia leads me to a booth in the back, and I sink into it. Miss Deveroux returns with several plates of food and a few drinks. She glances at Katia. Then she disappears, and I'm left with a pit in my stomach.

Has Miss Deveroux been instructed to keep her distance, too?

Did Mason figure out her involvement?

I want to be angry with him for making my circle even smaller, but I know he's trying to protect me.

In his infuriating, domineering way.

You don't even know what you're dealing with. When it comes to safety, better leave the details to Mason.

Shaking my head, I sink further into the booth and pull one of the plates closer. I sweep my eyes over the empty dance floor and ignore the neon lights pulsing from above. The toast is like ash as I chew it. I push that plate away and reach for the plate of fries. I'm halfway through when the hair on the back of my neck rises, and a tingling sensation spreads across my scalp.

I glance up, and my throat goes dry as I spot Noah across the room. He's wearing a button-down shirt tucked into a pair of dark jeans, and a scowl is etched onto his face. I scramble out of the booth as Katia shifts closer, following my line of sight. She scowls when she sees Noah, her hand moving to the dagger sheathed at her side. Katia looks at me, and I shake my head.

Inches away from the table, I stop Noah by placing a hand on his chest. "You shouldn't be here."

"I don't want to be," Noah replies tightly. "Your mom asked me to check in."

My heart misses a beat. "Is she okay? Is my dad okay?"

"They're fine," Noah says. "Just worried about you."

"Then they should answer the phone." My words come out a little harsher than I intended. "I'm sorry. I shouldn't take it out on you."

Noah shrugs. "It's not like I haven't been blamed for things I haven't done before."

I study his face. "None of this is your fault, Noah. I'm not blaming you for how things turned out."

"Maybe the kidnappers were trying to do us a favor. I mean, it would've been better if they'd kept you away from this place."

A sliver of unease races up my spine. "I never said...."

I trail off as a prickle of fear blossoms inside my chest.

No, it can't be. Not Noah. He wouldn't hurt you.

I take an involuntary step back, the unease and fear snowballing within me. "You're talking like... like you're almost glad you were bound and gagged."

"At least we're not in the dark anymore. They did do us a favor."

"They tied you up and kidnapped me," I point out. "They played mind games with me and tried to intimidate me. They starved me just to get back at—to make a point."

"I'm sure they wouldn't have hurt you." Noah reaches for me. "You and I both know you're in over your head. Now, I know you don't put much stock in my opinion anymore, but what about your parents? Do they deserve to have their life ripped out from under them?"

I swat his hand away, my fear replaced by cold, hard anger. "How dare you! You have no right to accuse me of endangering my family. All I've done has been to try to protect them, even at the expense of my safety!"

Noah snorts and opens his mouth to say something.

Over his shoulder, I see Mason leaning against a nearby wall, his expression giving nothing away.

I hold up a hand to Noah. "Don't say a fucking thing."

Noah frowns when he sees Mason. "Doesn't he ever give you any breathing room? Jesus Christ, Lo, what kind of leash does he have you on?"

"He doesn't have me on a leash," I snap. "Just stop talking."

Mason crosses over to us and fixes his bright eyes on Noah. "You're not welcome here."

"I'm a paying customer."

Mason takes a step in his direction. "Do I look like I give a shit? Get out."

"I'm just trying to make sure she's okay. She has a family, you know. And a life. Well, she had one before you took it away. Aren't you the slightest bit sorry about what you're doing to her? About what you've taken from her?"

I place a hand on Noah's arm and squeeze. "Stop it, Noah."

Mason looks at my hand and back at Noah's face. "You should listen to her."

"I'm not afraid of you, and someone needs to call you out." Noah is defiant. "You've already broken us up. Are you going to drive her parents away, too? Is that your plan, to have her completely reliant on you and at your beck and call?"

Mason's hand darts out, and I gasp as Noah crumples to the floor, and Mason gets on top of him. He lands punch after punch as I stand there, my mind racing. I force myself to take one step, then another, and ignore the pounding in my heart. When I reach out to touch Mason, he freezes.

He stops punching Noah and looks at me.

Abruptly, he stands up and dusts himself off.

Then, he storms off, and I look back at Noah, who gingerly rises to his feet. Blood is pouring down his nose, and his hair is matted to his forehead. I hand him a wad of napkins and wait until he looks at me again.

"I'm not sure what you were hoping to accomplish, but that was stupid."

Noah tilts his head back and winces. "I meant every word I said, Lo."

"I chose him, Noah. And that includes all of this." I make a vague hand gesture and take a big step back. "I appreciate what you're trying to do, but I don't need you to save me. You should leave before something worse happens."

And then, I race after Mason.

CHAPTER FIFTEEN

Mason

I storm into the office and throw open the door with such force that it crashes against the wall behind it. I stop in front of the decanter, pouring myself a generous amount and picturing Noah's smug face.

I imagine letting him loose in the forest nearby and then hunting him down.

He needs to be taught a lesson, and I'm not sure why I haven't done it yet.

He needs a few days in a damp basement with nothing but his thoughts for company and fear of the unknown gnawing at him.

I frown at the spatters of blood on my knuckles.

Make the call. You know you want to. All it would take is one word to Carlisle, and you could have Noah at your mercy in less than an hour.

I take a few more sips of my drink and mull over my options.

The door creaks open, and London appears in the doorway. Music spills in behind her as my frustration rises.

She will never forgive you if you do anything to him.

She stops a few feet away from the desk. Then, she pushes her hair out of her face and looks at me.

Maybe if you make it so London doesn't find out.

I shove the thought away and set my glass down with a little more force than necessary. "Shouldn't you be making sure Noah's okay?"

London exhales. "He'll be fine. He shouldn't have pushed you."

I raise an eyebrow. "Are you telling me what you think I want to hear?"

"Would it help?"

I stare at her and say nothing.

Slowly, I down the rest of my drink, my eyes never leaving her face. Once it's done, I stride past her and toward the door. In one quick move, the lock clicks into place, and I wheel around to face London.

The whole thing feels a little too familiar, but I don't care.

"I am not going anywhere," London continues, in a smaller voice. She takes an uncertain step in my direction and lets her hands fall to her sides. "No one is taking me away. When are you going to understand and accept the fact I am not leaving you?"

"Not yet."

"Not ever," London counters, her eyes flashing momentarily before she exhales. "I don't know what I can do to make you believe me."

I stare at her and say nothing.

"I know things have been hard, and I know there's a lot going on…."

"Yes."

London takes another step in my direction, her eyes never leaving my face.

"What's your point?" I ask.

She covers the distance between us and reaches for my hand. "My point is you can trust me. We're in this together."

I glance down at our hands and back up at her face. "I want to."

She wraps her arms around me and exhales. "You can."

For a long moment, I hold her against me, terrified of doing anything else.

She feels solid and warm and far more real than anything else in my life, and I don't like how it makes me feel.

I hate feeling weak and like at any moment she can be ripped away, and I'll be left exposed, laid bare for the world to see.

I am not a slave to my feelings.

Slowly, I take a few steps back and let my eyes sweep over her.

"Take your clothes off," I order.

London's eyes widen, but she doesn't react.

Then her fingers move to the button of her jeans. She leaves them in a heap on the floor and steps out of them, revealing the smooth skin of her thighs. Her eyes stay on my face as she unbuttons her blouse and lets it fall next to the jeans on the floor. When her fingers hover over her bra, I nod brusquely, and she unhooks it.

Her breasts spill forward, and the blood pounds in my ears.

London hooks a thumb through her panties and pulls them down.

When she's done, she straightens her back and lets her arms fall to her sides as I drink her in.

Inch by glorious inch until my eyes move back up to her face.

Even the sight of her body, normally enough to drive every rational thought out the window, isn't enough right now.

I still want to hunt Noah down.

I still want to make him pay for not leaving well enough alone.

It's taking every ounce of self-control I have not to drag him back here and make him watch us.

Suddenly, all I can see is Noah hovering over London in her father's diner, his fingers gliding over her body. I blink, and I can see the gleam in her eyes as Noah peels her clothes off and lays her out on the counter. My heart is still hammering as I clench my hands into fists and remind myself to get a grip.

No one, least of all a pathetic coward like Noah, can make me lose control.

"I didn't know he was going to be at the club." London's quiet voice slices through the silence. "Katia told me you wanted us out of the house for a few hours."

"I did."

London clears her throat and shifts from one foot to the other. "Okay, so logically, how could I have planned something when I didn't even know we needed to leave the house?"

"Fuck your logic."

London's eyes flash. "Well, you can't be pissed at me. I tried to get him to leave—"

I bridge the distance between us, and the rest of the sentence dies on her lips. "You need to learn when to shut up."

London snaps her mouth shut and stares at me.

"Bend over the desk," I say into her ear. "Don't move unless I tell you to."

After a brief hesitation, London braces her arms on either side of the desk and turns, so her ass is in the air. I wrench the nearest drawer open and pull out a whip. Then, I run my fingers along the tip and roll my shoulders. It makes a loud cracking sound as it collides with her bare skin.

She brought this on herself. She knows who you are, and you've made it clear how you feel about Noah.

"I will n*ot* be made a fool of," I say into the back of her neck. I wind my fingers through her hair and tug. "Not in my club or anywhere else."

London's breath hitches in her throat.

"You are mine, and you would do well to remember that." My hand connects with her bare behind. London jerks against me, but I tighten my grip on her hair so she can't move. Then, I press myself against her back and exhale.

Abruptly, I spin her around, so she's facing me.

London's face gives nothing away as I cup her face in my hands and release the back of her neck.

She already has too much control over you. You shouldn't give her any more.

It doesn't matter how many times I tell myself otherwise, I already know what I'm willing to do for her.

London has no idea just how far gone I am, and I wonder if that's for the best.

Figure out a way to get yourself under control before it goes badly for both of you. London walked away from Noah. She needs you to do what needs to be done to keep you both safe.

I dig my nails into her shoulders and yank her toward me.

A gasp falls from her lips seconds before my mouth descends on hers, hot and unyielding.

Desire floods every part of me, prompting me to pull her closer.

She drapes herself over me, and groan as one finger stays in my hair, and the other traces a path down my chest. London fumbles with my belt until I hold both her hands tightly. Her back hits the desk, and I pause to hoist her up before settling between her legs.

I can already smell how much she wants me.

Fuck.

I want to lose myself in her for days on end.

London whimpers as I tug on her lower lip, and then plunge my tongue into her mouth. Suddenly, her fingers are grasping at my clothes and trying to tug them off. I grunt as she whips my belt off, and splays her fingers over my stomach. I wrench my lips away and pepper her neck with kisses, nearly losing control when she begins to rub herself against me.

Jesus fucking Christ.

She has no idea what she does to me, or how dangerous it makes her.

It's why they took her. They know she is the key to your undoing.

London pries my shirt free. Her eyes are half-closed, and there's a hint of color on her cheeks. A few wisps of hair are matted to her forehead, and her chest is rising and falling unevenly. Her eyes fly open the rest of the way when I step out of her embrace and leave a wide berth between us.

"Get dressed."

London blinks, myriad emotions dancing across her face. "I don't understand."

"I don't need to explain myself to you," I tell her. "Katia will escort you back to the house."

London's back is ramrod stiff as she pulls on her clothes. Then, she pulls her hair into a ponytail and shoots me a wounded look. I resist the urge to meet her eyes and instead turn to the fire and study the flames.

A few moments later, she brushes past me, and I ignore the need to reach for her.

To pull her against me and take her against every surface of this room, loud enough for the entire club to hear.

It's what we both need, but I won't allow myself that release.

I hate the look in her eyes, almost as much as the little show I made her put on, but I know it's necessary.

For both of us.

I can't let her have complete control over me, not now, not ever.

Carlisle appears in the doorway moments after London leaves. I step behind the desk and motion to him. He pauses to shut the door and crosses over to me. Then, he reaches into his jacket and places an envelope on my desk. I glance between the envelope and his face before I sit down and reach for my drink.

"Speak."

"Michael Everett and Lance Fitzpatrick have been sent out of the country," he begins. "Something about business overseas that needs tending to."

Shit.

They're trying to recruit more allies.

I wonder if my stunt at the dock fixed whatever fracture they had.

Goddamn it.

"I've reached out to a few of my contacts abroad, but we have a bigger problem on our hands." Carlisle gestures to the envelope. "I got a lead on who hired the contract killer, and I think you're going to want to take a look at that."

With a frown, I pull the envelope closer and rip it open.

Inside are dozens of pictures of Noah, many of them with Michael Everett and Lance Fitzpatrick, together and separately. A chill races up my spine as I leaf through the pictures before spreading them across my desk. I push my chair back with a screech and stand.

Fuck me.

"What's the connection here?"

"Noah's father is a mayor," Carlisle replies. "His family has a lot of connections and goes way back. His father, in particular, is tied to several well-known families."

I meet Carlisle's gaze. "I need better evidence than this."

If I'm going to go in, guns blazing, after the man who once held London's heart, I'd better be damn sure.

Anything less will cost me London, and it's a price I'm not willing to pay.

Carlisle nods. "Noah was in the neighborhood at the time of the car crash, and there's a paper trail that leads to him."

I fold my arms over my chest. "Not good enough. If I'm going to nail him, I need more."

This will kill London.

First, her parents want nothing to do with her, and now this.

Fucking hell.

Is Noah right?

Am I the one who's holding her back, taking apart the life she's worked hard to build?

Then again, I'm not the one scheming with criminals to get revenge on my ex.

Is Noah really trying to get rid of London and give himself a clean slate?

Or was he hoping that working with my enemies would drive her away and back into his arms?

The asshole even had the nerve to show up, act concerned, and try to paint me as the villain.

I should've had my men drag him out of the club and into my basement.

Do not start entertaining what the bastard said. He was trying to get under your skin, and you know it.

No one made London stay. At least, that's what I tell myself as I pull my chair closer and study the pictures. My blood boils as I stare at Noah's smug face and realize, with a chill, what I might have to do.

I don't know if London can forgive me for entertaining what the evidence is showing me.

I don't know if she should.

It might be the nail in the coffin of our rocky foundation, but I can't let this go unanswered.

London deserves to have people in her life who won't stab her in the back when things get hard.

This is the excuse you need to bring him in. London can't blame you for taking your precautions. She'd understand if she saw these pictures.

I know I'm grasping at straws.

A few pictures of him with the enemy doesn't make him guilty enough.

If I'm going to go after London's ex, I better be damn sure of what I'm doing, and as much as I hate to admit it, I hope I'm wrong.

For London's sake.

How many more rejections can she take?

"Find out everything you can about the dad," I say, after a long pause. "This needs to be airtight, and I don't need to piss off a man like that."

Carlisle nods.

"Boss, if his dad is as powerful as he seems, just looking into Noah could be a huge risk. Are you sure you want to do that with everything else going on?"

"Are you questioning my decisions? I would hate to have to find someone else to fill your position, but it wouldn't be hard."

Carlisle's jaw locks, and he says nothing.

"Get out," I finish. As Carlisle leaves, I brace my arms on either side of the desk and inhale. Olivia appears on my third exhale, the pounding in the back of my head having spread around my skull. Wordlessly, she steps into the office and shuts the door behind her. She stops on the other side of the desk and glances from the pictures to my face.

"I just passed London on my way here. Is everything okay?"

I push myself off the desk and press two fingers to my temples. "Does it look like it's fucking okay? You shouldn't have come back, Livvy."

"You and I both know that Dad would've found a way to bring me back against my will," she snaps. "At least this way, I got to do it on my terms."

"You know he's going to try and stop you from leaving."

Olivia's bright eyes flash. "I'd like to see him try. I still have a few tricks up my sleeve that even the great Jack Payne doesn't know about."

I snort. "He always did underestimate you."

It was how she got away the first time, and damn if I don't admire her all the more for it.

Even with all the dangers lurking around every corner, I can't imagine walking away.

This is the only life I've ever known, the only one I know how to live.

Olivia's eyes move steadily over my face. "You know, you could leave too. I could help you."

I chuckle humorlessly. "I think you've been gone too fucking long."

"You know Mathew isn't going to stop trying to undermine you and looking for ways to get rid of you. Why don't you just do him a favor and step back?"

I raise an eyebrow. "You honestly think it's that simple? You can't just walk away from this life. No one says no to Jack Payne."

I might have fought for the job, bled, and killed for it, but our father had options.

He chose me because he wanted to, and the minute he did, I turned my back on the life I could've had.

Jack Payne is many things, but if there's one thing he hates more than anything, it's feeling like he's two steps behind.

Carrying his name won't stop him from coming after me if he gets wind of this conversation.

And no matter where we went, London and I would never be safe from him.

He's already itching for an excuse to get rid of her, and I won't give him one.

Olivia leans across the desk and reaches for my hand. "I know that it seems that way, but I did it. I'm sure we could get you and London out. Her family, too. You could start over somewhere."

I shake my head. "She's already given up too much. What makes you think she'll agree to any of this?"

"Because she's still here. In spite of everything. That has to mean something, right?"

I stiffen. "Yeah, it means I'm a bigger bastard than I realized."

I saw firsthand how my father's life took away the life my mother imagined for herself.

Her love for my father got her killed.

London isn't your mother, and you know it. If that means you have to take care of every problem that gets in your way, you'll do what you need to do.

I won't let her suffer the same fate.

Olivia's eyes flicker to the pictures. "Do you want to tell me what's going on?"

I run a hand over my face. "What would you do if I told you that I suspected your ex was plotting to have you killed?"

Olivia exhales and takes an involuntary step back. "I'd say you better be damn sure before you tell me something like that."

I search her face, and something in me dips and hardens. "And if I'm sure?"

Comprehension dawns on Olivia's face. "Then you'll do what needs to be done. You always do."

I press my lips together.

"But you better be sure, Mason. There's no coming back from something like that, and you know what happens when you set the wheels in motion."

I nod tightly.

"A broken heart can make people do insane things," Olivia says. "Trust me, I know."

"I remember."

It had nearly cost Olivia her life, and I'll carry that weight around for the rest of my days.

I don't know Noah well enough to tell if he's doing this out of revenge, but I do know a desperate man when I see one.

And if the look on his face tonight was anything to go by, he's not ready to give up on London.

Even if that means the idiot gets in way over his head.

Gather your evidence, and when you're ready, bring him here and question him yourself. This needs to be handled discreetly and as quickly as possible.

Before he does any more damage.

God knows what kind of promises Noah has made to my enemies, and what kind of information he's given them about London.

"I know I don't need to tell you to be careful with her." A shadow settles over Olivia's face. "She's not built like we are. I give her credit for making it this far and not running in the opposite direction. Of course, I also don't know how much that says about her survival instinct."

I shoot Olivia a meaningful look. "I assume you had a point?"

"She already has enough to deal with. She doesn't need anything else, especially if it's just going to make things harder."

"Well aware."

Olivia steps forward again, and her expression turns resolved. "I know you're moving people to some of the more important warehouses, and calling in favors."

"Olivia, you need to find something else to do while you're here."

"I am going to find a way to help," she says flatly. "You can either let me figure out what that is and back me up, or you can keep having that little man-child follow me around."

I blink. "What gave him away?"

Olivia snorts. "I might have been away the past few years, but I still know how you think, Mason. You're still the kind of person who does whatever needs to be done to protect the people he loves."

I glance away and gather the pictures on my desk into a pile.

"Things have changed in the past few years."

Olivia nods. "I know, and you're a lot more like Dad than you want to admit, but you also have something he doesn't have."

I don't say anything.

"You have Oliver and me," she continues. "Dad knows how to push people away. He instills loyalty through fear, and you know how easy it is to flip someone with the right incentive."

I huff and turn away.

I know Olivia is trying to help, but she's been away too long.

The key to making sure my father doesn't get rid of us isn't to inspire loyalty.

It's to stay one step ahead and keep a cool head like I've always done.

It's served me well the past few years, and other than having to keep an eye on London, nothing has changed for me.

If anything, I'm more motivated to make sure the Paynes come out of this swinging for the fences.

I won't let Noah or anyone else threaten what we've built.

One way or another, I'll make sure the Paynes come out on top. I'll worry about London's reaction after we do.

She'll forgive you. What choice does she have?

CHAPTER SIXTEEN

London

I hold my hands up to the fire and exhale.

The sound reverberates inside my head before being drowned out by the pounding in my chest. Slowly, I shift closer to the fireplace and study the red and orange flames, leaping and dancing, the crackling sound filling the silence around me. I stand there for a long while, replaying the scene in the office in my head.

I don't know if going after Mason was a good idea, but I don't regret it.

Even as shame and humiliation burn through me.

You know this is how he makes himself feel better. It's how he exerts control, and you are no exception.

A small voice in the back of my mind tells me that it still isn't fair.

I'm not like other people. I wish I knew how to distance myself from Mason's anger and his frustration.

How can I show him there are other, healthier ways to cope?

How can I get him to let me all the way in?

Each time I think Mason and I are making progress, I catch a glimpse of the finely honed weapon underneath and am left doubting myself all over again.

It's been two hours since the scene in his office, and I still have a bad taste in my mouth.

I have the urge to step into the shower and scrub my skin raw, except I don't think it'll chase away my disgust.

And the worst part is knowing I'd let him do it all over again just to feel better.

Maybe Noah was right.

Being with Mason is chipping away at little parts of me, and as I stand there in the quiet of the library, surrounded by shelves of books, I'm forced to confront my greatest fear.

What if, when all is said and done, the version of me that remains is nothing like the one Mason wants?

What if I become a shell of a woman, unable to recognize my reflection?

You just have to make sure that doesn't happen. Focus on what you can control and compromise where you can. And keep one foot in front of the other.

A strong gust of wind rattles the windows, startling me. Silver moonlight pours in through the window, casting tiny particles across the hardwood floors. I rub my hands up and down my arms, but it does nothing to ward off the chill in my bones.

I'm not supposed to be here.

Katia has better things to do than lurk in the bowels of the library.

But other than a brief, bored look, she dismissed my attempts to get her to leave.

It's been a long day. You should get some rest. Mason will come and find you soon and make things right.

Shaking my head, I step away from the fire and take in the shelves stocked with pristine hardcovers and first editions. The tightness in my chest eases as I drift closer and run my fingers along the spines. Then, I wander until I'm standing under a portrait, half-concealed under a dusty, worn sheet.

My heart is pounding in my ears. I reach forward and pull the sheet off.

I recognize a young Mason almost immediately by the quirk of his lips and the gleam in his eyes. Mathew is standing next to him with a scowl on his face. Opposite them is a little girl in a dress with thick auburn hair, and a little boy who is leaning away.

Seeing the Mason family in such an intimate position is unnerving.

But not as surreal as seeing Mason's mother standing behind his father, her bright eyes tight around the edges, and the smile not quite reaching her eyes.

Shit.

"It's uncanny, isn't it?"

I drop my hand and wheel around, my stomach twisting into knots when I see Mathew. His shirt is half-tucked into his dark jeans, and his hair is sticking up in tufts.

Mason's warning rings in my ears as his twin takes a step toward me.

"I'm sure you've noticed the resemblance," Mathew continues. "It makes you wonder, doesn't it?"

I clear my throat. "If you're trying to imply that Mason is only with me because I look like his mother, it's not going to work."

"And yet, you came to that conclusion all on your own," Mathew says. "I guess Mason keeps you around for a lot more than your looks."

He's just trying to get under your skin. Mathew might not be as lethal as Mason, but he obviously enjoys mind games. He's trying to fill your head with doubt.

Mathew isn't wrong about the resemblance.

It's like looking at an older, more tired version of myself, someone who has been hardened and broken by life.

I look back at the portrait, and something hard and unfamiliar settles in my stomach.

"He's not going to be able to protect you, you know."

I clench my hands into fists. "You're wrong."

His chuckle sends another wave of unease through me. "Your loyalty to him is admirable, especially considering how much you've sacrificed. Tell me, how are your parents dealing with their darling daughter's fall from grace?"

I dig my nails into my palms. "That's not your concern."

"I'm sure they're not happy about any of it." I can feel Mathew's eyes on me, open and assessing. "It's not like you can take Mason home and introduce him to them, can you?"

I frown. "Are you really that insecure about your brother?"

Mathew's expression hardens. "Think of all the Thanksgivings, all of the holidays, all of the normalcy you've had to give up. On the wrong Payne man, too. If you are as smart as you seem, you'll find someone else to throw your luck behind."

An incredulous laugh falls from my lips. "I know you don't mean you."

There is a cruel calculation in Mathew's eyes. "My offer has an expiration date, London. I'd take it if I were you."

"You can shove your offer up your ass, Mathew."

His expression darkens, and a muscle ticks in his jaw.

I wonder if I've pushed him too far.

Then, there's a clamor of voices near the door, and we turn to it. Jack Payne's voice wafts in, and every muscle in my body tenses. I take a few steps away from Mathew and glance around, fear snaking its way inside of me. Slowly, I move toward the shelves until Mathew's cold voice stops me in my tracks.

"It's only a matter of time before he decides to take care of you."

I look at Mathew over my shoulder. "I know."

He raises an eyebrow. "Without the right Payne by your side, this is going to get ugly fast."

"I'm sure I'll survive."

Mathew's eyes flash. "You can do more than survive. You can thrive."

"And what do Oliver and Olivia think about this?" I ask.

Mathew doesn't flinch. "My siblings are too short-sighted."

"Is that why you haven't spoken to them in years? Because you're too short-sighted to realize that you're in the wrong?"

Mathew sneers. "I see Mason has been filling your head with nonsense. Tread carefully, London. You might have Mason wrapped around your finger, but I can wipe that fucking smirk off your face in a second. You think being here a few months has given you some kind of insight into the Payne family? You're even more pathetic than I thought."

I search his face. "But I'm not wrong. It doesn't take a genius to realize who the most powerful sibling is. I think you should be the one to reconsider your loyalties."

I know Mason loves his brother despite their tumultuous history.

He doesn't want to be at odds with him, but it's obvious Mathew is too blinded by greed and selfishness to see the bigger picture.

The two of them are never going to see eye to eye, at least not from where I'm standing.

Mathew is always going to want what Mason has.

How much of this is Mason's own desire and ambition, and how much of it is their father's voice in his head?

I feel sorry for Mathew, but not enough to let my guard down around him.

Together, the sibling Paynes can be a force to be reckoned with.

Mathew growls. "You're a little bitch."

"And you haven't learned to steer clear of her." Katia strolls out of the shadows toward us, one hand drifting to her dagger.

I offer her a small, imperceptible nod. "Like I said, I know what you're trying to do, Mathew, and it's not going to work."

Mathew throws his head back and laughs, but it's a cold and hollow sound. "I shouldn't be surprised that Mason's whores are banding together. If there's one thing my brother knows how to do, it's collect women. Tell me, does he know how to handle both of you, or does he only watch?"

Katia fixes her gaze on me. "Do you have what you need?"

I nod. "Yeah, I'm done here."

"It's a shame Mason doesn't know how to choose better. You both could use a real man."

I place one foot in front of the other until I reach Katia, and some of the knots in my stomach unfurl. We share a quick look before she steps behind me.

"You should ask your precious Mason why Oliver and Olivia left in the first place. I might not be on speaking terms with my siblings, but at least I'm not a hypocritical liar."

I ignore him.

"You'll come to me sooner or later, London. You'll see." His voice follows us to the door and rings in my head as we climb up the back stairs. In the carpeted hallway, Katia glances around before unlocking the door to Mason's room. She waits for me to step inside before pulling the door shut behind me. I perch on the edge of the bed, link my fingers together, and try to calm my racing heart.

Something about the certainty in Mathew's voice stays with me long after I've changed into my pajamas. I sit on a chair by the window and wait for Mason until my eyes grow too heavy and sleep finally comes for me.

CHAPTER SEVENTEEN

Mason

I swirl the liquid around the glass, only half-listening to the voice on the other end of the phone. A short while later, I toss the phone onto the desk.

"She's a bigger liability than you realized."

I glance up and find my father lurking in the doorway to the study, not a single hair out of place, and his outfit looking far too pristine for one in the morning. "Liability is part of the job."

Jack scoffs and steps into the study. "Not when it's something like this. I spent years teaching you, but I should've warned you about women like her."

I push myself off the desk. "I don't know what you're talking about."

"I looked into her," Jack continues. "She dropped out of college, you know, and worked at a diner of all places."

"You're not the only one who knows how to check on people."

Jack stands opposite the desk and reaches for my drink. He sniffs it, wrinkles his nose, and scoffs. Then he sets it down. "Then you know her father owes a substantial amount of money."

Fuck.

Of all the tactics I expected, having London looked into isn't the way I thought he'd go. Still, knowing what I know about my father, I shouldn't be surprised.

Jack Payne leaves no stone unturned, and London is no exception.

What did you expect? It's honestly a wonder he didn't do this sooner.

"A wise decision on your part to stay quiet," Jack continues. "The son I raised isn't stupid or pathetic enough to give up that kind of property for a fucking girl."

I ignore the lurch in my stomach and toss him a bored look. "You know about the policy I have enabling people to work off the debt at the club."

Jack's expression hardens. "Don't fucking lie to me, boy. I know that you wrote off the money owed months ago. I know she's not paying us back anymore."

"What's your point?"

Jack barks out a humorless laugh. "I see your brother was right. She has her claws in you. All that time I spent teaching you how to make an enemy pay, and I should've taught you how to make sure a woman doesn't have you by the balls."

I stiffen. "You couldn't be further from the truth."

He stops laughing, and his eyes sweep over me, leaving unease in their wake. "I'll admit I couldn't figure out how it all happened, but I see it now. She's using you, and you always were fucking weak when it came to women in distress. I blame your mother."

"Don't you dare talk about her that way," I snarl. "As I recall, she affected you, too."

"I should end you where you stand."

I let my arms fall to my sides and spread my legs. "You're welcome to try."

We both know he won't strike yet.

But even I know that everything I've done for the empire won't protect me for long.

I'm running out of time, and I have no idea how to stop what's coming.

All I can hope is that I'm able to protect London from the deadly fallout.

Just say the words. Make him believe London doesn't mean as much as she does. You know it's what he wants, and it'll make things easier for both of you.

A part of me still hopes he's going to leave us alone.

But I know him well enough to know it's going to be anything but smooth sailing.

Sooner or later, he's going to make his move, targeting London's parents is proof of that, and while he has softened considerably in recent years, I don't know if it's going to be enough.

"Your brother has expressed an interest in the girl," Jack responds. "I don't understand the appeal, but I'm willing to overlook a few things if you prove yourself to me."

Bastard.

"I will not hand her over to Mathew," I reply through gritted teeth. "Ask for something else."

There's a lot I'm willing to do, and lines I have no qualms about crossing.

I'll wage a war and leave destruction in my wake if that's what it takes, but London is where I draw the line.

I know my brother, and I've had enough complaints from women at the club over the years to know what kind of man he is to them.

London might forgive me for keeping secrets and for not doing more to protect her parents. She might even find it in her heart to understand if I have to bring Noah to heel.

But she'll never forgive me for handing her over to Mathew, even if it means not having to worry about my father.

I can't ask her to pay that price.

Jack turns away from me and walks over to the bookcase. He runs his fingers along the spine of an embossed first edition, and the flickering flames of the fire illuminate his face. I study him for a while longer and find myself wondering how everything spun out of control so fast.

Almost as if he'd been lying in wait all this time, waiting to swoop in and cast me aside.

That's not his style. Jack Payne is not underhanded. His approach is more direct.

Slowly, my father pulls the nearest book out and flips open to a random page. He snaps the book shut and turns back around. "It's a pity I wasted so much time on you. You've turned into such a disappointment, Mason."

I offer him a tight nod in response.

"If I find out her little friend was behind the kidnapping, you're going to wish you'd given her to Mathew instead," Jack says. Every inch of him is on edge like he's going to attack.

I choose my next words carefully.

How does he keep uncovering things I try to keep hidden?

It's almost like he knows exactly where to look.

"I have a business to run. You can see yourself out."

Carlisle rushes in as Jack leaves, and I don't miss the knowing look. Once Carlisle finishes relaying his message, I race from the office and into the car waiting outside. When we reach the warehouse on the outskirts of the city, Carlisle strides ahead of me, and the men there part to let me through.

A figure is tied to a chair with sweaty hair matted to his forehead, and one eye swollen shut.

I pause to roll up my sleeves. Then, I yank his head back and press a gun to his temple. "Have you heard of Eddie Yakovish?"

The man stares at me through his good eye, and a furrow appears between his brows.

"He was from this powerful family." I release his hair and reach for the kit Carlisle is holding out. I select a pair of pliers and yank out a fingernail with them, and his scream echoes around the room. "We had a brief alliance that ended badly. Do you know why? Because Eddie was a rat. Do you know what I do to rats?"

His eyes widen, and he bites back another scream as I pull out another fingernail.

I drop the pliers to the floor with a clatter. I reach for the hammer and examine it in the moonlight. "First, I went after his family. I'm sure you've heard what I did to them. And then, I made sure to hit the business where it hurt the most. In the end, not even his family was willing to stand by him."

The man swallows, and a flash of fear flickers over his face.

I hold out the hammer. "I took my time with it, too. Dragged it out for weeks. He held out a lot longer than I thought, but every man has a threshold for pain. Getting to know what it is, that's the fun part."

"*Please.*" The man's voice is hoarse. "They threatened my family unless I told them things. I'll tell you everything I know."

I hand Carlisle the hammer and snap on a pair of gloves. "Oh, you're going to tell me everything you know anyway. Starting with what you know about the car crash they orchestrated."

"I don't know anything about that."

I pull back the hammer and take a swing at the man's knee, and he folds in on himself. "That's not the answer I want to hear. Let's try this again. Who went after my sister tonight?"

I have no idea how the hell they managed to mess with my sister's car, causing her to nearly swerve out of control, but I'm suddenly thankful Olivia is a hell of a driver.

Olivia is, thankfully, being taken far away from any danger.

But losing control of her car like that still means she came too close for comfort.

My enemies need to be stopped before they cause some real damage.

I want whoever is responsible to pay, and I need to make sure it sends a message to everyone else.

It is not open season on the Paynes.

The man is lucky Carlisle was nearby and managed to track him down, because if it had been me, he'd already be dead.

It's taking every ounce of self-control I have not to leave him gasping for air six feet under.

"I swear I don't know anything." Sweat forms on his forehead and rolls down the sides of his face. He licks his cracked lips as blood pours down his face. "But I overheard them talking about someone else on the inside, someone more powerful, and something about another attack."

I set down the hammer and reach for the pliers. "You're catching on. Good."

He glances over my shoulders and back at my face. "How do I know you're not going to kill me anyway?"

I shrug and kneel in front of him, so we're eye level. "You don't. At this point, you should be glad this is all I'm doing. Keep talking, and I might be persuaded to leave your girlfriend and parents out of it."

The blood drains from his face. "The attack on the Payne girl. It was just a ruse. They're planning something else. Something bigger."

I glance over at Carlisle and nod.

He takes out his phone and steps away.

Shit.

Why hadn't I kept Olivia and Oliver closer?

Because their lives have already been uprooted because of you, and you know neither of them will take this lying down.

I stand up and flex my fingers. Then I punch the man in the face, hard enough to hear a crunch. Blood gushes out of his nose and drips onto the floor. I turn to Carlisle, and my stomach dips when I see the look on his face.

With a frown, I turn back to face the man in the chair. "See, I think this is the real ruse. You're lying, and you have one minute to tell me the truth, or I will have your girlfriend dragged here, and I'll make you watch."

He shakes his head slowly at first, then faster and faster. "I'm not. I swear—"

I hold up my hand and look over at one of the men to my left. "Bring me the girlfriend. Alive. I want her to be aware of everything I do to her."

"They're going to try to break into the Payne estate." The man's words pour out of him in a rush. "Tonight was a ruse; you're right. They wanted you gone, so they could break in. I don't know why. I was supposed to double back and help them."

My blood turns to ice.

There aren't enough men at the estate to hold off an attack.

Oliver and Olivia are being taken there, but a quick look in Carlisle's direction ensures they'll change route.

Fuck.

I'm halfway across town, and getting to London in time will be nearly impossible.

Other than Katia and a few men stationed outside, everyone else is spread thin.

She's a sitting duck because you weren't paying attention. How could you not have seen this coming?

"Send as many men back to the estate as you can," I yell to Carlisle. "Get in touch with the others. Have them move into formation. Nobody better fucking get into the house."

Abruptly, I turn to the man who is watching us through his good eye. Wordlessly, I slice his binds, and his fingers immediately move to rub the angry red on his wrists. He rises to his feet and clears his throat. There's a low pounding in my ears as I turn my back on him and stride back to the car.

"You'll call off the men watching my girlfriend, right? I kept up my end of the bargain, and I'll make it up to—"

I wheel around and shoot him between his eyes before he can finish. His mouth forms a surprised O, and he slumps to the ground, blood pooling around him. I pause to sheathe my gun and slide into the back of

211

the car. Before we pull away, I spot one of our men dragging the man's body away.

Time drags as my driver weaves in and out of traffic, honking and with tires screeching. My fingers fly over the keyboard on my phone, and through the window, I spot my father's car, tearing in the opposite direction. One of our safehouses has already been set up for him and my siblings, and I know I'll get an earful for not joining them.

But I have to get to London, consequences be damned.

Katia might be one of the best weapons in my arsenal, but even she can't stave off an attack and protect London.

We race through a red light, earning a few disgruntled honks from the drivers.

Suddenly, the car skids to a halt, and I lurch forward. When I spot the line of cars ahead of us, I frown and shove the car door open. Then I pull the driver out, and he stumbles onto the street, his eyes widening in fear. Without looking at him, I get into the driver's seat and pull on my seatbelt. Then, I place my hands on the wheel and back out of the tight spot until I'm out. I see red as I muscle through alleyways and down side routes until the estate looms in the distance.

The gates are open, and I press harder on the gas.

I'm out of the car before it comes to a stop, my gun ready.

Carlisle and a few other men follow closely behind, and my heart sputters when I see the front door ripped from its hinges. A few of the guards are lying on the floor, gasping for breath. I step over them and gesture to Carlisle, who relays an order to the guards. As they spread out, Carlisle inches closer to me, and we creep up the stairs.

A few more bodies are waiting at the top, but no one I recognize.

I stop to slit a few of their throats.

I taste bile as I reach my room and see the blood spatters on the floor and the door. I do a quick sweep of the room and find Carlisle taking care of another man when I emerge. As I work to calm my racing heart, I hear a scream that sends me sprinting down the hallway.

Katia is standing with her back to the wall, fighting off three men.

Her movements are quick, barely flashes in the dark, but one look at the gaping wounds on her thigh and arm lets me know that she won't hold out for much longer. I inch forward, shooting one man in the back of the head. Carlisle drags another one back by the scruff of his neck and ends him before the man's face finishes registering his surprise. Katia sticks a knife into the remaining man's stomach and twists.

He falls to the floor with a howl as she swats away a few errant locks of hair.

"London is fine," Katia replies gruffly. "She's in one of the rooms with the door locked."

I nod. "How much damage did—"

A loud crash has us all whipping around, our weapons drawn. Down the hallway, a dark-haired man's eyes widen, and seconds later, he hits the floor with a thud. London is standing behind him, holding onto the remains of a vase, her chest rising and falling unevenly. She glances from me to Katia and back again, her mouth moving soundlessly. I step over the man's inert form and reach for her, and she immediately releases the remaining piece of glass.

Once my arms close around her, and the warm, familiar scent of her washes over me, something in me cracks. I take in a smattering of bruises on her arm and a few to the side of her face. I pull her against me before turning to face Katia and Carlisle.

"Secure the parameter. Kill everyone except for one. I don't care who, just have him ready in the basement."

They disappear, leaving London and me alone in the hallway.

I tug her behind me as more of my men pour in and pop into and out of the rooms. When I'm sure my room is secure, I pull London in and lock the door behind us. I steer her into the bathroom and wait for the shower water to heat up. While it does, I kneel in front of her and run a warm towel over her skin.

"I'm fine," she whispers.

I stop at the bruises close to her throat and push back against the red-hot anger bursting through me. "You had to fight off some of them?"

London smiles. "Katia is a good teacher."

I pull her to her feet and push her shirt over her head. Then, I reach for her yoga pants and leave her clothes in a heap on the floor. She swallows as I run my fingers down her bare skin, and goosebumps break out. I reach for the towel again, and London shivers as my fingers inch up, skim the waistband of her panties, and linger near her heaving chest.

"They shouldn't have been anywhere near you," I whisper. "I was so focused on punishing them for going after Oliver and Olivia that it didn't even occur to me that they'd try something—"

She pushes herself up to her toes and presses a finger to my lips. "Don't blame yourself. You couldn't have known."

I meet her gaze. "I should have. I don't even know how you're still here."

"Because I want to be." London runs her fingers over my face and stops at my lips. "When are you going to accept that I'm not running away?"

She reaches behind her back and unhooks her bra, allowing her breasts to spill forward. Then she hooks a thumb through her panties and pulls them to her ankles. After she kicks them off, she reaches for me, and I crush her against me.

Her mouth is soft as she surrenders herself to me.

My fingers move down her body and pause at her hips. Then I hoist her up, and she wraps her legs around my waist. She moans, and it sends desire coursing through me. I yank the curtain open, and London's hands move to my pants. She unbuckles the belt, and her fingers move inside to reach for me.

I growl into her mouth, lean back, step into the shower and set her down.

She helps me out of my clothes, and the look in her eyes is almost enough to make me come undone.

Adrenaline pumps through me as I kiss a path down to her navel. Then, I throw one leg over my shoulders and angle myself so I'm nestled between her thighs. London's breathing sharpens as she shoves her wet hair from her eyes and looks at me. I don't look away as I trace a path along the inside of her thighs. Using my tongue, I lick a path along her wet crease, and she bucks against me.

London throws her head back and says my name.

I reach for her other leg and press her against the wall.

My tongue darts in and out of her over and over, alternating between establishing a rhythm and enjoying her sweet taste.

Her body writhes as her fingers thread themselves through my hair, sending waves of pain and pleasure through me. London heaves a shaky breath as I rise to my feet. We reach for each other at the same time, our mouths colliding as I press her against the wall. London runs her hands down my bare back and squeezes my behind.

I spin her around, so her back is pressed against me.

London glances back at me with a wild-eyed look in her eyes.

It makes me want her that much more.

The feeling grows as I bend her over and thrust into her from behind.

I ease in and out at a slow, even pace, but soon London's whimpers unleash the last of my control. I dig my nails into her hips, and press the other into the small of her back. Then, I change my pace, slamming into her in a frenzy.

It's still not enough to drive away the fact that I almost lost her.

London continues to chant my name, a plea and prayer on her lips as I drive into her.

She meets each thrust with a buck until I lose all sense of time and space.

Too soon, the release within me reaches a boiling point, and I throw my head back to shout. Pleasure rips through me as my body jerks, and spots dance in my field of vision. The tightness in my chest unfurls. As I come down, I realize the hot water is still cascading around us, and London is looking at me.

Her eyes are soft and unflinching.

She reaches for the bar of soap and runs it over my glistening skin.

Once she's done cleaning me, I return the favor, paying attention to every curve and dip of her body until she's shivering again. I switch off the water and scoop her into my arms. Water drips on the floor and forms a path into the room where I set her down on the dresser chair. Then I dart back into the bathroom and return with a towel.

I bundle her into it, and she reaches for my hand to pull me into bed.

She throws a leg over me and snuggles into my side.

I press a kiss to the side of her head and exhale. "I won't fail you again, London."

I can't meet her eyes. "You haven't failed me, Mason. I'm fine."

I squeeze her shoulders and press another kiss to her temple. Slowly, I swing my legs over the side of the bed and walk back into the bathroom. After towel drying myself, I see London in the doorway, the towel secured around her chest, and her eyes worried.

When I'm dressed, I spin around to face her. "I have to take care of a few things."

London nods. "I figured."

I cross over to her and whip off her towel. "I won't be gone long. I'll have someone bring you some food and water. Katia will be nearby if you need her."

"I'm fine," London repeats with a sigh. "We're fine."

My throat closes as she kisses my cheek. I smile before forcing myself to walk away. Carlisle is waiting for me in the hallway. I glance at Katia, whose arm and thigh are bandaged. Carlisle matches his pace to mine, and at the bottom of the stairs, we stop in front of my father.

His sleeves are rolled up to his elbows, and he's got blood on his knuckles. "How nice of you to join us."

"I had some matters to take care of," I reply, stepping past him. "The damage has been contained, and we didn't lose a lot of men."

"You're missing the point." Jack matches his pace to mine as we make a beeline for the basement. "They shouldn't have been able to break in to begin with."

I wheel around to face him and clench my hands into fists. "I'm using the same security company you did."

Jack snorts. "It takes a lot more than a security company to make sure the estate is a fortress. You should've had more men stationed here, not out trying to put out fires."

I narrow my eyes. "Fires that will turn much worse if we don't nip this in the bud."

Jack's expression darkens. "I warned you this would happen. You've let your guard down, and our enemies are going to be gloating."

"We're still here, and they aren't."

"Have I taught you nothing?" Jack is exasperated. "It's not about the last person standing."

I turn away from him.

"This won't be tolerated."

Jack's voice makes me stop in my tracks. "Thatcher is waiting for you in the office. The prisoner will be taken care of."

I look over at him and frown. "Fine."

I storm past him and toward my office. The door is propped open, and Thatcher Thayer is sitting by the fire, his features illuminated in the crackling embers. He does nothing to acknowledge my presence other than offer a brief head tilt.

I let the door close behind me and stride over to the desk. "I'm sure you've heard what happened tonight. In light of recent events, we're going to need to renegotiate the number of men stationed at the warehouses."

Thatcher eyes me over the rim of his drink. "I want something in return."

I step behind the desk and reach for the decanter. "Naturally."

He rises to his feet, the streaks of silver in his dark hair glistening in the firelight. He covers the distance between us and sets his glass on the table. Then, he strokes his chin thoughtfully.

"The tabloids can't get enough of you and my daughter. They're calling you a power couple. Interest in our brand has gone up. We need to keep the momentum going."

"You want me to attend more events?"

"I want a lavish engagement," Thatcher replies, his eyes glittering. "I want anyone who's someone to be on the guest list. You will be by my daughter's side the whole night, and you will make everyone in that room envious."

I study him intently and press my lips together.

It's not an unreasonable ask, but the thought of spending a night glued to Elise's side doesn't sit well with me.

Not when I know London will be watching.

It's bad enough that her life is in danger, and now she has to watch me fawn all over another woman in public.

Fuck me.

"Your special friend shouldn't be anywhere near the festivities," Thatcher adds. "I'm sure you can understand why it would be better if we keep the focus elsewhere."

"Of course."

He smiles. "We have an understanding, then?"

I set down my drink and straightened my back. "As soon as your men are in position, I'll make the arrangements."

"You and Elise," Thatcher says. "My daughter has impeccable taste, and it must be worthy of the Thayer name."

I ignore the pounding in my head and nod.

Thatcher says something else, but I don't hear him.

For half an hour, he launches into great detail about the guest list and curating the kind of event people will talk about for days, but all I can think about is London.

Will putting a label on my relationship with Elise be the thing that pushes her away for good?

I'm on my third drink when Thatcher's phone rings. He takes it out of his pocket. "I'll tell Elise the good news. I'll see to it that she stops by tomorrow, so you can get started."

I set the drink down. "And the men?"

"I'll make the phone calls. You'll have the reinforcements you need," Thatcher replies. "I look forward to our continued partnership. I can already tell we'll do many great things."

With one last cryptic smile in my direction, Thatcher Thayer saunters off.

I brace my arms against my desk and swallow.

I call Carlisle into my office, and he listens intently.

A short while after he departed, Carlisle calls, and an ache settles in the pit of my stomach.

Thatcher has kept up his end of the bargain far faster than I anticipated.

Now I have no choice but to allow them to parade me around like a prize.

It's just another act. You and Elise know it, so as long as you keep putting on a show, everyone will get what they want.

There's a bad taste in my mouth as I climb up the stairs and find London in my room, wearing a silk black nightgown that falls just past her knees. She takes me in and frowns.

"What's wrong?"

My fingers move to the buttons of my shirt. "We need to talk about what happened in the hallway earlier, with that man who was fighting Katia."

London is confused. "Okay."

I let the shirt fall to the floor with a flutter. "You shouldn't have intervened. Katia can handle herself."

"You're mad because I helped? I thought you wanted me to take a proactive role in keeping myself safe."

I raise an eyebrow. "I meant by using a gun, not a vase."

"It was the closest thing I could find," London replies. "I know it's not your weapon of choice, but it got the job done, didn't it?"

I cross over to the nightstand, yank the drawer open, and pull out the gun. "This isn't a prop, London. You need to learn how to use it."

"I know."

"Then why haven't you asked Katia to teach you?"

"You mean besides the fact that I'm worried she might let me shoot myself a few times before she teaches me anything?"

I give her a pointed look.

London's hands flutter at her sides. "I know I need to learn to protect myself, and that's fine, but I'm not comfortable using a gun."

I set it on the dresser table. "You need to learn how, though. For your safety."

I need to know she can handle herself if things go sideways again.

What happens the next time they lure me into a trap?

Or if Katia is outmaneuvered?

London doesn't waver. "I've already given up a lot, Mason, and I know I made that decision when I decided to be with you, but can't I have this one thing for myself?"

I don't know what I'm supposed to say to that.

London searches my face. "I know things got a whole lot worse, and I will ask Katia to teach me. Just… not yet."

I nod.

"There's something else." I'm choosing my words carefully. "The terms of my alliance with Elise Thayer have changed."

London clears her throat. "I had a feeling they would."

"There's going to be a party," I continue, slowly reaching for her hands. "It's just for show, and I'll slip out as soon as I can, but it might be a while."

London stares at me for a long moment. "It's an engagement party, isn't it?"

"It means nothing," I stress before tugging her against me. "It's all part of the arrangement. You're the one I'm coming back to, London."

Her expression shifts and falls. "Okay."

My stomach lurches. "I'm trying to arrange for you to see your parents at a neutral location. It won't happen for some time, not until all of this dies down, but I'll do what I can."

I'm not even sure they'll agree to visit London, not with how coldly they've been treating her, but I owe it to her to at least try.

London throws her arms around me. "Thank you."

My arms come up around her. "You shouldn't thank me. I'm the reason you can't see them in the first place."

London stirs. "It's been a long day."

I lead her to the bed, pull back the covers, and wait for her to settle in. Then, I pull down my pants and climb in next to her. London tucks herself into my side, and I spend a long time stroking her back and planning what to do next.

If the Fitzpatricks and Everetts want to play dirty, I'll give them what they want.

And I won't stop hitting them, even when there's nothing left.

CHAPTER EIGHTEEN

London

"Can't I—"

"No."

"But it's just—"

"No."

"You haven't even heard me out." My tone rises. "It's just the library, for fuck's sake. I'm not asking to step foot out of the house."

With everything else happening, I know that any temporary freedom I've brokered is on hold.

I can't blame Mason for it.

I spent the night tossing and turning and replaying what it felt like when the electricity cut off and the sound of gunshots sliced through the air. In the morning, as I stood under the showerhead, I tried not to shudder as I remembered what it felt like to take cover in the walk-in closet in Mason's room while Katia fought outside the door.

Mason is right about hand-to-hand combat not being enough.

What good is learning how to use my fists if our enemies don't play fair?

You're not there yet, anyway. Besides, with Katia around, it's unlikely you'll ever have to fire a gun.

There is no love lost between the assassin and me, but if the past few months have taught me anything, it's that her loyalty to Mason runs deeper than whatever jealousy and resentment she harbors toward me.

Despite all the trouble I keep causing her.

Still, I don't like knowing I'm back to square one when it comes to my freedom, and I've spent the morning pacing and eavesdropping whenever I can.

I feel guilty for not trusting the information Mason gives me, but I know something has changed.

Sometime between the attack last night and when Mason woke up this morning, there's been a shift.

There's tension in the air, and everyone is on high alert.

I have no idea what it means for the Paynes moving forward.

They can't just be reacting anymore. They have to figure out how to retaliate before the others come after them again.

Katia clears her throat, and I snap back to the present. "After last night, you should be thankful he hasn't locked you up somewhere."

I fold my arms over my chest. "He wouldn't."

"Not yet."

"Not ever," I maintain. "Mason and I have an understanding."

"I don't care what lies you tell yourself, Blondie," Katia replies. "After last night, whatever understanding you have no longer exists."

Shit.

I know she's right, but I still want to hear it from Mason.

I frown and move back into the room. "Can I at least have something to eat?"

Katia nods and looks away. I retreat into the room and slam the door shut.

While I'm tempted to go back out and fight my way down, there's no point when Katia will just drag me back up. As I pace the room, I think back to the early hours of the morning, when bright sunlight poured in through the open curtains and illuminated Mason's face.

I don't know how to get him to be honest about everything, and I'm not sure I want to.

How will knowing how badly things are spiraling make me feel better?

I should be thankful he's keeping me in the dark.

All those bodies, and the smell of blood in the hallways, are going to haunt me for the rest of my days.

I don't realize how hard I'm digging my nails in until I draw blood.

I blink and stare at the crimson drop that falls to the floor.

I yank the nightstand drawer open and rummage through it. When I pull out the burner, my heart is racing. I dial the number and put the phone to my ear.

My mom's phone goes to voicemail after the eighth ring.

I listen to the message, sick to my stomach.

Once I hear the familiar beep, I suck in a harsh breath and press two fingers to my temple. "Hey, Mom. It's me. Look, I know you and Dad aren't happy with me right now. I know you don't understand the choices I've made, or the life I've chosen for myself, and that's fine. You can be mad at me all you want, but *please* just listen to me. I need you both to leave the city for a while. Maybe go abroad for a few weeks or something…."

I stand in front of the window and take in the sprawling estate below. "I know it all sounds crazy, and I can't tell you what's happening. I wish I could, but things just got worse, and I need to know that you two are safe."

I hang my head and go quiet.

"Please don't send Noah again. It's for his own good. I love you both so much, and you have no idea how sorry I am about everything. I'll reach out again when I can."

Slowly, I take the phone away from my ear and swallow past the lump in my throat. After placing the phone in the nightstand drawer, I move to the window.

How can I appreciate the beauty of this place when each step forward feels like five steps back?

It feels like one wrong move sends me back into the darkness.

There are worse places to be stuck. And at least your Mom and Dad are safe.

Tears spring to my eyes as I unexpectedly yearn for my old life, for Sunday night dinners when I sat across from my parents as we swapped stories. In my mind's eye, I see them seated side by side underneath dim fluorescent lighting as the waiter lingers in the background. When I blink, Noah is sitting next to me, his hand on mine.

I exhale sharply and try to push the image away.

Longing for simpler times won't do me any good.

I've burned my bridges with Noah, and although I hope he'll understand someday, part of me knows he won't.

As far as he and my parents are concerned, I've made the wrong choice.

You could've kept your head down and worked off your debt. Mason would've kept his word and kept his hands to himself, and it would've been just another Wednesday for you.

I could've been in the club, cleaning up whatever mess the patrons left behind.

And I would've ended the night with an ache in my bones and knots in my stomach.

Having to go through that kind of loneliness and isolation, with the crushing weight of what I had to do settling around me, still takes me by surprise now and again.

I don't think I'll ever forget how it felt.

Nor am I sure I want to.

It's too late to walk away now. Even if you could negotiate your safety and your parents', you have nothing to offer in return. Jack Payne is a businessman, and after all the trouble lately, he'll want something concrete.

Convincing him won't be enough.

Appeasing one enemy doesn't remove the rest of the targets on my back.

I need to find something to offer our enemies that will make them forget about me, but I know I'm grasping at straws.

However, it's the only thing that's been keeping me sane since the night Mason rescued me.

You won't leave Mason. You can't, so why even entertain the idea? The minute you realized he came for you instead of leaving you to rot, your decision was made.

With a sigh, I run a hand over my face, surprised when it comes up wet.

I blink and turn away from the window.

In the tile-floored bathroom, I splash cold water on my face and grip the sink. Back in the room, there's a low din of conversation outside. Then there's a loud scuffle, and a shout, and fear coils in my stomach.

I glance from the door to the nightstand, willing my feet to move.

The door creaks open, and I throw myself across the room.

My hands are sweaty as I wrench the gun from the drawer and grip it with both hands. Then, I wheel and find Mason's sister, with her long, auburn hair pulled into a braid. She glances at my gun.

My feet are unsteady as I force myself to stand and clear my throat. "I know you."

"Do you know how to use that?"

I lower the gun. "No, but I probably should learn."

Olivia glances over her shoulder at a scowling Katia. "Aren't you in charge of her training?"

"I'm not comfortable holding a gun," I say quickly, throwing it onto the bed. "She's a good teacher."

Olivia steps further into the room. "You must be going crazy being kept up here. Why don't we go and sit in the library?"

I blink. "Katia said I wasn't allowed."

Olivia waves dismissively. "We'll be fine."

I reach for my shoes and hurry after Olivia. She takes the stairs two at a time, pausing at the bottom to tilt her head. She motions to me, and we creep forward, and the pounding in my chest grows. We stop outside the library, and Olivia presses her hand to the door.

She then leads me to the armchairs by the fire.

I sink into one and look over at Katia, who is scanning the room intently. A few moments later, she shifts and disappears, and I turn to find Olivia stoking the flames, the light casting shadows across her face. She turns to me once she's done, and a tense moment passes. Then, she takes the chair next to me and crosses her ankles.

"I thought it was time you and I met and talked."

I square my shoulders and exhale. "Okay."

"When I first heard about you, I thought you were made up."

I stare at her. "Oh."

Olivia chuckles. "When your brother is Mason Payne, and he has the preferences he does, you learn not to expect much."

I'm not sure what she expects me to say.

She leans forward, and her expression turns serious. "I know about the contract you entered into with my brother in exchange for your father's life being spared and his debts being paid off. I think what you did is brave."

My throat is dry as I nod, and tears sting my eyes.

My contract has been called many things, but this is the first time I've heard anyone refer to it in glowing terms.

"I'm not sure I would've done the same," Olivia continues, "but my father and I have a… complicated relationship."

I swallow and link my fingers. "Why are you telling me this?"

"Because you can love a person and still want to keep your distance," Olivia tells me. "Sometimes, love isn't enough."

I press my lips together and say nothing.

"I know you were aware of who my brother was before you agreed to his terms—or at least you had some idea—but it's different to experience the reality."

I exhale. "It is."

Olivia leans back and tilts her head to the side to study me. "No one would think less of you for walking away, London. Not after everything that's happened."

I suck in a harsh breath.

She's not here out of curiosity.

Olivia Payne is here to size me up and see if she can make the problem go away.

I'm a nuisance, and that realization hurts more than it should.

I don't know why a part of me was hoping to find a friend within these walls.

It's pathetic, and it makes me feel ridiculous.

Why would Olivia want to be friends with the woman who helped ruin her life?

I wouldn't like me either if I were in her shoes.

"I'm not going to offer you money or make threats," Olivia continues. "I'm sure you've already thought of all the reasons why you should go."

"I have."

"I've never seen my brother act like this," Olivia murmurs. "I want him to be happy, but I'm not sure either of you knows what you're getting into."

"We're well aware. I didn't make this decision lightly. I know what I've given up, and I know it won't get easier."

I am not going to sit here and let her pass judgment, no matter who she is.

I don't need her to understand what Mason and I are to each other.

Olivia looks as if she's seeing me for the first time. "I wasn't trying to imply that you didn't."

I lean forward. "What are you trying to say?"

"He was right. You look a lot like our mother. I wonder... well, anyway, look, I know this must seem like I'm trying to ambush you, but I just wanted to meet you."

I frown. "You've got a funny way of showing it."

I wonder if coming down here with her was a good idea.

She's not plotting something like Mathew is, but that doesn't mean she isn't up to something.

I hate not knowing how I fit into the bigger picture, and which of the Payne siblings are willing to sacrifice me for the greater cause.

I take a deep breath and lean back into the chair. "I'm sorry about how everything's turned out. I know your lives have been affected, too, and I didn't mean for any of this to happen."

Silence stretches between us as I gather my nerve.

"But I'm not sorry about how I feel about your brother. I wish things could've gone differently, but I can't control any of this."

Olivia nods.

"I'm sure you've made some bad decisions too," I continue. "But at the time, I'm sure it felt like the right thing to do."

Olivia's expression hardens. "You don't know anything about me, or the decisions I've had to make."

I level her with a pointed look. "Exactly."

Olivia stands up, but before she can say anything else, Mason's voice drifts in. He strolls into the library and stands in front of his sister. A glance passes between us before she walks away. He turns to me with a look that would scare anyone else away.

"Good chat?"

My arms fall to my sides. "She came to me."

"We were careful," I add without looking away. "Were you going to tell me about the security changes?"

Mason's eyes flash. "Yes."

I raise an eyebrow. "Like you were going to talk to me about the fact that I look like your mother?"

"What does that have to do with anything?"

"I'm sorry you couldn't save her, but I'm not your mother," I say. "And if that's why you're keeping me around…."

I've danced around the topic long enough.

I need to know the truth.

Mason's hand darts out, and his fingers close around my wrist. "I won't dignify that with a response. You should know better."

Then, he tugs me out of the library and up the stairs.

The protest dies on my lips when I see the look on his face.

Once back in the room, I perch on the edge of the bed and turn the information over in my head.

Still, I can't keep my thoughts from wondering.

Am I a substitute for Mama Payne?

Is Mason trying to rewrite history by protecting me?

My heart aches at the thought that what he feels for me might be based on a lie.

CHAPTER NINETEEN

Mason

"I'm perfectly capable of handling this on my own."

My father snorts next to me but doesn't move his gaze from the glass. "Given how your last few meetings have gone, it's better for everyone if I'm there."

My head swivels in his direction, and I frown. "You would've done the same thing."

My father raises an eyebrow. "I wouldn't have taken so many men and left the estate undefended. I also wouldn't have put my fucking life on the line for that woman."

I clench my hands into fists. "That woman is not going anywhere, and the sooner you can accept that, the better it will be for all of us."

I'm goddamn tired of rehashing the same argument with my father.

I don't expect him to approve of London, and I don't need him to.

But I do need him to make his peace with her presence because it'll make things a hell of a lot easier, especially when it comes to presenting a unified front.

There are too many messes, too many fires to put out, and while I thrive under pressure and the chance to show everyone why our family is not to be messed with, I can't be everywhere at once. Between the attacks on the warehouse, the mole in our midst, and having to plan an

IVY BLACK AND RAVEN SCOTT

engagement to Elise, I'm ready to snap.

The Fitzpatricks and Everetts should've been brought to heel by now. The old you would've had this taken care of already.

I shove the thought away and focus on my father, who is watching me intently.

I don't like the gleam in his eyes or the pursing of his lips.

Something is up with him.

I'm getting a headache considering all the possible ways he might be trying to screw with me.

Jack Payne always has a plan, and today is no exception.

A meeting brokered by the Thayers with the intent of bringing all the major players to the table isn't the kind of thing he'd be caught dead going to.

He doesn't believe in truces.

He thinks you've failed to hold up your end of the bargain, and he's not wrong. The Fitzpatricks and Everetts are even more dangerous and unpredictable than before, and just because it's been a week of silence doesn't mean it's over.

Even this meeting doesn't mean anything if we can't get them to stop the mayhem.

"Besides," Jack continues, "I'm curious how Thayer got them to come to the table to begin with. Unless he's offered them something else."

I make a noncommittal sound but don't reply.

Thatcher must've made a deal with them.

It's the only thing that makes sense.

With a growl, I turn away from my father and turn my attention to the window, and the world rushing past, a blur of shapes and colors. At the traffic light, I hear my father sipping his drink. Then there's a clicking sound, and I move to see a puff of smoke shrouding him. I glance away from the cigar dangling from his mouth.

Taking my anger out on him isn't going to solve anything.

He's not the most pressing issue at hand.

232

He's always responded to initiative, and pushing back in the past has earned his respect. Maybe that's what he's trying to do now. Show him that the monster he created and unleashed is still there. Give him something to work with.

Except my father has always excelled at being able to spot a ruse.

He already disapproves of the shred of humanity I still possess and has been trying to push it out of me for years.

The last thing I need is to have him scrutinize me further.

When the car pulls up outside a nondescript building on the edge of town, flickering streetlamps are the only sign of life other than a few cars parked across the street. Carlisle gets out of the passenger seat, and a few more men pour out of the car behind us and join him. Once they're done sweeping the perimeter, someone opens the door, and my father steps out.

I exhale and join him.

Four men are standing guard in the entryway to the door.

After a quick search, one of them unlocks the door, revealing a dark carpeted hallway.

I shift, favoring the leg that doesn't have a gun tucked into the sock.

Bright light flicks on, and the hallway lights up, revealing Thatcher in a striped pantsuit. He motions to us to follow him into a large room with an arched door, a mahogany table in the center, and a smattering of chairs. A few men are standing with their backs against the walls, and their eyes sweep over us before looking away.

"Forgive the dust and disarray; the place is under renovation," Thatcher says. "Shall we begin?"

"We're missing a few people," I point out. "Unless Everett and Fitzpatrick got some cosmetic surgery."

Thatcher shakes his head. "These are the representatives that each of the families sent. Michael and Lance are otherwise occupied."

A burst of anger shoots through me.

Fucking bastards.

This is a power move if I've ever seen one.

"You can't be fucking serious—"

"Now, now, Mason. Play nice," Thatcher interrupts. "It doesn't matter who came as long as they did. Isn't the point of this negotiating the terms of a new alliance?"

"I wasn't done talking," I tell Thatcher. "The next time you interrupt me, they'll be finding your body parts for days."

Thatcher's face loses some of its color as he turns away and clears his throat. "Yes, well, on that note, I thought it was important to remind you all of why we're here. Our families go too far back for this misunderstanding to continue, and let's not forget how well the alliance worked before everything went sideways."

I snort.

Thatcher stops in the center of the room and spreads his arms. "It's time to put the past behind us and bury the hatchet. I think we can all agree that enough damage has been done."

"Not even close," I say. "We won't be satisfied until they all bleed and are begging for goddamn mercy. Even then, it won't be enough."

Silence stretches across the room.

Thatcher winces. "Yes, I'm sure reparations can be made on both sides."

I look over at my father, but he says nothing.

I hope he's already plotting how to take down every single one of these motherfuckers.

Slowly and painfully.

As Thatcher launches into the next part of his rehearsed speech, I take another look around the room, and the hairs on the back of my neck prickle. Thatcher drones on in the background, but I don't listen to a word.

They're not here to broker a truce.

The men in attendance look like they couldn't care less, but other than the quiet voice in the back of my head yelling at me to get out, I have nothing else to go on.

The certainty in my gut is telling me this is a trap.

I look away from Thatcher and glance over my shoulder at Carlisle.

He nods and quietly retreats.

I'm on edge while he's gone, my mind jumping between scenarios, each involving having to fight our way out.

Katia knows what to do if you don't make it back. She'll make sure London gets to safety, and Carlisle has orders for Oliver and Olivia.

By the time Carlisle returns, Thatcher has been speaking for ten minutes, and the pounding in my skull has intensified. I swing my attention to Elise's father, who pauses to wipe his forehead with a napkin. I advance on him, and a flicker of fear moves over his face before he stamps it out.

"I think this is all bullshit."

Thatcher blinks and puts away his handkerchief. "I beg your pardon?"

"Something is clearly happening. I don't know why you lured us here, but I don't like having my time wasted, Thayer."

"We have an agreement," he says.

"One I'm sure your daughter will be happy to honor should anything unfortunate happen here," I respond. "The question is, how much do you trust your new friends?"

Thatcher doesn't look away. "I have no idea what you're talking about."

I remove the gun from my sock and point it at him. "I'm not in the habit of shooting my allies, but if there's one thing I hate, it's rats. I'm sure Elise told you what we did to the last one since I made sure to share that story with her."

Thatcher's eyes widen. "I resent the implication. I am not a rat."

I point the gun at one of the representatives, and they all stiffen. "Your new friends are planning something. Either you're too stupid to see it, or they made you a better offer. Which is it?"

"I can assure you that this meeting was put together with the best of intentions—"

I remove the safety. "Once I start shooting, you're going to wish you'd told me the truth when you had the chance. I might even be persuaded to make your death quick."

Thatcher looks over at my father, whose expression remains blank. "Aren't you going to do something? He's going to derail everything."

"My son has killer instincts," Jack replies. "I taught him myself, and he's right to question all of this."

Thatcher throws both hands up and swallows. "The last thing anyone in this room wants is for things to get out of hand again. There's still a chance for us to salvage—"

I point the gun at Thatcher again, and he snaps his mouth shut. "Don't you ever get tired of hearing yourself talk? I know I do."

"Elise will never honor an agreement with the man who killed her father," Thatcher warns.

The phone in my pocket rings, slicing through the tension in the air.

I use my free hand to whip it out and answer without looking.

A few moments later, I slide the phone back into my pocket and press the gun to the side of Thatcher's head. "Let's go. You're coming with us. Carlisle, take care of the rest."

A shout goes up, and there's a scuffle as I drag Thatcher off, knowing my father is close behind. Gunshots ring out before we get into the car. I push Thatcher into the back seat and slide in after him. We peel away from the curb a few moments later, tires screeching in the stillness of the night.

"I just received a phone call informing me that a warrant has been issued for our club."

Thatcher holds his arms in his lap to hide the tremor. "A warrant?"

"The premises are being searched for illegal activity," I continue. "Your ambush didn't work, Thayer. Now, give me one good reason why I shouldn't dump your body on Elise's doorstep."

Thatcher glances from my father to me and back again. "I had nothing to do with this, I swear."

"Why don't I believe you?"

"I don't know," Thatcher responds. "Tell me what I can do to make you see that I'm not your enemy."

I grunt and lower the gun.

Slowly, I reach into the compartment in the center and pull out a few zip ties. Thatcher's hands are shaking as it takes a few tries for him to put them together. While he does, I call Carlisle, who is on his way to the club with reinforcements. The search won't yield any results, but I know we can't afford the added scrutiny.

I hang up on Carlisle and dial Katia, who answers on the third ring. "Has it been taken care of?"

"Yes."

I switch the phone to my other ear. "Good. Get back to London once you're done."

The line goes dead, and I tuck the phone away.

When we arrive at the Payne estate, the gates are wide open, and there's a swarm of reporters in front of the club. Red and blue lights flash as a few uniformed cops stand behind yellow tape. As the car pulls up, everyone gathered erupts into a frenzy, and several cameras flash in our direction.

My father gets out first.

I shoot Thatcher a warning look before my fingers move to the buttons of my shirt. "One sound, one wrong move, and you'll be begging me to have Elise honor our agreement."

Thatcher gives me a tight nod and stiffens.

I tuck the gun away and hurry out of the car.

There's a loud ringing in my ears as the cops clear a path for me, and I walk right up to the club, where my family is waiting at the top of the stairs. We turn to face the camera, and the cacophony of voices grows.

Carlisle sidles up to me, and I lean into him. "How the fuck did this happen?"

"Some reporter," Carlisle says. "We're working on figuring out who it is."

I offer the crowd another wave. "Make sure our people on the inside help. Double their pay."

Carlisle nods and disappears through the double doors.

Once we're inside, Oliver and Olivia start talking over each other. Our father stands near a booth in the corner, nursing a drink. I spot Thatcher being brought in, his hands tied behind his back, and a panicked look in his eyes. I stalk over to him, yank him forward, and throw him into the nearest booth.

"Are you ready to talk?"

Thatcher stares dumbly. "I already told you; I don't know anything. The Fitzpatricks reached out to me. I didn't even—"

I cut him off with a low, humorless laugh. "You fucking idiot. You didn't think to make sure it was legit?"

Thatcher scowls. "Why would I?"

"Because you allied yourself with us, which means you're probably next."

Thatcher sputters. "We have an agreement. If they try anything—"

"Our agreement is void if you fuck us over," I interrupt. "You should be thankful I haven't already killed you."

Without waiting for a response, I turn on my back and retrieve a bottle from the bar.

When Carlisle returns, my siblings are still arguing, and my father is bent over Thatcher. I know he'll make him break. I motion to Carlisle, and we retreat a few steps. He waits a few seconds before he reaches into his jacket for an envelope.

"The lead reporter on this is Noah's brother."

I snatch the envelope and rip it open. "You're fucking kidding."

Carlisle shakes his head. "He has a different last name, and there's some kind of falling out. I reached out to some people, and he's been

238

working on a story about corruption."

I rifle through the pictures, growing angrier by the minute. "Let me guess. Noah pointed him in our direction."

"Noah has been meeting with his father a lot lately," Carlisle adds. "We're working on killing the story before it gains any traction."

I nod to Carlisle. "I think it's time we paid Noah a visit. It's long overdue. But before we do, make sure accommodations are prepared for our guest. Mr. Thayer will be staying with us for a while."

Until I put all of the pieces of this puzzle together, I don't want any more fucking surprises.

CHAPTER TWENTY

London

"It's insane out there." I let the curtain swish back into place, but I can still hear their voices, clamoring to be heard over each other.

Mason is leaning against the kitchen counter with a furrow between his brows. It's been twenty minutes since he's looked up or said anything.

I have no idea what's happening, but the fact that we're standing in the living room, instead of sequestered in his room, doesn't make me feel better.

It means his father is no longer the biggest threat.

Jack Payne might be dangerous and unpredictable, but Mason knows how to handle him.

The media frenzy outside is another matter.

Mason frowns. "I'm sorry about all this."

I frown. "Why are you apologizing? None of this is your fault."

This kind of scrutiny must be bad for business, but Mason has barely mentioned it, and I don't want to push.

I'm not sure I want the answers.

"I'm not apologizing for them." Mason's expression hardens as he looks at the front door. "They'll be gone soon enough."

My frown deepens.

"I'm apologizing because I'm going to do something you're not going to like."

I take a step in his direction and pause. "Okay."

"You're not going to have that kind of reaction when you find out what I have to do," Mason says.

"Whatever it is, it can't be that bad."

Mason laughs humorlessly and turns away from me. "I have no idea how bad it is, or how deep it runs, but if what I've uncovered is right, we're all screwed."

"How bad is it?"

Mason turns to look at me. "What do you know about Noah's brother?"

I tilt my head and blink. "Ryder? Not much. They had a huge falling out when their mother died a few years ago, and they haven't spoken much since. Why?"

Mason stares at me for a few seconds longer. "Did you know he was a journalist?"

"Noah mentioned something about that, but what's that… no. I know what you're thinking, and no."

Mason takes my hands in his. "I'm sorry."

I wrench my hand away. "No, Noah wouldn't do that. He wouldn't go to his brother."

The man I loved, the one I spent years building and envisioning a life with, wouldn't hurt me like that.

He couldn't.

"I can't take the chance that you might be wrong."

My heart misses a beat. "Is that what you were talking about just now? The fact that you have to question Noah?"

Mason nods.

"I know what your questioning looks like." My voice is barely above a whisper. "Mason, please. It's not the kind of thing Noah would do. I know he's angry and hurt, but...."

I still refuse to believe he's involved in any of this.

He doesn't want anything to do with me, and he's trying to leave all of this behind.

Having his estranged brother dig into Mason isn't something he'd pursue without good reason.

Like the fact that you broke his heart and left him for another man? Or the fact that you humiliated him? Come on, London. Open your eyes. Hasn't the past few months taught you anything?

Mason searches my face, and the gleam in his eyes turns to pity. "You're not even one hundred percent sure. Getting hurt makes people do crazy things, even if they are out of character."

I take another step away from Mason. "No. Not Noah."

"There's more."

My heart misses a beat as my hands clench into fists. "What are you talking about?"

"I have evidence linking Noah to my enemies. He's been seen meeting with them, and he was nearby the crash site the day of your accident."

There's a low whistling sound in my ears as I struggle to make sense of his words.

But they still don't make sense.

Why would Noah want to come after me?

Are you kidding? After what you've put him through? You can't be that surprised.

Except I still can't wrap my head around it.

"I..no. There has to be another explanation. I'm sure if you to talk to him, he'll clear all of this up."

Mason's expression hardens. "Well then, he should have nothing to worry about when I approach him."

My stomach churns. "You're going to go after him anyway? Why did you bother asking me if you don't believe me?"

Mason's eyes flash. "This has nothing to do with me not believing you and everything to do with the swarm of reporters outside. Noah is involved in something, and I wasn't going to say anything until I was sure, but he's out of time."

"Mason, please—"

"I'll try and make this as painless as possible," Mason adds in a softer voice. "I'm telling you because you asked me to be honest."

I lurch into action and stumble in his general direction. He catches me, and the pounding in my chest drowns out everything else. "What if we made them a good offer? What if we gave them something they wanted?"

Mason's hands move to my waist. "What are you talking about?"

"The people who kidnapped me." The words pour out of me in a rush. "I overheard Katia talking about it the other day. They wanted the diner, didn't they? It's in a prime location, and you wouldn't give it to them."

Mason's expression turns blank. "You should know better than to eavesdrop."

"The diner is struggling anyway. It won't survive without a miracle, and the last time I spoke to my dad, I got the sense he'd be glad to lose it."

Mason doesn't say anything for a long time.

Finally, he releases me, and I feel cold all over.

"Are you sure that's what he said, or is that just something you want to believe to make yourself feel better?"

I stiffen. "Feel better about what?"

"About the role you think you played in all of this."

I fold my arms over my chest. "It's not wrong for me to try and make this right."

"None of this is your fault. If it wasn't the diner, it would've been something else. They've been trying to find a way to take us down for a while."

"I thought you were allies?"

"That means nothing in my world. It just means they wait longer to figure out where to plant the knife to make it bleed."

I swallow. "So, offering them the diner won't help?"

An hour ago, after catching my dad in a rare moment of vulnerability, I felt hopeful. Not only had he taken my call, but we'd fallen into familiar rhythms when I brought up the diner, and I heard the deep ache and resignation in his voice.

He didn't need to say it.

He didn't have to.

I know my father well enough to know when he is at his wits' end.

Giving them the diner might prevent an all-out war, and in the long run, I believe my father would be better for it.

At least that's what I tell myself.

Now, there's a sinking sensation in the pit of my stomach, and the vicious voices in the back of my head have only grown louder.

You knew better than to hope for a miracle, but you did anyway.

Mason exhales. "It's too late."

My stomach lurches. "What if I made them the offer? I could offer to work for them for an agreed-upon amount of time. Something to appease their egos or whatever—"

"No."

"It's at least worth trying." Fear and frustration flood my senses. "You should at least consider the possibility that—"

Mason places his hands around my waist. "I'll burn every last fucking one of them to the ground before I let you willingly go to them."

"But—"

"Listen to me, goddamn it." Mason's fingers sink into my waist, and his expression is one of cold fury. "You are not going anywhere near them. The second they get their hands on you, any contract you think exists won't do a fucking thing. Do you even know what they'd do to you to get back at me?"

A chill races down my spine. "I can figure out a way to make it work. I'm sure we can come to an agreement."

Mason releases me and growls. "You will not put your life in danger to end a war that you didn't start."

"I have to help." I work to keep the frustration from my voice. "I can't stay locked up in here while everyone I love is in danger. I have to do something."

Anything is better than being cooped up here every day with nothing but the voices in my head reminding me of all the ways I'm failing.

"You want to know how you can help? Keep yourself alive and out of harm's way. Knowing you're safe helps me focus on what I need to do."

My stomach sinks further, and I ignore the lump rising in my throat. "That's it?"

"I had my lawyers draft up a deed for your childhood home. It's in your name."

"What?"

"I can't stop the diner from going under, but if your dad sells, I made a deal with an old friend of mine to buy the place. Your dad is a proud man, so I know he won't accept anything else."

A low pounding starts in my ears, and my head begins to swim.

"But you—"

"I've also set aside some money for your family and you," Mason adds. "My lawyers know what to do."

"Why are you talking like that?"

Mason reaches for his phone again.

"You are not allowed to die," I inform him as I snatch the phone from his hand. "Not after everything we've been through. You will find another way."

Mason gives me the barest hint of a smile. "I can't control every outcome."

"Find a way, because anything else is unacceptable," I snap. "I'm all in, Mason, and I meant what I said. I don't want your money or any safety nets you have planned for me because I don't need them."

"It's just in case you do," Mason says.

Tears burn my eyes, and I shove them back.

"I will not need fake passports or whatever else," I repeat, stronger now. "You are going to come back, and we are going to get through this."

Mason cups my face in his hands and runs a thumb over my jaw. "You shouldn't have been dragged into any of this. If I were a better man, I would've let you go the minute I realized how much danger I put you in."

"I chose this, remember?"

Mason's thumb hovers over my lips. "It should've been about sex. I should've made sure it was only about that."

I stare at Mason for a few more moments while my mind races.

I don't like the way he's looking at me, like he's on borrowed time, and I'm the only thing keeping him from floating away.

Still, I stand there, trying to figure out the right thing to say.

How do I get him to stay?

I want him to turn a blind eye to the Noah problem, as much for my sake as his, but I know he won't.

He's got the resolve in his eyes that I love, the kind I want to drown in.

But it feels like everything is falling apart, and I'm standing in the middle of the debris with blood on my hands.

All those disruptions, and all those lives lost, no matter what Mason says, are at least partly my fault. While I don't regret staying with Mason, I know he's right about one thing.

Keeping it physical would've made it a hell of a lot simpler for both of us.

Mason wouldn't have enemies beating down his door, and I wouldn't be cooped up and afraid for the lives of the people I love.

We've let it go too far, but I don't know if realizing that now makes any difference.

I can't turn back time.

Despite my earlier protests, I know Mason is right about what they'll do if they get their hands on me.

Serving myself up to them isn't the answer if Mason has any hope of winning this.

That's assuming they don't gut you on the spot. That'll be a lot more merciful than what they could do. People like the ones who kidnapped you won't have any qualms about carving you up like a turkey and bleeding you dry for information and secrets.

There's no room for error here, and I know it.

My sacrifice would only make things worse, but I keep circling back to it as if the answer will magically present itself.

As if I think about it hard enough, I'll be able to bring this war to a screeching halt.

There's nothing you can do, London. You're just a girl who was helping her father and fell in love with his jailer in the process. You're not the first woman to lose her heart like this, but you need to tread lightly.

"I don't have any regrets," Mason says slowly. "Fuck all of them. Fuck everything. I wouldn't do any of it differently."

My heart swells to twice its size. "Not a single thing?"

"I wouldn't have wasted so much time fighting it, but that's about it."

A half-smile lifts the corners of my mouth. "I know what you mean."

I'm cold all over, and Mason's expression turns serious. "It's better if I get to Noah first. My father suspects he might be involved."

Terror floods my veins. "You told him?"

When it comes to the good of the empire, I know Mason has to put those interests first, but it still stings to know he didn't come to me.

"It wouldn't have mattered if I had. My father likes to stay in the loop. He had you checked out, but he did a more thorough background check. Learning about Noah's father probably tipped him off."

I furrow my brows. "What does his father have to do with anything?"

Mason straightens his back. "Nothing or everything. We'll see."

"Send someone else to take care of it," I respond. I reach for him, but Mason steps out of my reach, and his expression turns stony. "It would be better. Noah is more likely to fess up if it's someone he doesn't know."

Mason's eyes sweep over my face, tight and calculating. "You don't trust me to be objective?"

"Honestly? No."

Mason nods and turns away. "I see."

I place a hand on his arm and wait for him to look at me. "It's an impossible thing to expect given the circumstances. I wouldn't be objective if it were one of your exes."

He pries my fingers away and strides out of the room. I stare at the space he occupied for a long time, the tightness in my chest only growing worse. Then I take the stairs two at a time until I'm standing in the doorway to his room. I wrench open the nightstand drawer, my fingers trembling as I take out the phone.

My mom's number rings a few times, and I leave her a message.

I leave my father a similar message and ignore the bile rising in my throat.

Panic creeps in as I frown at Noah's number. A few moments pass when I wrestle with the idea before I dial. Noah's voice is thick with sleep when he answers. I clutch the phone tightly, but the words won't come.

I can't warn Noah without losing Mason's trust.

You're not just going to leave him unprepared, are you? No matter what's happened between you, you still care about him.

I will not let his life be derailed any further than it already has.

Not on my account.

But I can't bring myself to say anything, with Mason's face in my mind and his words reverberating inside my head.

After a long pause, I press my lips together and listen to Noah's confused murmurs.

When he hangs up, I lower my head and blow out a breath.

Why couldn't I have told him the truth?

You're trying to build trust with Mason, and no matter how well-intentioned this is, he'll view it as a betrayal, and you won't be able to blame him.

Offering Noah the chance to cover his tracks won't help anyone.

I have to trust that he's not involved.

I throw the burner back into the drawer. I pace the room a few times as an idea takes root in my head. After shoving my feet into a pair of sneakers, I grab my jacket off the hooks on the back of the door and find Katia outside. We exchange a glance as I push the door open the rest of the way and clear my throat. Then, I make my way down to the library.

Using the pale light of the moon, I pretend to peruse the books.

My heart is in my throat, and there's a niggling sensation in the back of my skull.

I see Katia turn away and move behind the nearest bookcase.

I flatten myself against the wall and hold my breath.

A few seconds later, I inch closer to the back, in the direction of the secret door I stumbled across a few weeks ago. I try to keep my breathing as quiet as possible as I creep around the library. As I reach the farthest corner, I pause and glance over my shoulders. Then, I crouch and pat around for the lever I saw Mathew pull, hidden behind an old portrait. The kernel of hope inside my chest blossoms as my fingers close around it.

It soars when the portrait slides to reveal a hidden door.

"Did you honestly think that would work?"

I sigh and refuse to look behind me. "I made it this far."

"Your adventure is over, Blondie. Let's go."

I whip around and find Katia leaning against the bookcase.

"We can't let him go like this."

Katia frowns. "You don't have a lot of faith in him, do you?"

I clench my hands into fists. "I have plenty of faith in him, but there are too many variables. Too many odds stacked against him."

Katia throws her head back and laughs. "He's going to interrogate your ex. I know you don't think Nolan can take him."

"It's not about whether or not *Noah* can take him," I snap. "It's about the fact that he shouldn't have to. This is my mess. I should be the one to clean it up."

Katia looks directly at me and raises an eyebrow. "I don't disagree."

"I should be the one to question Noah," I add. "I can get him to tell me the truth."

"And how, exactly, do you plan to do that?"

I blink. "I'm going to talk to him. I'll reason with him and—"

Katia cuts me off with another laugh. "So, you planned to sneak off and—in the unlikely event you don't get caught in the crosshairs—just have a little chat? Spill your hearts over tea and candy?"

Color creeps up my neck and onto my cheeks.

Katia makes it sound ridiculous.

She doesn't know Noah the way I do. Nor does she know how many nights we stayed up pouring out our hearts to each other, or how many parts of myself I've shared with him.

Noah knew me better than I knew myself, and I refuse to believe he would throw it all away so easily.

Katia's expression turns cold. "And what were you going to do if Mason saw you, huh? Were you going to braid his hair, too?"

I glower at her. "I hadn't gotten to that part of the plan yet."

Katia shakes her head. "I have no fucking clue how you haven't gotten killed yet. I thought you had a good head on your shoulders."

"I do," I protest hotly. "Just because I don't operate the way you do doesn't mean I'm any less smart."

"You're going to get yourself killed," Katia tells me flatly. "Or worse. You'll get other people killed."

"Come and keep an eye on me then," I say. "We both know you'd rather be going with Mason anyway."

Katia tilts her head to look at me. "I'm beginning to think you have a death wish."

I keep my eyes on her face. "What's your point?"

Katia sighs. "My skills are wasted on you; you're right about that. He could be walking into a trap."

My heart jumps into my throat. "So, you'll come with me?"

"Let's get a few things straight, Blondie. I'm not doing this for you; I'm doing this for him, and you will do as you're fucking told, or I'll take care of you myself. I hate liabilities. Is that understood?"

I nod. "Yes."

This isn't the girl who was forced into this life, and it's not the one who fell in love with Mason when she knew better. None of those versions of her exist as she studies me. The woman in front of me is all business and pure lethal precision, the gears in her mind turning as she considers her options.

Without Katia, I'm not going anywhere.

She darts out her hand and snatches my wrist. "I could just leave you here."

I ignore the thudding in my chest. "You could."

Katia's eyes narrow into slits. "It would be easier."

I force myself to hold still. "Until you get to Mason. What happens after that?"

Katia inches close enough that I can feel her breath on my face. "Are you threatening me?"

Bile rises in my throat. "Just stating facts. We both know Mason won't be happy if you go after him and leave me."

Katia draws her lips back into a snarl. "I don't like threats, Blondie."

"I know."

Katia releases my hand, and I let it fall to my side. "Seems like we've rubbed off on you after all."

I shrug.

A muscle ticks in Katia's jaw as she turns away from me. A heartbeat later, she whips a phone out of her jacket and presses it to her ear. A low pounding starts in my ears as I inch away from her and rub my wrist. She speaks in a guttural language I can't place. I study her face and wait.

Have I overplayed my hand?

The next few minutes are agonizingly slow.

I almost want Katia to put me out of misery, and the longer she takes, the more convinced I become that she will drag me back upstairs. While I hate being locked away, I'm not ridiculous enough to think that convincing Katia will be easy.

Not when trouble has a habit of finding me.

How can she focus on helping Mason if she has to stop me?

You should just let her go. She'll be more useful to Mason if she doesn't have to worry about you.

Except I know she won't be of any use to Noah.

And although a trickle of guilt is building inside of me, I know I need to be careful because Mason will never understand.

Regardless of how I act, there will be consequences.

But for the first time in months, I'm tired of sitting around and waiting for a better option to fall into my lap. Noah might no longer be in my life, but that doesn't mean I can turn my back on all our history, laughter, tears, and all the times he's been there for me.

You were going to build a future together, remember? You can't just stand aside and do nothing.

Even when I know Mason will turn his wrath on me.

Just as I'm about to venture further into the secret exit and take my chances, Katia hangs up and swivels to face me. Wordlessly, she reaches out and binds my hands. My eyes widen as I look at the restraints. Katia steps in front of me and tugs me after her.

Fear and uncertainty rise within me.

Have I pushed her too far?

The passageway is barely lit, forcing Katia to stop every so often and glance at me. I focus on quieting my breathing and placing one foot in front of the other. The damp, moldy smell fills my nostrils, making me want to gag until I spot a beam of light ahead. I stumble, but Katia hoists me up before I fall. My forehead is drenched in sweat as we stop in front of another door.

She pulls another lever, and the door creaks open.

Mason's right-hand man is waiting for us on the other side, with a gun in his hand that he's examining intently. Every inch of me grows cold as I stand there and wonder if our mission is over before it's begun.

Has someone betrayed Katia?

"You know this is a bad idea."

"I can handle whatever punishment he comes up with," Katia replies tightly. "We both know that none of this is like him. He needs people out there who know better. Who are loyal to him."

"You're taking a big risk," he says.

"So are you."

He sheaths the gun. "I was never here. You, on the other hand, are walking right into trouble."

Katia presses her mouth into a thin line.

"Taking her with you will only make things worse," he adds. "Sure you want to do that?"

"I don't have a choice," Katia replies.

He raises an eyebrow and looks at me, a flicker of amusement moving across his face. "Not many people can handle Katia, you know."

I swallow past the lump in my throat. "I know."

"You're both insane." He's no longer blocking the exit, and I see a beat-up Chevy bathed in the pale light of the moon, parked on the side of the road. Another look passes between him and Katia, and I glance away. Then, he says something in the same language I heard earlier.

Katia's response is short, but there's no mistaking her impatience.

We're running out of time.

I don't know how much of a head start Mason has on us.

Suddenly, Katia yanks me against her, and I bite back my retort. She shoves me into the backseat of the car and motions for me to crouch low. I do as I'm told, knowing that each moment I waste arguing is another moment that trouble draws closer to Noah. As Katia slams the back door shut, I hunker further down and stare straight ahead.

A few moments later, the engine revs, slicing through the stillness of the night.

I can't believe I am doing this.

Mason isn't just going to punish Katia.

He has warned me about interfering, and I know he's hanging on by a thread.

The famous Mason restraint I've seen in action is about to snap, and I offer a silent prayer that it won't be for nothing.

I can't be too late.

Katia pauses at the main gate, and I hold my breath until the iron gates swing open. Katia keeps both hands on the wheel as I give her directions to Noah's. She races past several traffic lights and breaks at least a dozen driving rules as we race through the city streets.

On the outskirts of the city, Katia presses harder on the gas.

"Please don't let us be too late."

"Didn't take you for the praying kind." Katia swerves onto a smaller street and hits the brakes as a group of kids appears. "Still, I'd consider my last words carefully if I were you."

"Mason won't hurt me for interfering," I tell her with more confidence than I feel. "You said yourself that he needs us."

Katia snorts and turns her attention back to the road.

I lurch sideways when she presses on the gas again.

She pulls to a stop in front of Noah's parents' house, and I feel sick all over again. Katia unbuckles her seatbelt and reaches into her boots. She tosses me a gun and shoves open the driver's door.

"Don't do anything stupid," Katia snaps before disappearing behind the house.

My fingers close around the gun.

For a long while, nothing happens, and I wonder if we're too late.

Then I hear a gunshot, and I scramble forward.

Using the edge of the gun, I slice the zip ties open and scramble to open the door. I race up the driveway, every muscle screaming at me in protest. On the front porch, I stop and suck in a deep breath.

Then, I burst through the door with the gun held firmly in my hand.

Noah is sitting on a chair opposite the kitchen, and Mason is crouched in front of him, gun held in his hand The lights are dimmed, and there's no one else in the house, and the two of them turn to look at me.

Mason's expression turns from shock to icy fury.

I lower my gun and clear my throat. "I'm here to help."

Mason crosses over to me in a few seconds and leans forward, so I have to tilt my head to look at him. "What the fuck are you doing?"

"I'm here to help," I repeat.

Mason's expression darkens. "Me or him?"

"I... both of you," I stutter. "We talked about this. You know he's part of my past, and I can't just turn my back on him."

"Evidently not," Mason replies. "I never should've told you about

254

this."

His words feel like a punch to the gut, but I try not to let it show. "You did the right thing by telling me. It would've been worse if you hadn't."

Mason's expression remains blank. "Where the fuck is Katia?"

"I don't know."

Mason's nostrils flare, and his eyes flash. "Don't lie to me, London. You couldn't have made it here without help. I'm only going to ask you one more time."

"Leave her alone."

Mason levels Noah with a withering look. "It's not your turn. Mind your own damn business. The first shot was a warning. The next one will go into your skull."

"Anything that concerns London is my business."

I wince and look over at Noah. "Noah, you're just making this worse. Stop it."

Noah frowns. "But, I—"

"I'd listen to her if I were you." Katia materializes out of the shadows, a blank expression on her face and a gun in her hands. She presses it to Noah's head. "Otherwise, I might get trigger-happy."

CHAPTER TWENTY-ONE

Mason

Fuck me.

I have no idea what the hell Katia thinks she's doing, but it's only making me want to punish her more.

That's because you weren't hard enough on her the past few times.

Letting her off the hook for not stopping London when she wanted to see her father was one thing.

I can even understand why she didn't step in with Noah at the club since London insisted on taking care of things herself.

But bringing London here, to her ex-boyfriend's house, is almost like Katia wanted me to rain down fire and brimstone.

It is taking every ounce of self-control I have not to drag her into the nearest back alley and unleash my fury.

My fingers itch with the desire to inflict pain.

I haven't spent the past forty-five minutes telling myself to remain calm and collected just to have them barge in here and fuck it all up.

Any earlier fuzzy feelings I had toward London's selfless diner offer quickly evaporate.

You didn't honestly think she would stay put, did you? You know her better than that.

I should've known she'd get through to Katia, who has developed a soft spot for London, much to my chagrin.

What the hell do I do now?

"Katia, lower the gun."

"You're supposed to be helping," London adds. "What are you doing?"

Katia yanks Noah backward and forces him back into the chair. Then she towers over him, a familiar, deadly gleam in her eyes. "I'm taking care of the problem."

"That's not why we're here," London protests. She holds her hands up on either side of her and tries to remain calm. "He hasn't done anything."

Katia's eyes darken. "If that's what you need to convince yourself, that's on you, Blondie. You're too blinded by your feelings."

"But—"

"That's why you're here," Katia interrupts. "I'm here to bring a stop to this."

The color drains from London's face. "What is that supposed to mean?"

Katia raises an eyebrow. "You're not stupid, Blondie, so don't act like it. You know who I am and what I do."

London swallows. "But he's not—"

Katia taps the gun against Noah's temple, and he winces. "I don't give a shit what you think. As far as I'm concerned, he's a loose end, and I've been dying to get my hands on him for months."

I cover the space between us and wait for Katia to look at me. "I'm still questioning him. Now, lower the gun before I make you."

Katia quirks a brow. "He should be bleeding and begging for his life, and you know it."

Katia knows me better than most people, and she's been to her fair share of interrogations.

She knows every trick up my sleeve, and she knows why I'm holding back.

Because I can't stop replaying London's words on a loop in my head.

I'm terrified that if I lay a finger on him, that will be what makes her leave.

Even now, he can't stop screwing with us.

Fucking Noah.

You know what needs to be done. Quit stalling and do what you've been trained to do.

"I'm getting to that part," I respond. "But he's mine to question, not yours."

"He's going to deny it," Katia says.

"Yes."

"I didn't do anything," Noah sputters. "I don't know how reporters and journalists wound up at your estate."

I turn to Noah. "So, your brother looking into me is just a coincidence?"

Bullshit.

Noah is hiding something, and if I have to spend days waiting him out, I'll do what needs to be done.

But I can't do it with London standing a few feet away, looking like she's going to be sick all over the hardwood floors.

A muscle ticks in Noah's jaw. "I already told you that I didn't…"

He trails off, and a flicker of something jumps into his eyes.

In one quick move, I snatch the gun out of Katia's hand and inch closer. "You fucking said something."

Panic springs to Noah's eyes, and he swallows. "I was just venting about what happened between London and me. Ryder and I hadn't seen each other in years, and I was so angry…"

"Noah." London's voice catches toward the end. "What did you do?"

"I swear, I didn't think he was even listening, Lo. I told you how Ryder is. You know how self-involved he is."

I withdraw the gun and use the butt to smack the side of his head. "And you're a self-absorbed moron. What did you think would happen?"

Noah clenches his jaw and turns back to me. "I wasn't thinking."

I draw the gun back again, but London's sharp cry stops me.

I know what I need to do, but I can't bring myself to do it.

Noah has been a nuisance since the moment I first laid eyes on him, but of all the scenarios I expected, an accidental slipup wasn't one of them.

Jesus.

How can I enjoy making him pay now?

"I wasn't behind the kidnapping," Noah adds when the silence stretches on for too long. "But I remember overhearing them when they were holding your father and I, Lo. The kidnappers were talking about someone else. Someone on the inside—"

"You're not telling us something we don't already know, Nolan," I bite out. "If I'm going to let you walk out of here, you'd better give me something good."

Noah's eyes flash. "What the fuck do you want from me? *I don't know anything.*"

"You have until the count of five." I slowly remove the safety on my gun, roll my shoulders, and sigh. "One."

Noah throws his hands up in the air. "Jesus. Fuck, man. You won already. Isn't that enough?"

"Two."

"It's not enough that you got her." The words pour out of Noah in a rush. "Why is it so important to you that I'm out of the picture?"

"Three."

"Mason." London appears next to me and clears her throat. "He didn't mean to make things worse."

"Four." The word tastes funny in my mouth. "Time's running out, Noah."

A thin sheen of sweat breaks out across Noah's forehead. "Lo, I swear—"

"Time's up." I pull Noah to his feet and take two steps back so the gun is pointed at his chest. "Any last words?"

Noah's face is white now, and he's trembling. "Alright, fine! I pushed Ryder to look into you, okay? I knew a few slipups here and there would push him to dig deeper. He's like a dog with a bone when he gets a whiff of something big, and I knew that all I had to do was push him hard enough."

The anger inside of me floods my veins and melts everything in its path.

I clench my free hand into a fist. "What else?"

"Nothing, I—"

I point the gun at Noah's foot and pull the trigger. "Don't fucking lie. The only reason you're not already bleeding out in a basement somewhere is because of her. I will not hesitate to kill you in front of her if I need to."

London's worst fears are coming true.

You warned her about what would happen, and she came anyway.

Noah has tears streaming down his face and is biting back a few whimpers of pain. The color drains from his face as he shifts his weight to his uninjured foot. "My father suspects something, but I didn't tell him anything."

"We both know it wasn't out of the goodness of your heart."

Noah is panting now, and he sways a little on his feet. "I knew London wouldn't forgive me if I took things too far."

I curse and point the gun at his other foot. "I should cut off your fucking balls and hang you up—"

"No." London wedges herself between us and raises her chin to look at me. "The damage has already been done. Hurting him won't change anything."

"Get out of my way."

London holds firm. "No."

I turn to Katia, who is leaning against the nearest wall. "Take her back to the house and keep her there. I'll deal with you later."

Katia crosses over to London.

She grabs London's hand and pulls. London pulls away, and the women struggle. Abruptly, London draws her weight back and kicks free of Katia's hold, momentarily surprising the assassin. Katia recovers quickly and wraps both arms around London's waist. London throws herself back, and they crash to the floor with a thud.

Katia jumps to her feet and snarls. "Get your ass outside."

"The only way I'm going is if you drag me," London replies. "Don't forget that you're the one who's been teaching me to fight."

I growl, and they look at me.

"Katia, take care of him." I tilt my head at Noah. "I'll take care of London."

I cross to London, who doesn't hide her surprise as I throw her over my shoulder.

She bangs her arms against my back, but I don't loosen my grip until I reach the car. Then, I throw her into the back and pin one hand on either side of her as she bucks and thrashes, her face turning a bright red.

I wait for her to stop struggling.

She fights me longer than expected.

I'm jealous of the fierce loyalty and determination Noah inspires.

The little weasel doesn't deserve it.

How did he win her heart to begin with?

He sure didn't hesitate to throw her to the wolves to appease his wounded ego.

How could he live with himself knowing London would get caught in the crosshairs?

He was probably hoping she'd come back to him if he took you down. You know he still loves her.

I blink when I realize London has gone still and is regarding me with wide eyes.

"Can I trust you not to run out of this car?"

She narrows her eyes. "You can't expect me to just sit here."

"I can, and I do," I reply. "When are you going to learn to do as you're told?"

London's face darkens. "When it comes to the people I love? You can't expect me to do nothing."

I release one arm and growl. "You really think that little of me?"

"I know he caused problems you don't need, but he was hurt. We've all done stupid shit when we're hurt. He doesn't deserve to die because of it."

I release her other arm. "And what, in your opinion, is enough to pull the trigger?"

London frowns. "I don't know."

I lean back to study her. "What if he had told you he had done it on purpose? Would you have been okay with killing him?"

London winces and looks away. "Well, no. But I don't believe in violence—"

"That right there is the problem, Pigeon," I interrupt. "My world is surrounded by it. It is violence, and I've told you that it's the only way to survive."

London swallows audibly. "I know that, but—"

"But what? You expected me to make an exception because of your history? I made it clear that I wouldn't."

London clears her throat. "There's got to be some other way to clean up this mess."

"Noah needs to learn to keep his fucking mouth shut."

"I know."

Abruptly, I lean away from her and run a hand through my hair. "Katia will make sure he gets the point."

London loses a sharp breath. "I know that you need to make a point.

I understand..."

"She's not going to kill him."

"Won't it just cause more problems if… wait, did you just say she's not going to kill him?"

The relief in London's eyes makes me want to hurry out of the car and hunt Noah down.

He doesn't deserve her sympathy.

"I just said I wouldn't," I snap. "Contrary to what you might think, I'm not fueled by bloodlust and impulsive decisions. As much as I would love to put Noah in the ground, I know better than to invite more scrutiny. His dad is a mayor."

London exhales, and her shoulders sag. "Oh."

"He still loves you," I tell her flatly. "The fact that he's the mayor's son gets him a pass this time. Next time, he won't be so lucky."

I already know I will regret this.

You were going to find a loophole anyway, and you know it. London can forgive an interrogation, but she would have never looked at you the same way if you had killed her ex.

Fuck.

When did I turn into a pathetic sap who agonizes over feelings?

When did London dull my sharp edges?

"Mason, I… thank you. I'm sorry."

"Sorry you ignored the fact that I told you to stay away, or sorry that you still care about him?"

"I never lied to you about my history with Noah," London replies. "I won't hide the fact that I still care about him. I'm always going to care about him. He was in my life for years…"

"Do you still love him?"

A part of her still has to. Why else would she be here, risking everything between us for him?

London shakes her head. "No."

I want to believe her, but when all evidence points to the contrary, I've learned to trust my instinct.

Everything I have is screaming to cut my losses and move on.

But the thought of facing a world without London is unbearable and unimaginable.

"Even if I hadn't realized how I felt about you, I wouldn't have gone back to him," London adds. "You know that, right? I loved Noah, but I wouldn't have been happy with him in the long run. It just took me a while to realize that."

Silence stretches between us.

London reaches for me again, but I push the back door open and get out. I straighten my back, exhale, and wait for a few seconds. Then, I get behind the wheel and lock the doors. I start the engine and adjust the rearview mirror so I can see London.

She's so fucking beautiful that it hurts.

As I drive back to the estate, the headache in the back of my head spreads to the rest of my skull. The wrought-iron gates part to admit the car, and I press down on the gas.

Olivia and Oliver are waiting for me by the front door.

Olivia takes one look at London's face and steps forward. Then, the women disappear up the stairs, and I'm left in the kitchen with my brother. I retrieve a bottle of bourbon from the cupboard in the back and pry the lid off with my teeth. I spit it out and take a long swig, but the smooth liquid does nothing to ease my upset stomach.

Oliver leans against the counter and stares at me. "How long are you going to keep us here, Mason?"

I take another swig, and my stomach lurches. "I'm not keeping you here. You're free to leave."

"You know it's not that simple."

"You weren't supposed to be involved in any of this," I reply. "I've done my best to honor the deal, but I can't control other people."

Oliver pushes himself off the counter. "I overheard Mathew talking about how you screwed up, and how it's your fault we're here."

I grip the marble counter and press my lips together. "He's not wrong."

"We have lives, you know. I know it might not seem like much compared to the life you're building here, but I have a good, quiet life."

I grip the counter more tightly. "I know."

"We deserve to be able to stay away from all of this." Oliver's voice rises in anger. "That was the deal, right?"

I release the counter and look at my brother. He looks so much like our mother in that moment that it sends a fresh wave of pain through me.

I wonder what she'd think of all this mess I've made in the name of love.

I doubt even she would've approved.

"I will make this right," I say. "It'll take a while, but I'm a man of my word."

Oliver studies me, his face tight. "You mean like you kept your word last time?"

I frown. "I did what I could."

It's not my fault they had to relocate several times because our enemies are resourceful.

They still think it's because of my screw up and not because of the fact that I was outmaneuvered.

It's better for them to believe I'm the villain than to have to live with the truth of the blood spilled in their name.

Oliver stiffens and shoots me another look. "We'll see."

"Where are Mathew and Dad?"

He shrugs. "Keeping tabs on people is your area of expertise, not mine."

"We need to have a family meeting," I say.

I'm glad Mathew isn't around to gloat, but it's worrisome that neither of them is here to rub my face in my latest screwup.

Neither of them misses a chance to criticize me, especially when it comes to London.

They'll have a field day when they learn about Noah's involvement.

Can you blame them? You've allowed London to cloud your judgment and blind you to the truth. Hell, you even made an exception for her by not killing Noah on the spot.

As painful as dealing with the mayor would've been, I've dealt with my fair share of irate politicians.

Noah's father would've been no exception.

You can still fix this. You know where Katia is taking Noah. You can get back in the car right now.

Olivia returns a short while later, heads to the fridge, and pours herself a shot of tequila. She downs it all in one gulp and grimaces.

"How are we going to fix this?"

"*We*'re not going to fix anything," I respond quickly. "Neither of you should be anywhere near this. All you need to focus on is making sure you're ready to go at a moment's notice."

"Go where?"

"Back to your lives," I say. "I know you don't believe me when I say this, but things were never supposed to turn out this way."

For the first time in a long time, I have no ace up my sleeve or backup plan in the works.

I'm not sure what I'm supposed to do next.

Between Noah, the Fitzpatricks, and the Everetts, I'm spread thin, and my head is spinning in a hundred directions, trying to figure out all the ways it could get worse.

Pretty soon, you won't be able to stop any of this. Come on, Mason. Think

I leave my siblings without a backward glance and storm off in search of Carlisle.

I find him lurking near my office. He follows me into the room and waits until I pour myself a drink. Then, I look at Carlisle, who is standing with his back erect and his hands fisted at his sides.

"Have arrangements been made for our guest?"

Carlisle nods.

I take a sip of my drink and eye him over the rim. "Good. My instructions are clear. He's not to come to any serious bodily harm."

A flicker of surprise moves across his face.

I know what he's thinking.

Why in the hell am I not ripping Noah limb from limb?

I've done far worse for a lot less.

I'm tempted to stride over to the closed-off section of the manor and take care of the problem, but I have to get under control first. The beast I keep under lock and key is too close to the surface, and he's itching to come out.

I don't trust myself to do what needs to be done with Noah, and I'm in no mood to face the man who has caused problems since I laid eyes on him.

"You'll take over for Katia until she's done," I tell Carlisle. "I want eyes on London at all times."

"I can assign one of the other men—"

I step out from behind the desk, cross over to Carlisle in a few strides, and pin him against the nearest wall. Fury radiates off me in waves. "I didn't fucking ask for anyone else. You will do as you're told."

Carlisle avoids my eyes. "Yes, sir."

"Make sure there are eyes and ears on Oliver and Olivia, too." I release him. "It appears we have another traitor in our midst."

Carlisle's fingers move to his throat, and he swallows. "How do you want me to handle this?"

"I'll handle it myself." I turn my back on him and step back behind the desk. "When I find out who it is, they'll beg for death."

Then, I dismiss Carlisle, who runs into Elise on his way out.

She does a double-take when she sees the look on my face before lifting her hand to rap and adopting a careful expression. Elise clears her throat and steps in, the light glinting off her dark hair, with not a single wrinkle in her expensive suit.

"I wasn't aware we were meeting today."

Elise stops on the other side of the desk to study me. "We were supposed to meet to discuss engagement preparations, but imagine my surprise when I heard the rumors about my father."

Shit.

In all the excitement, I'd almost forgotten I have him under guard in a guest wing.

"Elise—"

"What the hell are you doing?" Elise steps forward, her eyes bright with fury. "We have an agreement. We provided you with men, and this is how you repay us?"

I pour myself a drink without taking my eyes off her. "Your father is playing me for a fool."

Elise scowls. "You and I both know he's not stupid enough to cross you."

I lift the glass to my lips and study her. "Not even for the right price?"

Elise leans against the desk and levels me with a look. "Let him go."

"Not until I'm sure he wasn't involved."

Elise bristles. "Let him go, or I'll—"

I set my glass down. "Or you'll what? I don't think your dad would approve of all your secret meetings with the mob bosses."

"I have no idea what you're talking about."

I scoff. "You're not as careful as you thought."

"Mason—"

"Still, I imagine he could forgive a power move if it worked," I continue, in harder voice. "What I imagine will be harder to forgive is your relationship with his enemy's son."

268

Some of the color drains from Elise's face.

She opens and closes her mouth several times then straightens her back. "What do you want?"

"I have to admit, I was impressed that you've managed to keep it hidden," I continue, in the same even tone of voice. "Your father might be willing to forgive you. Your allies, on the other hand...it would be a shame if the information fell into the wrong hands."

Elise goes as still as a statue.

"I've heard stories about what they do to traitors in your family. I might even make it a point to swing by to see for myself."

"You son of a bitch. I can't believe you were having me looked into this whole time. I thought we had an understanding."

I narrow my eyes at her. "I make it a point to have the people I do business with looked into. It's common practice in our world. It's not my fault your father didn't bother to teach you."

Elise says something under her breath and clenches her hands together.

"For now, you're going to make sure your father's allies don't retaliate," I reply, before reaching for my drink again. "If you don't, I might start sending body parts. I'd say he doesn't need all his fingers."

Elise pales further. "How far do you think you're going to take this? My father's allies won't stay quiet for long."

I tilt the glass in her direction and smile. "That's where you come in. I think a little hands on experience will be good for you."

Elise mutters something under her breath.

I finish my drink and straighten my back again. "Perhaps a little demonstration is in order for you to—"

"No," Elise says, a little louder than intended. She swallows and blows out a breath. "I'll do what I can, but you know this isn't how things work in our world."

I set the empty glass down and pick up the phone on my desk. "It is a pity we couldn't keep being on the same side. I have a feeling you're going to grow into quite the leader."

Elise shoots me a withering look and says nothing.

Moments later, one of Carlisle's men comes in, dragging a sweaty looking Thatcher in tow. He blinks, and as soon as he sees Elise, his shoulders heave, and a sob falls from his lips. Elise steps forward and catches him before he falls to the floor. She holds him to her and says something into his ear. A moment later, my man steps forward and yanks Thatcher backward.

Elise's expression is tight when she twists to face me. "How do I know you're not going to throw him in a basement somewhere to starve? And don't tell me to take your word for it. We both know it won't work this time."

My smile grows wider. "Fair enough. What kind of proof do you want?"

"Three phone calls a day."

"Once a day, and he'll be monitored the whole time. If I find out either of you are trying to fuck with me, you'll never find his body."

Elise looks back at her father and hangs her head.

Slowly, she nods and looks back at me. "Fine."

I offer my man a nod, and he begins to drag Thatcher away. The man snivels and whimpers as he calls out for his daughter while disgust and frustration build within me.

Pathetic coward.

I have no idea how he wound up being the head of his family, nor do I care.

As far as I'm concerned, it's one less problem to deal with.

"When I'm satisfied your father has played no part in the attack, he'll be released," I tell Elise, after a lengthy pause. "As for the information I have.....well, as long as your family doesn't ally itself with our enemies, I'm sure we can come to an agreement."

Elise licks her lips and takes a step in the direction of the door. "What about our arrangement?"

"Your men will continue to do our bidding. As for the engagement, I'll leave you to deal with the press. I'm sure you'll figure something out. Make yourself into the victim for all I care."

Elise stares at me for a while longer.

I sit down. "I trust you can see yourself out."

She straightens her back, and a moment later throws the door open and storms out of the study.

I don't hate Elise for her father's cowardice, but I know it would make things easier.

Without warning, I rise to my feet. I throw Elise's glass against the nearest wall and don't react when a piece nicks my knuckles. When I throw another glass against the window, it drowns out some of the roaring in my ears. For a while, I stand in the middle of the debris, blood dripping from my hands, and a loud pounding in my chest.

I don't realize London is there until she curls herself against my back.

The warm and inviting smell of her, strawberries and vanilla, brings me back to the present.

I can't afford to wallow in anger when we've lost our biggest ally.

Even if Thatcher is innocent, keeping him here and threatening Elise into submission has burned the bridge between us.

I turn toward London and hug her against me. She melts, and I bury my face in her hair. Then, I hoist her up and carry her over to the desk. I set her down, push her legs apart, and nestle between them. London runs her fingers down my back and stops.

I grab the back of her neck and wait for her to look at me. "You're still here."

London's eyes widen. "Yes."

"You shouldn't be," I murmur. "This won't get any easier. You'll just get better at shutting it out."

London angles her head and says nothing.

I cover her mouth with mine and growl.

She tastes like hope and possibilities, everything I've spent my life running from.

I want to drown myself in her and forget about the world outside.

Even when a small voice in the back of my mind warns me that we can't.

When London moves her fingers to my hair, I wrench my lips away. Then, I step out of her embrace and leave a few inches of space between us. London's face is flushed. She pats down her hair and stares at me through hooded eyes.

"I'll be up later."

London lowers herself to the ground and picks her way through the debris from the broken glasses. "What can I do to help?"

"You're already doing it." I squeeze her hand on her way past. Then, I cross the room and open the door. Carlisle is on the other side, and he glares at London, who doesn't look fazed as he leads her back upstairs. Once they're out of earshot, I shut the door to the study and go off in search of Katia.

She's in the East wing of the house, which only a handful of people are allowed in.

Noah is tied to a chair in the middle of the basement, with a single light bulb hanging over his head, and the smell of sweat and something else in the air. Katia sees me, and we exchange a quick look. I pause to roll my sleeves to my elbows and study Noah, who is holding himself erect and ignoring the dried blood on the side of his face.

"She's never going to forget this, you know."

I stop in front of Noah and tilt my head. "I don't expect her to forget."

"You're only making things worse," he says.

I reach for one of Katia's knives and run it along the side of his face. "London might not forget what I have to do, but she will forgive me because she knows it's necessary."

Noah's expression is incredulous. "Is that what you tell yourself?"

I stop at the base of his throat, over his bobbing Adam's apple. "Why the sudden interest in what I do or don't do?"

Is he finally understanding who he's messing with?

Noah shrugs and looks away. "I don't give a shit, but you know London will. She might have... feelings for you right now, but all the money and power in the world won't change what you are."

I dig the knife into his skin and wait for him to flinch. "You're awfully confident for someone who is at my mercy. Tell me, Noah. Do you honestly believe this will win her back?"

His expression darkens.

"Did you think you could take me down and win her back? That I would be a footnote in your story?"

Noah presses his mouth into an angry line.

I chuckle. "I've dealt with men like you before, Noah. Do you know what you all have in common? You don't have what it takes. That's why London chose me. It doesn't matter what you do or what you try to take, she will never go back to you."

I hand Katia the knife and lean back to look at him. "You had her, and you fucked it up. How does it feel to know that *you're* the footnote?"

Noah pulls his lips back and glares at me with hatred in his eyes. "Fuck you."

I bark out a laugh and shoot Katia an amused look. "I think I hit a nerve."

"She will never accept who you are." Noah's voice climbs higher with each word. "You're delusional if you think this ends any other way."

My expression hardens. "I'll just have to make sure it does, won't I? Either way, I doubt you'll be around to see it."

Some of the color drains from Noah's face, and his shoulders sag. "You won't hurt me. London will never forgive—"

"She already knows I have you," I interrupt coyly. "She might have begged for your life, but she knows you betrayed her. And she didn't try to stop me from questioning you."

"I don't believe you."

I scoff and punch him in the stomach, and he wheezes out a breath. "I don't give a shit."

I land another blow to his stomach, and he coughs. Then I circle him, watching as beads of sweat form on his forehead and slide down his face. When I press myself against his back and yank back his head, he sucks in a breath, and I can almost taste his fear. I release him and move back to the front, eyeing him with thinly veiled disgust.

Noah is barely holding himself together, and I know the anticipation is killing him.

It's my most effective form of torture.

Let the bastard wonder what I'm going to do next.

I know I can't push him past a certain point, but I can at least enjoy watching him squirm.

He will pay for every bit of pain he's inflicted on London.

I reach out a hand, and Noah flinches and turns his head to the side. When he squeezes his eyes shut, I wait. As soon as one eye pries open, I land a punch to his jaw, and little pinpricks of pain dance up my arm. I throw another punch, and this time I hear a sickening crunch as bright red blood drips from his nose and onto the floor.

Noah winces. I hit him again, this time focusing on the side of his face. It isn't long before his face is covered in blood, and his breath is shallow and uneven. Still, it isn't enough to quell the bloodlust rising within me, and the image of London's hurt face playing on a loop in my head.

Rage pumps through my veins as I focus on the feeling of my fist connecting with his face.

I blink, and Noah's bruised, bloodied face swims into my field of vision.

The smell of blood fills my nostrils.

Noah doubles over as I land another punch to his stomach, and he coughs, spittle and blood staining the floor at his feet. Then, I yank Noah's head back and wait for him to focus. As he does, he offers me a grim smile that surprises me.

He's harder to break than I thought.

I'd be impressed if I weren't so livid.

Most men would've broken down in tears and offered me everything they owned by now.

How have I underestimated Noah?

I lower myself, so we're at eye level. "You're going to tell me exactly what you told your family about me."

"Or what?"

I raise an eyebrow. "Or Katia's knife might just slip."

Noah's eyes flash as he glances over at the assassin, who is leaning against the wall, examining her nails, and then back at me. "You're bluffing."

I release his head and stand up. "Don't say I didn't warn you."

Katia strolls over to us. She whips out a knife and runs it along the length of Noah's arm. The silver glistens in the dim light as she reaches his shoulders. Then, her expression hardens as she presses hard enough to draw a thin welt of blood down his forearm.

Noah turns green, and a shiver ripples through him. "You don't want to do this."

"This is taking too fucking long," I tell Katia, shaking my head. "He's a waste of space."

Katia digs the knife in harder, and Noah hisses. "Give me a few hours with him. I'll make sure he tells me what I need to know."

I shrug. "Make sure you clean yourself up after. London won't want to smell his blood on you."

Katia's smile is a flash of white in the darkness. "I'll tell you all about it after."

I chuckle. "I look forward to it. When you're done with him, bring me his brother."

"No! Leave him out of this. Ryder hasn't done anything."

"We'll need a plan to get to his father, too. I don't want any loose ends."

Katia levels Noah with a withering look. "I'll take care of it."

I turn my back to her and shove my hands into my pockets. Noah calls out to me, but I ignore him. Once I reach the top of the stairs, the door swings open, and Carlisle appears, smiling. He lowers his voice and leans back to look at me.

"Get the car ready," I tell him in response to what he shares. "And tell Katia there's been a change of plans."

A short while later, Katia and Carlisle are waiting for me by the front door, wearing identical grim expressions. I don't look at either of them as we step out into the cool night air, and then into the black car waiting for us. Katia gets into the back with me, and Carlisle slides into the passenger seat. As the car drives away from the estate, I lean back against the leather seats.

"What do you want to do when you find them?" Katia asks.

"Leave Everett to me," I say. "You can have some fun with Fitzpatrick first."

As long as I get to deal the deadly blow, I don't care what Katia does to either of them.

Not when I finally know where they are.

All I need is to get close enough, and it's only been a few minutes since our guy at the airport tipped us off.

Fucking amateurs.

I can't wait to see the looks on their faces when I cut them off on the way out of the airport.

They won't see me coming, and it's almost enough to make up for the disastrous night I've been having.

Don't forget that you still have the Noah problem waiting for you.

I pour myself a drink and picture returning to Noah, who is on his hands and knees, begging for mercy.

For London's sake, I might even consider it.

Knowing that Noah will sleep with one eye open for the rest of his life is tempting, but it's not enough.

He needs to be taught a lesson.

Carlisle's phone rings a while later. He presses it to his ear and says nothing. Once he hangs up, I recognize the glint in his eyes. "They've got the journalist."

I eye Carlisle over the rim of my glass. "Good. And the security company the mayor hired?"

"Working on it," Carlisle replies. "Should I tell the men to bring the journalist in the usual way?"

I take a long sip and nod. "Yes, but keep him bound and gagged. I want to greet him personally after I take care of this problem."

Carlisle reaches for his phone again.

Halfway to the airport, as I'm envisioning all the ways to make Michael and Lance pay, the car begins to skid. With a frown, the driver grips the steering wheel with both hands and swerves out of the way of an incoming car. He lets out a steady stream of curses when we almost collide with another truck, its bright headlights nearly blinding me. I glance out the window at the world racing past on either side of us.

"Someone messed with the brakes." The driver raises his voice to be heard over the clamor outside. "I'm trying to find somewhere safe to crash."

"Just fucking do it." I ignore the pounding in my chest. I glance out the window again and stare at the asphalt below, and then yank on the door handle. When the door doesn't open, I scowl and try again, but it's no use. Fear claws through me as I throw my shoulder against the door, but it doesn't budge.

What the hell?

Katia is trying to pry the other door open with her knife. "Get us the fuck out of here."

The car skids again, and we're all thrown forward. The impact rattles my teeth. Then, the car swerves out of control and spins in a circle. A few seconds later, we crash into a tree. Pain blossoms behind my eyes as I grit my teeth and push back against the searing pain. Slowly, I open my eyes to see Katia hovering over me.

She shatters the window and crawls out.

As I climb through behind her, I spot Carlisle with one arm hanging limply by his side and his pant leg drenched in blood. His eyes widen as he looks past me. I wheel around, but my gun is kicked out of my hand before I can shoot.

Katia's grunts pierce the fog.

I crouch, throw out my leg, and kick my assailant onto his back

Then, I retrieve the gun hidden in my sock and open fire.

Two bullets lodge themselves in the man's legs, but they only slow him down. His face is half-hidden behind a mask, and his all-black outfit makes it harder to make out his outline. Something sails past me, and I turn to see Katia throwing another man through the air, his face contorted in fury.

Carlisle is shooting blindly now, and bullets race past in either direction.

One of them hits another man in the arm, and he yells as a streak of lightning illuminates the night sky.

I grip my gun tightly and fire again. This time, the bullet lands in the man's chest, and he crumples to the ground. He sputters, and his eyes widen and fill with panic as I aim between his eyes and shoot again. His blood soaks the ground beneath my feet as the skies break open, with rain pouring down around me.

When the light leaves the man's eyes, I step over him and frown.

Then I shove strands of hair from my face and look around.

Another bolt of lightning streaks through the sky, offering me a glimpse of Katia with one arm around the back of a man's head, and the other holding a knife to his throat. Her knee comes up, and she hits him in the groin. A heartbeat later, she slices through skin and releases the man, his hands moving immediately to the gash on his throat.

I shift closer, and the man's sputtering fills my ears.

Carlisle joins us a moment later, breathing heavily.

"Where the fuck is our backup?"

Carlisle shifts on his feet and winces. "I don't know."

"It's your damn job to know," I snap. "Get us the hell out of here, or there will be one more body to join the rest."

The anger coursing through me means that no one, not even my right-hand man, is safe.

My mind is still reeling as Katia steps out onto the road, her dark eyes scanning the cars that rush past, bright headlights momentarily illuminating the dark. One hand remains clenched at her side, and the other is holding her knife, still dripping with the man's blood. With a frown, she glances down and wipes the knife on the thigh of her pants.

She looks over at me, and our eyes meet and hold for a brief second.

I know she's thinking the same thing I am.

The crash wasn't an accident.

How the hell did they get to you so fast? Only a handful of people knew about tonight, and two of them are with you.

It's not Katia. She wouldn't betray you, but even if she did, she would go for something far more subtle. Crashes aren't Katia's style.

Whoever did this wanted a show.

It would've been the perfect setup, too, with the pouring rain and no witnesses.

My blood boils at the thought of what I'm going to do when I find out who's responsible.

"We've got company." Carlisle's voice barely carries over the sound of the rain. "They're only a few minutes out."

I curse and rifle through the bodies, retrieving a few more guns.

I toss one to Carlisle, one to Katia, and keep one for myself.

"There's been an attack on one of the warehouses," Carlisle adds as he steps beside me. He grimaces and shifts his weight again. "There are men on the way."

I wipe the gun on my pants and roll my shoulders. "We'll just have to make sure we give them hell. I want everyone driving by to hear their screams."

Carlisle nods.

Katia appears by our side, her hair pressed to her face. She steps closer, and I see a figure huddled behind her. It takes me a second to place the face, but as his hat and button-down shirt shift into focus, I point the gun at the driver and let out a stream of curse words.

He shrinks and hides behind Katia, who offers him a disgusted look. "I figured you'd want to deal with him yourself."

Slowly, the driver raises fear-filled eyes to me and swallows. "Mr. Payne, please. I didn't have a choice. They were going to hurt my family—"

"I don't care if they held a fucking gun to all of your heads," I interrupt. "You should've thought twice. I'm going to make it my mission to hunt down your family once we're done."

His eyes widen, and he wrings his hands. "What if I gave you the name of the person responsible for all this? The guy who's been pulling the strings behind the scenes?"

I stare at the man for a few seconds and weigh my options.

He's a lower-level hire, a nobody in the grand hierarchy, but there's something about the hint of panic in his voice.

He's telling the truth, or at least he thinks he is.

Katia pulls him by his hair and forces him to his knees. She presses the knife against his throat and scowls. "Speak."

"I... I don't have a name." The man is trembling violently. "But I do know it's someone close to you."

I glance over at Katia. "How fast can you get rid of the body?"

"It's a Payne." The man's words chill my blood. "I didn't catch the first name, but it's another Payne, I swear."

I nod to Katia, and she releases the man, who lands face-first on the wet ground. His eyes are filled with relief when he looks up at me, but the relief is quickly replaced by fear when he sees the gun still pointed at him. The protest dies on his lips as I pull the trigger.

Katia steps over him to stand next to me. "We'll hold them off."

I stand up straighter. "Paynes don't run from a fight. Just make sure it hurts."

"We will," Carlisle vows. "Those fuckers are going to pay."

There's a rustle somewhere to our left, and we shift as one, turning to face the stream of men pouring out from behind the trees.

Sometime later, the smell of blood fills my nose, and I ignore the stabbing pain in my ribs as I limp forward.

When I collapse on the side of the road, all I can think about is revenge.

Images of London's face flicker in my head as I move in and out of consciousness until I see Katia hovering over me.

CHAPTER TWENTY-TWO

London

"Are you sure you're not going to get in trouble for this?"

I gesture vaguely at the armed man behind me, and frown. "He can drag me back anytime, but since he hasn't, I think I'll enjoy this while I can."

I know it won't last.

Whatever illusion of freedom I have is quickly fading, and each incident, each death, ensures the walls are closing in tighter.

I'm not sure how much longer I have before there's no way out, and the urge to keep glancing over my shoulder has been with me for the past few hours.

I can't shake the feeling that I'm being watched.

Even within the confines of the Payne club, I know I'm not safe.

You're not safe anywhere, London, but at least here, you're safer.

The man left to guard me hasn't said two words all night, but I have a feeling he's a lot more lethal than he looks. He's coiled tightly and has made no effort to hide the guns under his jacket, but the sight of them is oddly comforting. As is being back in the Payne club, leaning over the counter with Miss Deveroux on the other side, eyeing me intently.

I take another sip of my drink as I take in the empty corner of the club and the low din of music.

"Business hasn't picked up at all?" I frown at Miss Deveroux.

She shrugs. "Some of us are allowed to work here for now, but since the rumors broke, we lost a lot of our usual clientele."

I grimace. "That's bad, isn't it?"

Miss Deveroux leans closer and drops her voice to a whisper. "Some people are getting too close to the truth. I have a feeling it will get a lot worse before it gets better."

I sigh. "You should get out while you still have the chance. If you need money…"

Miss Deveroux squeezes my hand. "I've got enough stashed away for a clean break if I need it."

I lean back to study her face and the unfamiliar gleam in her eyes. "Why don't you? Leave, I mean."

Miss Deveroux blinks and stands up straighter. "I know this is going to sound crazy, but this place… it's my home. I'm not as young as I was, and the idea of starting over somewhere new isn't as appealing as it once was."

I frown. "Miss Deveroux—"

"Delilah," she interrupts. "I think we've known each other long enough to be on a first-name basis, don't you?"

I swallow and instinctively reach for my drink. "Delilah. If things get bad, I don't think anyone will be safe."

I don't want her anywhere near the club or the Payne family if things fall apart.

She's the closest thing I have to a friend around here.

I just hope the foundation the Paynes have built is sturdy enough to withstand a full-on assault. Otherwise, we're all on borrowed time.

Miss Deveroux nods and reaches under the counter for a glass. She pours herself a drink and tips it back. "Like I said, this is my home."

I blow out a breath. "You're a lot braver than I am."

"Having second thoughts?"

"No, but I wish I had done more to protect my family. They won't return my calls, and I can't go and see them for obvious reasons."

Miss Deveroux pats my hand. "I'll reach out to them."

My shoulders sag with relief, and I swallow past the lump in my throat. "Thank you."

Miss Deveroux glances over her shoulder at my bodyguard. "I see you're keeping different company tonight."

I glance over my shoulder. "Yeah, I don't know what's happening. He won't say a thing."

Miss Deveroux clears her throat. "I hate to be the one to say this, but you need to have a backup plan, London. In case things go to shit."

My stomach lurches. "What do you mean?"

"You can tell them he's been keeping you here against your will," Miss Deveroux says. "Tell them he threatened your family, and that you owe him money. They'll go easy on you. He won't contradict your story."

I search her face and pause.

It's not like the thought hasn't crossed my mind, but betraying Mason and abandoning him when he needs me, even to save myself and my family, doesn't sit right. The mere thought of it sends a fresh wave of pain through me.

I know it's the smart choice, and I know Mason would forgive me, but I can't bring myself to do it.

There will be no turning back if you don't turn on him. Remember that. You still have a chance.

"I'll keep that in mind," I respond. "But I—"

"You." The voice makes the hairs on the back of my neck rise. I swivel on my stool and easily find the source of the voice. Steven is making a beeline for me, his hair plastered to his forehead, and a murderous gleam in his eyes. My bodyguard steps in front of him and gives him a long look.

"Of course, you hide behind him." Steven leans sideways to look at me. "Call off your dog or I'll tell this whole club what you did."

I jump off the stool and ignore the twinge in my chest. "I don't know what you're talking about."

Steven's lips twist into a sneer. "Oh, I bet you don't, Princess. Is that why you won't call off your bodyguard?"

I reach Steven. "He's here to make sure assholes like you don't step out of line."

His expression tightens. "I always had a feeling about you, but I never knew what it was. I told Noah that he wouldn't be able to handle you, and it turns out, I was right."

At the mention of Noah's name, my stomach lurches again, and guilt courses through me.

What the hell did Noah tell Steven?

I ignore the blood roaring in my ears. "You're wasting my time. I've got better things to—"

"I know you did something to Noah," Steven hisses. "Don't bother denying it. There's more to the story than what Noah told me. You wouldn't have just left him like that unless it was someone powerful or important or both. Women like you like to upgrade."

I offer Steven a blank look. "I never took you for a conspiracy theorist."

Steven takes a step in my direction, and my bodyguard throws out his arm to stop him. "If you have nothing to hide, why is he here?"

I step closer to the bodyguard. Then I lean in, so my mouth is next to his ear. "I know you have your orders, but I'm pretty sure you don't want a scene, and that's exactly what he's going to cause if you don't back off."

A muscle ticks in the bodyguard's jaw.

"There are enough problems as it is," I add. "You don't have to like me to know I'm right."

Given how powerful a client Steven is, the last thing I want is to draw attention to myself. I have no idea where Mason or Katia are. While my new bodyguard seems to take his job seriously, I have no idea how far or how deep his loyalty goes.

Or if one word from Jack Payne is enough to call him off.

After a tense moment, the bodyguard steps to the side. I move to stand in front of Steven, and I don't miss the cruelty in his eyes. He glances from the bodyguard to me and back again. Then, without warning, he lashes out, and I throw myself sideways, so his hand misses my face by a few inches.

"I'm going to find out what you did to him." Steven's face is one of fury. "Don't bother denying it. I don't care who you're fucking. These walls can't protect you forever."

He tries to punch me again, and I sidestep again, tasting fear on my tongue.

Several of the people in attendance are staring at us, and a few are whispering.

The hairs on the back of my neck rise when Steven gets a little too close, and my bodyguard intercepts him. He twists Steven's arm behind his back and holds him still. Steven releases a litany of curse words, his face turning red as he writhes. I swallow past the lump in my throat and let my arms fall to my sides.

"I don't owe you anything, Steven. We both know you're a shit friend. Now, I don't know what game you're playing here, or why you're putting on a show, but you and I both know that what Noah and I had was real."

"Lying bitch." Steven is bristling now. "I should've taken care of you when I had the chance."

"I don't care if you believe me," I say. "I still care about Noah, and I wish him nothing but the best."

Steven mumbles something unintelligible.

I motion to the bodyguard, who releases him.

Suddenly, Steven charges me, and I spread my legs shoulder-width apart and stand my ground. Once he's close enough, I punch him in the stomach. He doubles over, and I knee him in the groin, forcing him to crumple to the ground. His eyes are filled with hatred as he glances up at me.

"I'd suggest you leave before you get yourself into even more trouble."

Steven lunges at me again, but he's pulled back by the scruff of his neck. I blink and realize that Katia has both his arms pinned behind his back. She presses him against the nearest wall and says something into his ear. Steven stops squirming, and the color leaves his face. Abruptly, Katia releases him, and he scurries past without a backward glance.

"I was beginning to think you'd found someone else to…" I trail off when Katia moves closer, and I see the bruises on her face and the marks on her arm. Terror slams into me as I step forward. "What happened?"

"You need to come with me." Katia's eyes dart around the club before she looks at me. "Unless you want to find some other way to get yourself in trouble."

My throat closes as I fall into step beside her.

We take the back door out of the club and cross the lawn and path separating it from the estate. My mind spins as I imagine all the things that could've gone wrong. When we reach the estate, there are even more guards patrolling than usual, and they center around Katia, who has her arms by her sides, her steps long and measured.

Olivia is waiting for me near the door to the manor.

She and Katia exchange a quick look before the latter disappears.

My throat is dry as I follow Olivia down a series of dimly lit, carpeted hallways.

We stop outside a set of double doors, and when I see Oliver leaning against one wall with Mathew and Jack against the other, my heart jumps into my throat.

Olivia turns to face me. "Mason was ambushed."

My stomach drops. "What do you mean he's been ambushed? Where is he?"

Olivia exhales. "The doctor is taking a look at his wounds right now."

"Here? Shouldn't he be in a hospital?"

"That's what this wing is for." Oliver's voice is hoarse. "And the doctor has the equipment he needs, and a discreet team that knows what to do."

I'd seen glimpses of the room, but it wasn't enough.

Not as far as I was concerned.

My anger rises. "I don't think this is the time to be worried about discretion. If it's serious enough to need surgery, he should be in a real hospital."

Olivia places a hand on my arm. "He's going to be fine, London. He's in good hands."

I shake Olivia's hand off and step away. "I want to see him."

"I don't care how much leeway my son has given you," Jack says. "If you don't stop being a nuisance, I'll do what I should've done when I first learned about you."

"You're not going to risk Mason's wrath," I reply. "Despite your claims, you need him."

Shut the hell up, London. Have you forgotten who you're dealing with?

Olivia steps between us and fixes her gaze on me. "Let's go for a walk."

"I don't want to go on a fucking walk." My eyes never leave Jack's face. "I'm staying right here."

I don't trust Jack not to finish the job himself.

An ambush is a good way for Jack to get rid of Mason without getting his hands dirty, and with a war raging at our doorstep, it's the perfect opportunity to lay the blame at the enemy's feet.

You cannot take Jack on, and you know it. Keep your mouth shut and pray that Mason makes it out of this alive.

Olivia tugs on my arm again, and I look at her. "You'd be doing me a favor."

After a brief pause, I reluctantly let Olivia lead me away.

We go back the way we came, and each step away from Mason feels harder than the last. When we make it to the living room, Olivia releases my arm and releases a shaky breath. "Listen, I know I said you were brave, but there's a fine line between being brave and being stupid. Are you trying to get yourself killed?"

"If Mason was ambushed, Jack was behind it."

Olivia presses one finger to each of her temples and rubs in slow, circular motions. "Look, our father is an asshole. He's conniving and manipulative, but he wouldn't kill Mason."

"He tried to shoot him when we first got here."

Olivia exhales. "He never would've hurt him. Trust me on this."

"How can you—You sound so sure."

Olivia runs a hand over her face. "I am. He's punished us before, and once or twice, he's taken it too far, but he wouldn't seriously hurt us. In his own twisted way, he does love us."

"I'm sorry if I'm finding it hard to believe that when he's repeatedly threatened us, assaulted Mason, and is having my family watched."

Olivia blows out another breath. "That's fine. I understand why this is a hard pill to swallow, but I'm telling you our father's bite is worse than his bark. At least when it comes to us."

My stomach lurches as I stand up straighter. "We still shouldn't leave Mason alone with him."

"When Mason pulls through—"

"If he pulls through." My voice catches on the last word. "How are you so sure?"

Olivia's hand falls to her side. "Because my brother is an arrogant and annoying jackass when he wants to be, but he's also stubborn and tough as nails. He's going to want to hang on to punish whoever did this himself."

I swallow. "I hope you're right."

Olivia steps closer to me. "I know this is all new to you, but you need to be smart about this."

I nod.

"If you really want to help, you can help me send a message to someone."

I stare at her for a few seconds. "Does this have anything to do with the rumors I've heard about how you were involved with someone from this world?"

Myriad emotions dance across Olivia's face, and she stiffens. "How much did Mason tell you?"

"He didn't tell me anything, and I didn't push."

Olivia's eyes move over my face. "It's true. I was involved with someone. I don't know if our history will help end this war, but I think it's a worth shot."

"Mason doesn't approve, does he?"

Olivia grimaces. "You know how he can be. Overprotective to a fault, but he needs help, and he's too proud and stubborn to admit it. He'll be keeping a close eye on me, so you'll have to help me establish a line of communication."

I taste bile in the back of my throat. "You want me to lie to him?"

"Unless you have any other suggestions."

I blow out a breath. "That depends. What do you want me to do?"

CHAPTER TWENTY-THREE

Mason

"I'm fine," I repeat. "You need to stop hovering."

"I'm your sister," Olivia snaps. "It's part of my job to hover."

I snort, and my hand moves to my ribs, where a tender bruise has been stitched together. "How long have I been out?"

"A few hours," Olivia replies after a brief pause. "You gave us quite a scare."

I sit up straighter and frown. "How did you know I was in trouble?"

Olivia pauses, and her eyebrows draw together. "What do you mean?"

"The men who got us here—"

"We didn't send anyone, Mason." Olivia shakes her head. "We would have if we had known, but we had no idea anything was wrong until Carlisle and Katia showed up carrying you, all three of you covered in blood and looking like death warmed over."

I press my lips together and say nothing.

"You were pretty out of it when I saw you. Mathew said you were rambling about another traitor." Olivia's voice is hushed. "Do you have any idea who it is?"

"No, but it's only a matter of time before I find out."

The fact that it might be someone I share a last name with only makes things worse.

Especially after the ambush that I barely escaped.

Whoever is helping the enemy is out for blood, and they're not pulling any punches.

Are you really going to pretend it's not Mathew? You know he wants to get rid of you, and this is the perfect way to do it. Lay the blame on Michael and the Fitzpatricks, and give him an excuse to launch a full-scale war. It's exactly the kind of he would do. The real question is whether he acted with Father's support.

I'd seen the look on my father's face when he'd stepped out a few minutes ago to take a call.

It hadn't looked like the face of a man who had suffered defeat.

I'd even caught the worried gleam in his eyes seconds before he snuffed it out.

Jack wouldn't kill you. He'd probably just hide you away somewhere till he smoothed things over.

"London is waiting for the right moment to come and see you," Olivia adds. "She's been steering clear of Jack."

I nod. "Good."

A heartbeat later, the door swings open, and Jack steps in, not a hair out of place. He keeps one hand in the pocket of his pants, and the other holds the phone to his ear. He hangs up and moves closer to me, and a shiver of unease races through me.

"Since you've managed to screw up the alliance with the Thayers, I've been on the phone trying to secure another alliance."

I raise an eyebrow. "You've convinced the Harrisons to come to the table."

The Harrisons haven't been at the forefront of anything for years, and while the thought of allying myself with an ill-prepared family doesn't sit well with me, it's better than the alternative. Now that our understanding with the Thayers has gone up in flames, we don't have another choice.

Tonight's ambush is proof of that.

Time is no longer a luxury we have.

Jack's eyes sweep over me. "I've also managed to convince the Fitzpatricks and Everetts to restart negotiations. You should be thankful they're still willing to come to the table after the shit you pulled."

"The shit *I* pulled? They tried to have me killed."

A shadow settles over Jack's face. "And they'll be brought to heel. We've already compromised several of their locations."

I clench my hands into fists. "It's not enough."

"I'll be the judge of that."

"Like fuck you will. I'm the one who was almost made into roadkill."

Jack scowls. "A Payne doesn't let his feelings get in the way of business. This needs to be dealt with—"

"Fuck you."

Olivia wedges herself between us and throws one hand up on either side of her. "Stop it. Mason almost died. Instead of bickering about that, we should be trying to figure out how the hell they keep flipping people from the inside. You can worry about revenge later."

"Your sister makes a good point."

I stare at my father and say nothing.

A short while later, he leaves, the phone pressed to his ear again, and I glance at Olivia. She nods and leaves the room. I press two fingers to my temples, the bright fluorescent lights making the pounding in the back of my skull worse. With a frown, I let my eyes dart around the room, taking in the table under the window and the patches of silver light pouring in from outside.

The hospital bed dips and creaks as I sit up, and a sliver of pain races up my side.

Carlisle pokes his head in a short while later. His arm is in a sling, and he's favoring one leg. There's an angry red welt on the left side of his face, and it comes into harsh focus when he stops a few feet away.

"What's the news?"

Carlisle shifts from one foot to the other. "There's no chatter. It's too quiet."

I scowl. "Find me whoever did this, Carlisle. In the meantime, see if you can reach out to any of your contacts to find out about this other traitor."

I open my mouth to say something, and Olivia comes in with London in tow. Carlisle's hand darts out to hand me an envelope. in one quick move, I shift to hide it under the pillow. London waits until Olivia's gone before she approaches me, her red-rimmed eyes drinking me in.

When I pull the cover back, London looks at the white wrapping around my side, and a sob falls from her lips. I pat the bed and shift. After a brief pause, she kicks off her shoes and carefully perches on the side. She lets out a low, startled noise when I pull her against me and exhale, some of the knots in my stomach unfurling.

London got me through the fight.

Even in my delirium, she remained clear and focused, a beacon guiding me back home.

London stirs. "I wanted to come sooner."

I cup her face in my hands and blow out a breath. "I know."

London shudders and leans into my touch. "You're not allowed to die on me."

"Likewise."

Slowly, London inches back to look at me, and her eyes move steadily over me. "I mean it, Mason. We've been through too much for you to be taking risks like that."

I give her a quick, rough kiss and pull away before she can deepen it. "I'm a survivor, and I'll always find a way to come back to you."

London reaches for my hand. "Katia would only give me highlights about what happened, and that was after I wouldn't stop nagging her."

I huff a laugh. "She didn't tell you because you nagged. I think she likes you."

London makes a face. "I think what you meant to say is she'd like to kill me."

I tuck London into my side and drape an arm over her shoulders. "Katia doesn't want to kill you, but there's no shortage of people who do."

I have to add one more name to the list.

"Our alliance with the Thayers is no longer at play," I add, in a low voice. "Thatcher will be staying with us for a while."

London sits up. "You're keeping him as prisoner? Is that a smart thing to do?"

"It's the only thing I can do to make sure the Thayers don't turn on us."

If they haven't heard already.

London blows out a breath. "I'm sure Elise is pissed."

I wave her comment away. "She'll get over it. There's something else."

"What is it?"

"Those men who ambushed me were hired by someone on the inside, and one of them told me it was a Payne."

London goes still and swallows. "You believe them?"

"How else do you explain the attack? And how they've managed to stay one step ahead this whole time?"

I don't want to believe it, but there are too many coincidences to brush off.

Too many close calls not to look into it.

London takes my hands in hers. "There's got to be another explanation. Something that makes sense."

"He was seen meeting with several associates of the Fitzpatricks and the Everetts," I reply in a gentler voice. "I know this is a hard pill for you to swallow."

"Me?" London squeezes my hands. "How are you so calm after... everything?"

I shrug. "I don't have a choice."

Dwelling on what it means isn't going to do me any good.

There will be plenty of time for me to feel the bitter sting of betrayal later.

Now, I need to focus on getting rooting out a name, even if it means having to take them on directly.

London's frown deepens. "Well, I think it's Jack. I know you have a complicated relationship, so he is the most obvious choice, but you should've seen the look on his face when Katia came to get me."

"I'm looking into him, too."

London sucks in a harsh breath and leans in closer. "It's too dangerous. What if he finds out?"

"I'll take care of it."

I've gotten myself out of worse messes, and although I don't relish the idea of confronting Jack, I know I have to cover all of my bases.

"I want to help," London says. Her eyes flick over the scar on my cheek. "There's got to be something I can do."

"If I tell you to stay out of trouble, will you listen?"

London pauses. "Not if I feel like there's something I can do."

I grimace. "I'm going to regret this, but I need to know what Noah told his father and his brother. I've been in the dark for too long, and if I'm going to come out ahead of this, I need to have the full picture."

London stares. "You want me to talk to him?"

"You're not going to like what you see," I warn, my stomach lurching. "Just remember that I'm keeping us safe, and Noah has threatened that."

London nods and says nothing.

When I pull her against me again, she doesn't resist.

For a while, we lay there, her head pressed against my chest, and my arm draped over her shoulders, the smell of her washing over me.

It is a rare moment of peace before the storm.

Eventually, London's breathing evens out, and she goes slack against me. Using my good arm, I pull the blanket over us. Then, I sink further against the bed and squeeze my eyes shut. Unfortunately, the harder I try to sleep, the more elusive it becomes. When I finally drift off, my body feels heavy, and everything is tight. I keep replaying the car crash in my mind, seeing Katia and Carlisle's faces as they fought to protect me, and the steady stream of people pouring in from the forest.

Only in my dreams, I couldn't stay on my feet.

Rain poured, and endless darkness spread around me.

When I raised a gun to shoot, it was replaced with a knife, and it went sailing through the air before I realized I had thrown it at Oliver. I scrambled to my feet as his body crumpled. My heart pounded as I ran over to him, and his face was replaced with Mathew's, his bright eyes wide and accusing. I propped his head up and ignored the tremor racing through me when the face changed again. This time, I was holding London.

Her expression changes as she stares up at me, the life slowly bleeding out of her.

I open my mouth to scream, but no sound comes out.

Suddenly, I sit up in bed, drenched in a cold sweat, and my heart galloping unevenly. Gray light pours in through the open window, and I hear birds chirping in the distance. My vision clears, and I see London sitting next to me, wisps of hair plastered to her forehead and a furrow between her brows.

Wordlessly, she takes my hands in hers.

"I'm okay." My voice is hoarse. "Just a stupid dream."

London kisses my hand and swings her legs over the side of the bed. "Why don't I get you something to eat?"

"Katia should be outside, or Carlisle. Make sure one of them is with you."

London turns to face me. "Okay."

I raise an eyebrow. "That's it? No arguments?"

London lets her hands fall to her side and straightens up. "Let's just focus on getting you better. That's all that matters now."

I tug on her hand, and she leans forward, breath hitching in her throat when I move my other hand around the back of her neck. My mouth descends on hers, hot and unyielding, and the sigh that falls from her lips makes something in me unfurl. London slides onto the bed and links her fingers through my hair. When she angles her head and parts her lips, red-hot desire pulses through me.

She's all I want in that moment.

Everything else can burn for all I care.

My tongue plunges into her mouth, and I draw slow, lazy strokes, the moans falling from her lips erasing every voice of doubt in my head. I use my hands to frame her face and growl into her mouth, smirking when a shudder goes through her. London throws one leg over me, so she's straddling me, and suddenly, the small bed doesn't bother me as much.

I keep one hand on the back of her neck, and the other glides down her bare arms.

London makes another noise in the back of her throat, and my fingers move under her shirt and splay across the bare skin of her stomach. She grinds against me, and I growl again, needing to feel more of her.

Someone clears their throat, and London stills.

I wrench my lips away, finding Oliver standing in the doorway. Slowly, I untangle myself from London and tuck her into my side. She pushes her hair out of her eyes, and I feel her stiffen when she spots Oliver. His hair is in tufts on top of his head, and when he steps into the room, I see the wrinkled clothing and dark circles under his eyes.

"I can come back later." Oliver's voice is low and uneven. "I thought you'd be resting."

"I was."

Oliver's eyes dart all over the room, and he swallows. "I thought I'd check on you."

"Came to see if they finished the job?"

Oliver snaps to attention. "What?"

"The medical team," I say. "I won't need more surgery."

Oliver's expression is relieved as he slides his eyes away again. "Good. I'm glad."

Silence stretches between us.

Oliver shoves a hand into his pocket and drifts closer to the window. The first patches of yellow light illuminate his features. Every time I'm around him, I'm reminded of how much he looks like our mother, and it's like losing her all over again.

I know he's been itching to get back to his life

I swallow past the bile in my throat and square my shoulders. "I'm getting close to finding out who was behind this."

Oliver doesn't turn to face me, but I see the subtle straightening of his spine. "I'm guessing it's someone from the inside."

"Higher up this time," I reply tightly. "I don't care who they are. When I get my hands on them, I'll gut the traitor myself and hang him by his balls."

Oliver turns to face me, and his expression is smooth and unreadable. "You'll want to interrogate him first."

"I have something special planned."

Oliver's mouth moves, but no sound comes out.

A kernel of doubt takes root and blossoms in the center of my chest. *What have you done, little brother? What do you know?*

London clears her throat, breaking the tension. "I was going to get us breakfast. Oliver, do you want me to get you something?"

Oliver doesn't look at her.

"I'll be right back." London stops in the doorway to shoot me a meaningful look. Then she steps outside, and the door shuts behind her. Oliver remains rooted to the spot, his eyes dancing around. He looks at me again, and a long moment passes between us.

He opens his mouth, and I clench my hands into fists.

The door to the room bursts open, and Oliver jumps up, fear flashing across his face before he stamps it out. Carlisle spares Oliver a cursory look before he stops in front of me. I don't take my eyes off Oliver's face as Carlisle leans forward and whispers something in my ear. I offer him a curt nod, and Carlisle leans back again.

"Duty never sleeps," Oliver comments in a strange voice. "I'll leave you to it."

"It shouldn't have come to this."

Oliver stops in the doorway, every muscle poised and tense. "I'm sure you'll find a way to make things right."

"I meant you and Olivia being here," I continue in the same measured voice. "For what it's worth, I am sorry."

A heartbeat later, he looks away and leaves the room.

Once he does, I press two fingers to my temples and exhale. Carlisle wordlessly steps into the room and folds his arms over his chest. "He knows something."

Carlisle clears his throat. "It's a little more than that, unfortunately."

I drop my hand and stare at Carlisle for a moment longer. Wordlessly, I take the envelope out and rip it open. My heart sputters and speeds up as I leaf through the pictures and realize two things at once.

The first is that how easy it was to find the paper trail leading directly to the traitor.

And the second is that Oliver is the one who hung me out to dry.

Confusion, anger and fear roll up into one and rise within me.

Out of all the scenarios I imagined, my little brother being the one to twist the knife in my back isn't one of them.

He wasn't even on my list.

How could I have been so blind?

Is he really so eager to get back to his life that he's willing to do whatever it takes, including sell me out?

Whatever blood is on his hands, you might as well have put it there yourself. You know you're the reason he got dragged back.

Suddenly, I wonder if Oliver came to see me to finish what my enemies started.

Would he have taken London out too?

I go cold all over as I force myself to glance up from the pictures. "How sure are you about this?"

Carlisle straightens his back. "As sure as I can be. I used all my usual channels."

I frown. "That's not good enough. I want you to look into this yourself."

"Boss—"

"No one else can know that Oliver is the traitor," I hiss, turning wild eyes on my right-hand man. "Do you fucking understand? Whatever *this* is, he's still a Payne."

I desperately need Oliver to be innocent.

I need another explanation, but I can't let myself be blindsided again.

The last thing I need is more my problems on my plate.

Carlisle will dig as deep as he can, and when he finds proof, I'll make sure to deal with it personally.

I'm sorry, mom.

I lower my voice further. "No one else can look into this. You need to handle this as discreetly as possible. Only go to Katia for help."

Carlisle nods.

London returns as Carlisle is leaving and ignores the look he gives her. She carries the tray over to the table by the bed and sets it down. Then, she waits until the door shuts and Carlisle is out of earshot.

"What was that about?"

"What was what about?" I lean sideways and snatch a croissant off the tray and rip it into pieces.

London drops her hands. "You and Oliver. I thought you two were good."

I pop a piece of the flaky bread in my mouth and chew. "It's complicated. Oliver has been here too long."

London reaches for my hand, and I let her hold it. "I'm sorry."

I stop chewing. "None of this is your fault."

"I'm still sorry." London's eyes never leave my face. "What happens now? How many people do we have to keep an eye on? People we're supposed to be able to trust."

The croissant suddenly tastes like ash in my mouth.

"As many as it takes. We won't let on that we know. We beat them at their game, so they don't see us coming."

London stands up and blows out a breath. "This makes things worse, doesn't it?"

I stare at her for another moment and then nod. "Yes."

London walks over to the window and looks out. "We can handle this. We just have to get through it together."

My heart twists at the optimism in her voice.

"The food is going to get cold, Pigeon," I say. "Let's eat."

I don't want to take away her hope just yet.

I'm coming for you, you bastards. You'd better be ready to throw every damn thing you've got at me.

Ready for your next swoon-worthy escape?

Check out these other captivating love stories!

Dark Mafia Romance

Feathers and Thorne Series
His to Claim Series
The Umarova Crime Family Series

Motorcycle Club Romance

Dark Pharaohs Series
Blazing Rebels Series
Steel Knights Series

For a complete list of new releases and best-selling romance books, visit IvyBlackRomance.com or scan the QR code below!

www.ingramcontent.com/pod-product-compliance
Lightning Source LLC
Chambersburg PA
CBHW050924030726
47503CB00007BB/2450